Michael Levey contributed to *Winter's Crimes, 1979*, and to *The After Midnight Ghost Book*, edited by James Hale. He has also written some non-fiction. At present he is Director of the National Gallery. He is married to Brigid Brophy.

MICHAEL LEVEY

Tempting Fate

ROBIN CLARK

To Ted Willis
in gratitude for generous encouragement

Published by Robin Clark Limited 1983
A member of the Namara Group
27 Goodge Street, London W1P 1FD

First published in hardcover in Great Britain
by Hamish Hamilton Ltd, 1982

Printed and bound in Great Britain at
The Camelot Press Ltd, Southampton

British Library Cataloguing in Publication Data

Levey, Michael
Tempting Fate
I. Title
823'.914 [f]   PR6062.E/

ISBN 0-86072-065-9

1

'Kick us,' he murmured fondly, as he knelt at my feet.

By then I was not just tired but positively shagged out, so it was an effort to oblige (yet I'd been brought up with excellent manners, and not solely because they make men). I managed a softish push with my free bare foot, only to see him look up surprised, though still soppily fond, while he went on tying my other shoe lace.

He murmured again. This time I heard it as 'kickers' and realised he was admiring my rubber-soled green, blue and orange canvas sneakers that, somehow, in my resolutely untrendy way, I preferred to think of as plimsolls.

The being-dressed-afterwards aspect of an afternoon with Dennis was probably one reason why I felt irritable as well as exhausted. Usually I'm cool about all these things – and certainly by now reasonably experienced – but this putting one's clothes on for one always made me feel unpleasantly like a corpse. Not that poor old Dennis had the glimmerings of murderous impulse in him, I was sure. At best he might have auditioned as one of nature's 'second' murderers – the sort that stumble on in Shakespeare like some Jacobean plumber's mate and are lucky to be allowed to chorus 'we shall, my lord,' before exiting.

Almost more unpleasant than feeling dead under Dennis's clumsily loving hands was the implied regression to child-hood. I suppose I'm simply not old enough to get any pleasure out of that sensation; it's too easily recoverable to hold anything but embarrassment for me, though perhaps I'll grow into it if I live long enough.

Of course I recognise how sexy clothes can be and the part clothes play in every form of sexual attraction. Indeed, I think I may have discovered a principle here that most of the pundits have missed. Everyone at school (all the schools I've been at) used to go on about how much they'd like to see so-and-so – probably one of the maids – without any clothes. That was thought really lecherous. People just laughed when I said I'd much prefer to see them wearing a whole series of different clothes. Some fool once suggested it was because my mother was an actress. I was tempted to reply that I didn't mean *her* clothes, but it wasn't worth it. Before I'd finished somebody else would have said either that I was fixated on my mother (oh God) or that I favoured transvestism (which is actually one of the few things which never seriously attracted me, even when, or even because, I took girls' parts in school plays).

There doesn't seem much glamour in going around naked, unless circumstances give it piquancy, and certainly there isn't in seeing other people naked. Not much is left for suggestion, as became only too clear in the school showers, whereas the combination of the right flesh and the right clothes is endlessly intriguing. I've rarely wanted – or felt any necessity – to be naked to get my effects. Most adults are incredibly naïve, and even while you're appealing to them, in your suit, surplice, running shorts or swimming trunks, your clothes are helping to re-assure them that this sensation can't exactly be lust.

I think I had always sensed this, anyway since the days of being a boy of about nine when I abruptly realised the charm all our clean necks rising from our clean shirts had for our form-master as we bent over our desks, and he bent over us. The point is that he could barely have spelt paedophilia – it wasn't fashionable, and anyway he took us for maths. He appeared happily married to the matron, who was unexpectedly young and pretty (we were all in love with her ourselves); but the warmth of his lingering hand on one's shoulder, thinly covered yet covered, of course, by shirt, revealed far more than his brusque efforts to explain simple equations.

Dennis now had one hand on my knee – perhaps that's why I'd sleepily drifted into thoughts of Mr Gresley-Fox and times past – but it was merely to lever himself upright, I noted, none too pleased.

Then Julian put his bald head round the door. 'Tea's served,' he announced excitedly. 'Come and get it.'

I was planning to go out to dinner with my cousin Mopsa,

and after a fatiguing afternoon being both photographed and played with the last thing I wanted was the sort of scrumptious school-boy spread that this Julian person had obviously prepared. Let him eat it. He was quite obese enough to suggest that was how he spent his time when he wasn't doing what he called art historical research. He'd told me, unsurprisingly, that Caravaggio was his favourite painter. I managed to stop him dead in the midst of his resumé of Caravaggio's grubby life and loves by saying that my own taste was for Ingres (actually a painter Dennis, with his francophile passions, had not only shown me pictures of but taught me to name with a tremendous, almost Southern accent).

We went into Julian's aubergine-coloured kitchen, where under the strings of suspended fake-looking onions the table groaned, as I did audibly, weighed down with cakes, buns and even a green jelly which at least looked cucumber-cool and wetly luminous.

'You sit here, Nicky,' Julian said, patting a slatted pine chair positively promising discomfort. 'Gosh, I'm hungry, aren't you?'

'Nick hasn't really got a large appetite,' Dennis replied, subtly re-establishing his claim on me, like something he repented of having lent out.

'Not after that strenuous afternoon? Well, I'm famished – and you always look as though you need feeding up, Dennis. So sit you down.'

'I should love some jelly,' I said carefully, sounding to myself irritatingly prissy and just a touch too gracious: Prince Handsome takes tea with the peasants in a tinted story-book for tots thirty years ago. Julian was bustling about in his striped butcher's apron (at least it wasn't floral) and didn't notice, but I saw Dennis's narrow face sharpen briefly with a parental pang. I pushed back my hair, flushing slightly to my annoyance.

'It's dreadfully hot in here,' Dennis said at once, jumping up from the cane contraption he was seated in at the other side of the table. 'May I open a window?'

'This kitchen's far too small.' Julian shook his head at it, as though he'd been handed the wrong size in a shop. 'Still,' he turned brightly to me, 'buggers can't be choosers, can they?'

Not in Brixton, I thought, as I looked out of the grimy

window Dennis was still struggling to open, and at the flat roof and strip of guttering beyond. In the strong late sunlight some pots of presumably herbs on the kitchen window-sill seemed sparse and oddly forlorn, foster-children of Julian's who just wouldn't grow up properly out there behind the glass, however much he fussed over them.

Abruptly I sensed under the too-lavish tea-time spread that emptiness I was always detecting in so-called adult lives: their awful need for something – God knows what – to fill them up, like cars driving in for celestial grade petrol at some sempiternal garage. I could almost taste grit permeating the spoonfuls of jelly I dutifully scooped up, putting my elbows on the table and making an effort now to be the great guzzling schoolboy Julian no doubt dreamt of pampering. In many ways I had preferred my earlier role of latter-day boy Bacchus, stripped to a sheet off one shoulder and clasping a debased Venetian glass goblet Julian's sister had bought for him on her weekend trip to the city. She'd not be seeing the photographs of me, increasingly out of the sheet as the afternoon passed, though still toying cheekily with her gift. At one point I had seriously thought I might be part of Julian's research into Caravaggio's compositional effects; that was an unusual naïvety which I wasn't going to reveal even to Dennis (I felt he'd not laugh, just be annoyed and then loving).

'Milk or lemonade, Nicky?' Julian buzzed in my ear. 'And do have an iced bun. I'm going to.'

'Haven't you any coffee?' I drawled, no longer much caring what I was meant to be. I glanced at my watch as Julian turned hastily to fetch the teapot (defective hearing or conditioned reflex), and gestured at Dennis who frowned back over-proprietorially.

'I mustn't be too late,' I said loudly, not quite addressing either of them. 'My aunt and uncle are expecting me back.'

That made Julian nervous, despite his big smile at me as he settled into something rush-seated which looked far too fragile for his bulk. I shifted my elbow away from the horribly hairy arm – like an arm clothed in thick seaweed – which made my flesh goose-pimple at the prospect of contact. I'd been careful throughout that he never touched my bare skin. He could fondle his Pentax, or whatever it was, I thought, privately grinning. Anyway he was in awe of Dennis not only for having found me but – I expect – for having seduced me. And Dennis would never reveal that it had been the other way round.

'I'm off to Rome in September,' Julian told me, 'and then Sicily.'

'Is that for research?' I asked idly, licking the icing off the bun he had placed on my plate.

He giggled. 'That's one word for it. No, truly, I've got to take a good look at Caravaggio's work once more. I'm giving some lectures on him next term.'

'Better be careful you don't get your slides muddled,' I said.

He felt relaxed by that, I could see, as he giggled again. It was something he'd ensure never happened (though I had no objection to being flashed on to a large screen in front of his doubtless absurdly docile students, labelled 'an early master-piece') but the slightest prospect of real scandal, hinted interrogation by parents, guardians or just busybodies had him worried. Although it all seemed so silly to me, I didn't blame him for getting nervous.

I could always testify he was harmless enough – a bit sad really, since he looked so grotesque and had fairly awful taste – but it wouldn't be my evidence they'd listen to. After all, nobody blamed me over Dennis; they merely kicked him out of the school, along with his classically pure French books, his records of Rameau and Lully, and his collection of illustrated catalogues of boys modelling pullovers and grey flannel shorts.

'And at least you're not too bad-looking,' I told him musingly in the car as we drove away from Julian's depressed road of bravely painted brick villas (Aphra Avenue) shrivell-ing in the oven-hot glow of the summer evening. Julian had not accompanied us downstairs; he thought that could look rather obvious, and also we might bump into his landlady who came back from work about that time. Upstairs he had decided to shake my hand briskly, and no less briskly I had pocketed his three ten-pound notes.

'What's the logic of that remark?'

Dennis couldn't turn to look at me, as he concentrated on getting us out of Brixton (and he didn't drive well), but his tone was as sharp as his pointed chin. I'd often noticed, and

5

been glad of, Dennis the true pedagogue who usually took over after a bout of sentimental pederasty.

'Does it have to have logic?' I answered sulkily. 'If you must know, I was comparing you and Julian – to your advantage. He looks a lot older,' I added.

'I suppose in return I'm meant to compliment you on your appearance?'

I casually draped my bare arm along the back of the driving seat. He knew I knew what intense pleasure that innocent-looking, utterly discreet gesture always gives him, just because it says much but tells nothing. If he had been a king of France, he would have been called Denys the Discreet.

'Are you taking me all the way to St John's Wood?' I asked, gazing calmly into the driving mirror.

'Of course I am.'

'I'm sure I could always hitch a lift. If you dropped me at Victoria, I'd pick up something. Or maybe better in Piccadilly; I could exercise my charm.'

He narrowed his eyes, possibly at the admittedly heavy traffic we were encountering.

'Sometimes,' he said shortly, 'you're a silly, smutty, spoilt and stupid brat.'

'I thought that was my appeal for you and people like Julian.'

'Julian and I are not Siamese twins.'

'Just what I was trying to say when you began about logic. I was really using instinct rather than logic, Dennis, wasn't I? Please don't try and overtake that lorry; I'm fairly all right for time, so far.'

'Is your aunt giving a dinner party tonight?'

'Not that I'm aware of.'

'But you have to be back for dinner?'

'Yes.' I wanted it to sound neutral yet unapologetically firm. 'I do.'

He made no response, letting the silence build up around us atmospherically until I decided to take my arm away and open the window. As I cranked it down I thought – much as I dislike slang terms – what a crummy car Dennis's was. Then I felt that wasn't fair. I suppose Dennis was poor – well, I knew he was – but the fact is that in his wretched vehicle (an ancient Morris miniscule I called it) I'd had some good rides, both at school and in the holidays. One Easter we'd actually gone to France in the old chariot, and somewhere near Châteaudun ('remember one of Charles d'Orléans' poems, Nick?'), after a thoroughly enjoyable too-rich dinner the previous evening, I was disgustingly sick over the upholstery and the dashboard. Funny to think that then, smelly as I must have been, was the first occasion he dared kiss me properly. Even now I couldn't quite understand it. It all seemed a long time ago.

'Look.' I decided to bust the accumulating silence. 'I'm quite serious about not dragging you all the way up to ma tante at Bois Saint-Jean. Drop me at Marble Arch and I'll get a cab.'

'No,' he said grimly, staring ahead as at last we crossed the Thames (Lambeth Bridge? Vauxhall? I never know). 'What are you doing tomorrow?'

'Tomorrow?' I paused to think and he recognised the pause, though I went on to tell the truth. 'I'm going down to Spenn. Philip expects me back.'

'I thought you found it dull there with him. Isn't he out a lot? And you've always told me Spenn itself is deadly.'

'It is – deadly pretty and pretty deadly. But I did say I'd spend a few weeks there, and then Mother will be back from filming – and, oh, I don't know ...'

'Don't know what?'

London looked so fierily beautiful in the setting sun that I was tempted to do what Dennis most despised in conversation and make an admittedly irrelevant, even temporising, remark about it.

'What,' he repeated, 'don't you know?'

'My French irregular verbs, sir, to begin with. Look, Dennis, I've had a tiring afternoon with you and your bald chum – '

'Obliging us instead of hanging around some filthy amusement arcade, I suppose, where you might have got beaten up or arrested. And you got some money from Julian. Don't you have any feelings at all?'

I was relieved to notice St John's Wood church appearing palely at the end of the road ahead of us. Even my Aunt Margot would be a welcome sight and her drinks cabinet definitely would be. And I'd take Mopsa out to dinner;

7

usually she paid, though I called for the bill, and tonight Julian's tip ought to cover it. And then there was after dinner.

Dennis drew up awkwardly outside the wrong block of mansion flats (they're all hideous and look alike, I admit). Nor was it easy to park there. Before, it had been in my mind to ask him up for a drink: 'Margot,' (naturally never 'aunt'), 'you haven't met Mr Rickard who used to teach me French. I just happened to run into him in – Harrods. I hope you didn't mind my bringing him back ... Yes, he really helped us all a lot, specially me. It was rather rotten when he decided to leave.' And afterwards she would express astonishment that he appeared quite presentable, so much younger than she expected schoolmasters to be: rather a pity he wasn't taller but there was something artistic about his long fingers – she was surprised he didn't play the piano. He might almost be invited to dinner sometime; the odd man was always useful.

Dennis still gripped the steering wheel with those sensitive hands. I hadn't forgiven him for his last melodramatic remark. It seemed worthy not of him but of the old, trite, tear-stained movies that people even of his generation love seeing again and again. I had actually meant to leap out of the car – slamming the door maybe, if he wanted a big farewell scene – and I burnt angrily under the dark mournful gaze he now turned on me. He looked like photographs of Kafka (even to the ears), but of course it was Baudelaire he wanted to resemble.

'Don't you understand – or won't you?' he began, in a way that increased my resentment as I sat there, trying to appear as crisply cool as a new-laundered shirt (I had to change before going out with Mopsa). 'All I'm asking is, when do I see you next. I could stay on in London with Julian if you'll come up again. Or would you come down and stay with me and my parents? – but I know that's awkward. I wondered if maybe there was any chance of a trip to France next month.'

'My plans are vague. You might get a postcard from me. Anyway, take care – and have fun.'

'Nicholas.' That usage was like a warning flash – igniting not him but me.

'Oh stuff France and you and the whole bloody thing.'

I stepped out swiftly into the path of a swerving Mercedes which was driven by a man unpleasantly like my uncle

Hugh. I quite failed to close – let alone slam – the door of Dennis's car, whose prolonged stay had now attracted the uniformed porter from the flats on to the pavement, to peer suspiciously at it and its occupants. I gave him the sort of smile Mopsa always gave him, but I got nothing back except a surly, humiliating glance which made me shake with rage as I ran by, banged the lift cage to and stabbed the button for the second floor. I nearly went up to the fifth floor just to calm down.

It's so unlike you, I told myself as I took the longest possible time shutting the lift and taking the key of the flat out of my jeans. That foul porter was one of the exceptions to my rule that healthy good looks and honest boyish charm, carefully controlled, are the *laissez-passer* to everyone's heart. I hadn't wanted the porter's heart: just an indication that the route was open should it ever be convenient to walk that way.

While I fumbled with the lock the door swung inwards and I half-fell on, half-embraced the hard, sleek, scented shape of Margot.

'My dear boy,' she said, kissing me even as she extricated herself and the folds of her silk dress from any real contact. 'How impetuous you still are, but you're just in time for a drink. What does that amusing badge say?'

I had forgotten, in the stress of events, that I had set out that morning with a denim jacket (brown, *not* blue) bearing my 'I love paedophilia' badge. Dennis was taking me to the Reform Club for lunch, but nobody there had seemed to notice precisely what I was proclaiming, though they had noticed me.

Margot thought the message vaguely funny, perplexed though she obviously was about whether it was in good taste (haemophilia she didn't approve of). She took me into the upholstered Chinese hell of her drawing-room where I hoped to find Mopsa but it was empty, apart from a couple of tall, gilded *bodhisattvas* who had been reduced to serving as lamp-stands.

Whatever her faults, Margot was never mean with the alcohol. She and Mother had that in common, perhaps through both being short-sighted. From the belly of a red lacquer shrine she produced a giant iced gin and tonic (no time-wasting proposals about coca-cola) which tinkled and glittered like a chandelier, and went down rather like swallowing glass.

She had planted herself, plus drink, at the centre of the dragon-infested carpet, while I sprawled boyishly on the colossal feather-bed-soft sofa. She thought she looked good, but to me she seemed all bone, fleshless bone, polished and covered by paint and tied up with a jewelled bow. You might have thought she was an old-style distinguished actress – she had the sort of bony face that photographs conventionally well. Beside her, Mother usually looked more like her mother, not her younger sister, with crumpled back-of-a-bus features and crazy-lady clothes that suggested a vast, disintegrating patchwork quilt.

It was just that Mother could act and would go on acting as long as there was a demand for old bags, ancient or modern, comic or serious. Her career only got going when she ceased to look young. With a battered felt hat, a teaspoon and a tin kettle she could have infused a brew even more nauseating than the one she currently advertised on television ('Warms me on the coldest day – *Tee-caff* – double flavour in a single pack') and somebody would have bought it, if only to try on the charwoman. She made a wonderful royal frump too: neglected, despised and constantly divorced by characters like Henry VIII or Charles II.

Margot had been on the stage, very briefly, long before I was born – before Mopsa was born, come to that. She'd just got into a posh production of *The Winter's Tale* when she discovered she was pregnant. It didn't matter, as she had only to appear in Act IV as Mopsa, one of the two shepherdesses (I can't remember if she actually speaks, and I doubt if Margot remembered either). Her daughter commemorated her career: it made a story, I suppose, if people commented on the name. And somewhere she'd acquired and married much older, merchant banker Hugh; although I'd never said this to anyone, I had for long felt sure he couldn't possibly be Mopsa's father. I didn't somehow see him and Margot in bed at any time.

'Mopsa's changing,' Margot said, 'but I know she'll love to see you.'

'I ought to go and change,' I said, struggling up from the slippery cushions.

'I feel rather awful,' Margot was beginning when Hugh

came in. He was wearing a dinner jacket and looked like an apoplectic American senator – a resemblance increased as he poured himself, with medicinal care, an exact dose of whisky from a square, cut-glass decanter with a silly silver label round it.

He grunted a greeting, tacking on his usual 'How's your mother?'

'She's in Portugal.'

'Darling,' Margot said lightly, 'you know we had a card from her on Monday.'

'Forgotten. Can't remember everything.'

Margot smiled round the room. Somewhat annoyingly, I saw a fleeting resemblance to Mother, though Margot's eyes were greener, paler, lacking that sapphire depth which (thank God) had passed on to me.

'Hugh's got to go out,' Margot said. 'Isn't it a sort of bankers' dinner, darling, in the City?'

'Brooks's at eight-fifteen. Oliver's retiring; I told you.'

'And I promised to have dinner with Pamela. The awful thing is, Nicholas darling, we're all deserting you, but I know Mrs Eckstein has left something in the kitchen because I asked her to. And, Hugh, surely there's some perfectly good hock, isn't there? Or is it riesling?'

'It doesn't matter,' I said. 'I'm taking Mopsa out to dinner. I've just drawn some cash.'

'How lovely.' Margot's brightness flickered, then suddenly failed. It was as if she'd noticed my fly unzipped – and I even glanced down hastily, just in case.

'Actually,' she went off in a desperately over-animated rush, 'I think Mopsa's got something on; I'm not absolutely sure, but I know Simon Sinclair was meant to be dropping in for a drink.' She paused.

'Oh, darling. There you are.' Real relief showed in her tone and face.

I knew Mopsa must have come into the room but I didn't want to turn round, didn't want to look at her at all. I wanted to tip the rest of my drink all over the floor and hurl the glass into the fireplace occupied by some oriental arrangement of dried grasses; or, better, to unzip my fly and savagely pee over the blue and cream carpet – only no doubt to leave them less furious than stiffly embarrassed on my behalf.

11

I felt embraced by a fabric cloud as Mopsa kissed me, murmuring, 'Hello, Nicko, angel boy. Sorry I was so long.'

'You're going out,' I mumbled, still not looking up, as I watched the hem of her black and white dress swaying and faintly glinting.

'Not till later,' she said, holding on to my arm. 'So don't fuss. I asked Simon to come late. But I want you to see him: give your verdict.'

'I don't want to see him,' I burst out, immediately horrified at the childishness of my rising voice. I took a deep breath (as though about to embark on a long speech) and the room seemed to ring with the resonance of my declaration about our dinner.

'I ought to fly.' Margot said it so flatly that I half expected her to go out through the open window. 'Pamela hates people arriving late. And you'll be late too, Hugh, if you aren't careful. Isn't the car coming for you?'

Although they were going their separate ways, they seemed glad at least to be leaving the room together. Perhaps Margot felt a tinge of cowardice, because she called gaily from the hall about my having the second spare room, and about towels, while Mopsa and I stood close, not speaking.

'Eh bien, mon cousin,' she said at last, as if testing that we were now alone.

I was meant to reply, 'Eh bien, ma cousine.' The exchange was my invention but I felt too totally miserable to respond.

She dropped my arm and moved slowly, cloudily, to the lacquer shrine where she poured herself a bitter lemon.

'Care to lunch with me tomorrow?'

She turned quite suddenly as she spoke, and the metallic threads or whatever they were in her floating, stencilled dress glinted momentarily in the gradually darkening room.

I put my head in my hands and sank down on the carpet.

'I love you, Mopsa,' I groaned.

'So we *are* lunching tomorrow, I hope?'

'I hate lunch. Please, please, have dinner with me tonight. I won't be here tomorrow evening. I love you so much – and this time I could give you dinner.'

'Tonight I'm going out with what you'll call this Simon person – which I happen to want to do. Give me decent notice next time and we probably can have dinner together.'

I stared at her across the shadowy space, straining my dry but aching eyes as I knelt upright. Already I was tense from the threat of the doorbell, and tense with the problem of getting back into proximity to Mopsa, to bury myself in her lap and then let her raise my head with her wonderfully small, starfish hands, push back my hair and kiss me fiercely.

I had her on the sofa in the drawing-room, I heard myself telling someone, a mythical best friend; but as I gazed at her fading figure, shimmer of pale hair and pale dress I felt desperate uncertainty about how it could happen. Did I begin by taking her clothes off, or my own? Grabbing each other, aroused (bland word for our urgent, pulsing sensations) and heaving around, would we find our clothes melting from our bodies? I wanted her, but that seemed a barrier rather than the solution. It would be too easy to disgust her. Her physical presence was an actual check – like an expanse of swimming pool seen from the highest diving board, even to me who swam well. I needed time: that meal together, our drifting afterwards through the streets or park, her slowly twining around me until, without clumsiness and certainly without rape, I became lost in making love to her.

'Do you sleep with – Simon?'

'Not yet – as you ask.'

'Sleep with me,' I pleaded, shuffling on my knees across the carpet. Now I could see her features, but not her expression. I stretched out my hand, as if I really had swum exhausted to her side, and she took and held it tightly.

'I can't, Nicko,' she said, with a gentleness far more despairing to me than violence.

'What's wrong with me? Am I so horrible? I thought you loved me. You go to bed with other people, don't you?'

'You must find a girl of your own age, or perhaps an older woman. You're very attractive indeed – and you know it. I like you enormously, Nicko. Good God, do you think I usually go out to lunch with schoolboys? Anyway, Simon'll be here any minute and we must stop this Victorian proposal-scene.'

There were so many replies I wanted to make, it was confusing. I decided I wouldn't tell her now about my intending not to go back to school. I meant to pay her out, be silent in fact, but I found myself for some reason asking about her other lover, her boss, Sir James, as I got reluctantly to my feet. He was well over forty, almost twice Mopsa's age, though according to her he still had good looks and a sort of glamour. Since I'd heard about him from her I'd often noticed his name in the newspapers, expanding this and disposing of that, putting a stake out here and squeezing a margin there in a way that must have absolutely bewildered old Hugh who had (as described by Mother, who really cared about money) a dreadful gilts-complex. Mopsa was Sir James's personal secretary; it was as banal as that.

'He's on his yacht with his wife and children,' she said.

'Have you finished with him?'

'Why should I? Do you mean because of Simon? I'd no idea you could be such a puritan. I thought you claimed to be H.R.H. the Prince of Darkness, utterly amoral and all that.' She too got up, smiling at me.

'I am Lucifer, son of morning,' I chanted, forgetting my annoyance.

'But even better-looking?'

The doorbell rang. Mopsa put her silver-ringed hands on my shoulders. I gazed into her green eyes and insolently down at her breasts as if I had spent the evening fondling them.

'Send him away,' I suggested. 'Say you've got a headache. Or tell him your cousin's unexpectedly arrived from Aleppo.'

'Does it still exist?'

The bell rang again. I thought of Simon the suitor standing out there, in dark clothes and striped shirt, probably holding a bunch of roses he'd bought on his way from the City.

'Who the hell is he, by the way?' I asked quietly, as if he could hear.

'He plays tennis,' she answered, moving away. 'Mummy sweetly talks about his playing *for* Wimbledon. He is quite good. Might be picked for our Davis Cup team next year.'

'So might I.'

But she had left the room. There wasn't time to get another drink and I didn't want to be forced into acting as their cupbearer. I drank the remains of my giant gin and listened. Did he kiss her yet? Would they feel, in the end, they had to ask me to dine with them?

'Your bloody bell's out of order,' I heard an unexpectedly deep voice saying. I adjusted my expression from neutral to one suitably quizzical for the son-of-the-house, *in loco parentis.*

Mopsa entered entwined with a hefty blond figure who looked to be about my age, wearing an open-necked blue shirt and white jeans.

'God, it's dark in here, Mopsa,' he said.

'Nicko prefers the darkness. You don't know my cousin Nicholas Gonville, Simon; he's just back from – where is it, Nicko?'

'Brixton,' I said.

'What on earth were you doing there?' he asked.

Like a fool, I began virtually stammering, still rather disconcerted and feeling obscurely defeated. Mopsa went and switched on the *bodhisattva* lamps; their gilded faces, with lowered eyelids and demure lips, seemed to endure the absurdity of fringed lampshades over their heads like Ascot hats with a dignity I really envied. Then she brought Sinclair a drink – bitter lemon again, I noticed.

The three of us stood close, too close for ease, while I used the opportunity to scrutinise him. We should have been rivals (hussar officers in a smart regiment and tight jackets coldly quarrelling over the next polka with the same partner) but he lounged there very casually, not bothering with me and confident enough of Mopsa's attention. I wished I had seen or played more tennis; apart from wondering if he knew Björn Borg, I could think of nothing to say.

He was, I realised, actually several years older than me. He wore his blond curly hair long, much longer than Mopsa's, in the way that used to be fashionable, and there were very slight lines around the brown eyes in his tanned face. Pretty was the word I should choose to describe him, when Mopsa asked me. He had on some sort of expensive gold necklet and matching bracelet which added to the prettiness. Some time ago I'd decided that for men personal jewellery was out.

'I booked our table for nine,' he said, finishing his bitter lemon with a gulp.

'Smashing,' Mopsa replied inanely. 'Oh, Nicko, do get yourself another drink, if you like.'

They were going out, and I was staying in. It made me feel ludicrously aged. I felt I ought to say gruffly, Hugh-style, 'take good care of her, young man – and don't stop out till all hours.' Don't sleep with her either, I might have added, surveying him as though his tendency to bulge out of his

15

clothes conveyed a threat to my little girl. Would Dennis have fancied him, I abruptly wondered, ten years ago? Extra coaching in tennis and talk of his being in the French play? I could see him as Néron in *Britannicus*.

'Look, don't let me keep you,' I said with suavity, unsure whether to go and take another slug of gin while they were still there.

'I do hope there's some supper for you, Nicko.' Mopsa made it a very final-sounding sentence. As if in extenuation she kissed me rather theatrically. 'Be as good as you can, angel boy.'

I almost expected a scowl from Sinclair but he seemed sportingly amiable now the real decision had gone in his favour.

'Nice meeting you, Nicko,' he said, extending a braceleted hand.

The familiarity of it required a killing bow, and I bowed as killingly as I could, though unclear how the effect so apparent when read about was actually achieved.

It was a relief that they had gone. I breathed in the emptiness of the large flat. A few telephone calls would rapidly alter that, of course, and I was briefly tempted by the prospect. But better was to explore it, unenviously, just wondering at the vacuity of it all, despite its long, carpeted corridor of numerous rooms. I found it hard to think of anything I called living going on in this atmosphere.

The kitchen was aseptic – rather too much so, I thought, as I noticed the semi-monastic still-life of plain white plate, tumbler, knife and fork set out for me. The plate was very different from Margot's green and gold dinner service; it might have borne on it the word 'Doggie'. Nor did Mrs Eckstein's idea of supper – cold ham in a plastic envelope and a rudimentary salad – seem any more alluring. In the fridge was an amoeba-like cluster of tins of lager; I tore one open and took it round with me on my inspection.

I knew there were no books in the flat. I bet there weren't many either in the adjoining flats. The occupants were mostly Margot and Hugh type people: just too busy, darling, for reading, except on holiday – and then the books could fortunately be abandoned once an amusing couple was encountered at the hotel.

Even sudden death wouldn't alter lives like theirs. Everything had been double-glazed and upholstered against noise

16

and sharp intrusion of any sort. Mopsa was too bright not to see it, but she hadn't moved out, had she? Instead, she still accepted a sort of rosebud décor for her room – I saw, as I peered in – that would have seemed soppy to Amelia Sedley.

Not rosebuds but something rich like rosewood, I presumed, plus heavy velvet and pseudo-tapestry characterised the furnishing of the bedroom Margot and Hugh shared. It was exactly the kind of room that Maigret instinctively enters on tip-toe, impressed somehow despite his distaste for it, and where the body of the shot husband is lying waxen and peaceful on the thick, embroidered counterpane. Someone has put a chaplet into the corpse's clasped hands, and it strikes an incongruous note in a setting that otherwise exudes an oddly Protestant air of prosperity.

I could see Hugh laid out there; and Margot, tearless and sleek as ever in something dark yet not black, making the Chief Inspector conscious of being out of place even while she deliberately put him at ease in her drawing-room.

That cheered me up a lot. I debated whether Margot had actually shot Hugh and if Simon Sinclair ought to be worked into the plot. Mopsa I didn't want involved except in so far as she caught my eye when, as his young assistant (younger than Lapointe), I accompanied Maigret on a return visit to interrogate Margot, who remained aloofly polite: 'Monsieur le Commissaire, permettez-moi de vous présenter ma fille.' I don't expect she concerned herself with me.

I was occupied looking into the other rooms, gathering atmosphere rather than searching very seriously for clues ('Rien de définitif, patron ...'), but by the time I reached the bathroom I had abandoned hope of even atmosphere. I was rather tired, in fact, and it seemed sensible to have a bath.

I liked the way the wall of mirror partly folded back, revealing shelves of welcome white towels stacked in an Alpine array. Maybe this was where the household really came to life; certainly, as I poked among the bathside jars and flasks (a surprising number of essences turned out to be Hugh's), I caught a flavour of personalities off-duty and alone. And I suppose I responded, or even invented the sensation, because it matched a private feeling of pleasure when I confronted nobody but myself.

I don't mean I was drawn to any life-long love-affair with

my reflection in mirrors. I stripped and ran the bath, almost indifferent to the several images that flashed across the room. The promise of the towels, I may as well confess, excited me more. Already when I was very young I had devised at bedtime a sort of bathroom-orient of heat and steam, with myself turbaned or swathed in a burnous-style towel against which my skin showed darker. My hair was dark and water darkened it more; in those days I regretted my jewel-blue eyes not being dark.

It was possible – quite likely – that I would enjoy draping myself in several of Margot's towels when eventually I got out of the bath. Perhaps then I might gaze into the long expanse of mirror. But I had made it a rule not to be the sort of insecure person who is always looking for and into them, arranging or disarranging his hair. Better to look into other peoples eyes. I had often wanted to tamper with Kipling's 'If' (some camp friend of Mother's must have given me a pseudo-illuminated copy of it when I was about twelve) and include an extra line, 'If you can walk past mirrors without glancing ...'

The bath water nuzzled and sucked gently at my body as I lay feeling agreeably bleached and increasingly brainless. My day disappeared like a layer of grime floating off, but even more soothing was the recession of the future. So much of my existence, increasingly as I got older, seemed concerned not with the quite complex process of what I was doing but with what I was going to do. Sometimes I felt like a new Saint Sebastian, stuck all over with questions fired at me like arrows: my career, the future, a job. It is extraordinary the amount of unflattering curiosity one provokes simply by growing up. It was as though nobody had foreseen this happening, couldn't quite believe it and wanted the pheno-menon got under control as quickly as possible. Even Mother sometimes asked vaguely what I 'wanted' to do. At school people were always cheerfully swapping putative careers as if they were cigarettes or contraceptives ('a friend of my father's is in computers and he says ...'). They didn't understand my refusal to play. Few of them dared to declare that they had no idea what they would be. But then few of them enjoyed the advantage of being fatherless.

Of course I had, and had had, plenty of surrogate fathers:

from a paternal old judge in chambers all the way to Dennis, via several of mother's rather ineffective lovers. I even had a godfather in the Reverend Philip Kerr, living at Spenn. My real father committed suicide five years ago. He and Mother were already divorced, amicably. He was a professional golfer, who got cancer. He shot himself. It was in the newspapers, but I've never wanted to look up what was said. It gave me a strange status for a period at my preparatory school, exciting more awe than pity and sealing me off from the other boys as someone to whom something alien had happened. That was how I too felt about it, because I had never seen much of my father. Secretly I was ashamed of how little his death mattered to me, and what I longed to unburden was not my grief but my indifference.

Mother always kept photographs of him beside her in her peripatetic, usually confused existence. I think she tended to forget about the divorce and definitely about his re-marriage to some girl who now lived in Nottingham. The photographs showed him tall and good-looking enough in a craggy way but suggested he was rather dim. I could easily have found out more about him from Philip, who had been a close friend of his – they were both obsessed by sport of all sorts – but I preferred the freedom of not knowing. Altogether, I had long realised, freedom was what I wanted.

'I am,' I could have shouted to the wall of mirror when I climbed out of the bath, letting my shout echo like a warning up and down the well of the mansion block. I don't suppose it would have caused much disturbance to the inhabitants. And anyway it seemed too childish a thing to do.

2

Mrs Rainbow was no more pleased to see me than usual – in so far as she could see me, screwing up her nasty little eyes and adjusting her ramshackle spectacles which I always suspected lacked lenses, though they increased her general air of disapproval.

'I'm off and the Rev's still out,' she greeted me in her depressed Midland whine.

'You ratbag,' I replied, though not until I had reached the privacy of my own room, up the dusty, fret-work staircase and past the ever-crooked grey-mounted photographs of Philip on the College barge, Philip brandishing a scull and looking like the Michelin-man in layers of sweater and scarf, and Philip easily the beefiest in some beefy winning Eights group at Oxford or Mortlake about fifteen years before I was born.

From the window of my room – a bedroom which doubled as lumber-room, holding a tin trunk and a perishing bag of golf clubs (could they once have belonged to my father?) – I saw Ratbag retreat across the scrubby patch of waste land sown with bits of brick which separated Philip's house from the rest of spick-and-span Spenn. Out of the detritus accumulating on that ground a demented child might have assembled Mrs Rainbow: with a strip of sodden eggbox as body, rusty barbed wire for hair and a couple of bottle-stoppers for her squat legs. Engendered in a plastic sack and *née* Bilgewater (I theorised), she had found a perfect mate in Rainbow, a sour runt of a man with a limp: an ex-jockey who would have given a midden a bad name.

'She'll do for you, all right,' I had cracked back at Philip when he feebly explained her services for the fifth time. Among the more printable of her disgusting doings, aside from her vacuuming his shabby carpets with an overcharged cleaner that always spilt fluff as she and it thumped over them, was the leaving of meals prepared for him out of God knows what household sweepings. Suet boiled in her headscarf, I suggested, but Philip remained robust and laughingly indifferent. I was carefully living off yoghurt and fresh fruit, which she couldn't tamper with, and I usually bore them off up to my room to avoid even seeing the nightly concoction Philip sat down to.

Of course, he really kept her on because of Rainbow and Rainbow's racing knowledge. It was the last sport he had become aware of, I suppose, and almost the only one he'd never taken part in. Funny old Philip. In middle age, after bumming round the world, he'd discovered God and horses.

He had been ordained and given a curacy in Spenn where the church rose prettily as a postcard adjunct to the pink-and-white-washed houses near the high street, and a few people still thought of getting married in it, mainly at weekends during the summer. Luckily, the vicar was not only as picturesque as the lych-gate, and as pink and white as the local plasterwork, but he really bloomed at summer weddings, especially when the photographers arrived.

That left Philip free to go pooping off on his heavy, old-fashioned BSA, with Rainbow riding pillion, to Newbury, Newmarket or even Goodwood. Sometimes they'd get as far as Thirsk: I liked to think of them appraising what are billed as two year-old maiden fillies running in something called the Abbey Lands Stakes at 4.45 (why do races so often start at these odd quarters to and past the hour?). If you asked Philip about Fonthill he'd have thought you meant Fontwell. A mention of *Mansfield Park* would lead him to Sandown Park and regret that he had been misled by Rainbow's stableyard tip in the Solario Stakes two years ago. Personally, I'd never put any faith in an animal called 'Rose of Slough'. The only time I had gone with Philip to a ghastly steeplechase it poured with rain and some tout or lout stole my wallet (and, like Mother, I always carry a lot of cash).

'Look on the bright side,' Philip adjured me absently, when I finally discovered the loss as I zipped up my new blue anorak and pulled its hood gloomily over my head. He was occupied quite seriously with binoculars and with exchanging arcane gobbets of information with a whole series of unsmiling, Rainbow-like little men who never gave me a glance.

'Which is?' I said, doing rather a good imitation of Dennis.

'What?' Philip asked vaguely.

'The bright side of this damp and depressing afternoon.'

'Well, there are the horses to look at – and it's good to be in the open air. You'll enjoy it much more once the race begins, though the going may be a bit slow.'

'You know, Philip.' I spoke with measured, impressive vehemence. 'I am not one of your moronic, antiquated parishioners who'll swallow any cliché from a man in a dog-collar.'

'Of course you aren't.' He sounded cheerful rather than hurt. 'Anyway, we don't need to give them a thought this afternoon. The horse to watch is that light-framed colt – the bay one.'

I shut both eyes as he pointed, and either raindrops or tears of boredom genuinely soaked my cheeks. I longed to beat my fists against Philip's stained and smelly Burberry, but that would have made no difference to it or him. Standing there, shivering in the pervasive dampness, I had felt the impotence of being still a child in Philip's friendly, unfocused consciousness – where I hung as inertly as the leather case of his binoculars, just one more item of what he liked to call his paraphernalia.

On the spot, keeping my eyes tightly closed, I founded the Blue-hooded Hedonists, an order only for people of perfect physical beauty. No one over the age of eighteen was admitted. The order's distinctive uniform consisted solely of a sky-blue hood and single blue gauntlet; each gauntlet was embroidered in seed pearls with the device of a phallus rampant encircled by the motto *'à mon plaisir.'*

That was a year or more ago, when I'd been (I could now admit) almost an infant. Yet, though I'd outgrown the anorak, I had not entirely given up the Blue-hooded Hedonists.

'You need a spot of faith in something,' was one of Philip's favourite philosophical observations, usually proffered with a protective apologetic laugh of the kind he used for serving sherry or confessing his attendance at annual College dinners where the quite innocent appeal was meeting again some 'men'. Often though I'd wilted under Philip's breezy obviousness (lather as he mentally was to Dennis's razor), perhaps the poor sod was not so far wrong. I believed in myself – most of the time – but I wouldn't have minded a group of chevaliers of the Blue Hood, or even the odd devoted squire or two. The trouble with my Order was filling its ranks, at least from what school offered in the way of candidates. I could always go on fantasising about our select company, or anyway a select companion (fair where I was dark, maybe even a little plump rather than thin ...) but it was lonely work.

I felt it more than ever this afternoon, as I sat in a pudding way on my bed with the sticky, summer evening sunlight pouring over me like treacle. The thought of Spenn for August, September and beyond seemed nearly as dreary as a term at school, but really it was more than that: much more. Kicking at my suitcase instead of unpacking it, I knew it had all happened – even while little appeared to happen – when Mopsa talked to me at our lunch which was meant to be so special. From that moment, the meal had literally gone sour. I didn't want to eat any more, and on the train to Spenn I nursed a stomach-ache which made me less inclined than usual to divert and dominate the passengers. They were poor pickings anyway, but I hadn't stepped off the train as quite my usual Orpheus-self, charming beastly people.

I stooped under the baskets of petunias which hung too low at intervals along the platform, watching my carriage-load disappear. 'Spenn' was picked out as freshly as ever in white-painted stones on the high, poisonously green bank of dyed chippings which concealed the car-park. Toy farmyard fencing led up to the station-master's timbered office which lacked only a thatched roof and crooked smoking chimney to qualify for the picturesque label on something like processed homely cheese.

I wouldn't have minded the picturesque addition of a welcoming chauffeur in matching green livery, to take the young master's suitcase and guide him to the waiting, petunia-coloured Porsche. Nothing, of course. I had to walk up the hot, empty platform, past the open-plan Gents which no amount of green paint could disguise, scarcely bothering to embarrass the departing passengers by friendly waves. I left behind the carriage-sprinkling I'd started with at Paddington: a middle-aged American couple, a bespectacled schoolboy with a boil and two sheep-like matrons who had been to a matinée, in pale pink trousers and toning hair. It was only the Americans' belief that they would at Aylesbury be visiting the cathedral that inspired me to mention the tombs there of the three royal brothers Richard I, Richard II and Richard III. They were grateful, of course, but I preferred some of my earlier tips for foreigners – like advising them on the Underground to enquire for trains going through to Cocksuckers.

Philip was much more disapproving than Dennis about this sort of thing. His fat, cheerful, pink face would crease faintly into puzzlement when I described my latest misleading of mere mortals; and shouting 'Puck' at him, in an attempt to help, only made him pout like a baby and grow pinker.

'I enjoy a joke as much as anyone,' he would say protestingly.

'In that case,' I liked asking, 'why watch television comedy?'

If there wasn't racing, or at least show-jumping, Philip would sit any evening in front of the television screen, bubbling and chuckling over the comedy shows until he had a coughing-fit, quite drowning out the pathetic titters of the studio audience.

Dennis, of course, never watched television at all. He made a point of listening to the radio. Still, it was Dennis, not Philip, who understood if I suddenly collapsed shrieking over a new slogan like 'Blind dogs for the Guides', or even 'Harp-ic, your Excellency.' I suppose Dennis would never have been a schoolmaster if he couldn't, in however superior a way, smile even at such efforts as the Pubic Wars (not mine but a cricketing oaf's, unconscious that for Dennis there was anyway a touch of appositeness under the joke).

How stupidly joyfully I had gone that morning to meet Mopsa, dancing along the Knightsbridge pavements like someone out of an old American musical. I couldn't be bothered to see if heads turned or what I looked like mirrored in the otherwise unrewarding expanse of shop windows. I guessed the place Mopsa had chosen would be fashionable, though hardly Mother's idea of posh, if not that I'd find myself waiting for her and a drink at a scrubbed table in a khaki-painted cellar where service came with a scowl, if at all; I almost wished I'd appeared in an Edwardian sailor-suit to make a clear assertion of style amid the porridge-coloured pullovers and unpressed sub-combat clothes which character-ised the clientèle and the crop-haired waiters. I've sat wait-ing for Mother at enough café and restaurant tables, so that was no ordeal; but Mother looks for service of the sort Queen Victoria got from Disraeli ('he'd have made a marvellous maitre d'hôtel,' she once told me, having been Mrs Disraeli in a radio play). As for dressing up, I think my style when I was younger may occasionally have embarrass-ingly approached the waiter-cum-ballet convention. Even Mother hadn't quite carried off the evening we arrived at a restaurant to find the waiters were not merely young and pretty (as then expected) but also wore my costume of flame-red shirt and flared black velvet trousers.

For Mopsa's place I was wearing a dead plain white shirt and very dark grey, narrow, flannel trousers: youthful if you like, but cool, straight and quite cunning, even sophisticated, in its simplicity. I felt angelically pure, clean and compact, down to my black and white canvas shoes and my zebra-striped underpants which Dennis had found for me in Mono-prix at – of all places – Auxerre; I hadn't worn them before. Most schoolboys would have dressed up, I bet, or aped the vicarage jumble-sale rubbish worn by the cellar-lot around me. Looking at them, as I kept signalling for a drink, I realised that at last Philip had accidentally stumbled into fashion, thanks to his effortlessly unstructured clothes, whereas Dennis would here have looked as quaint and provincially foppish as one of those funny, two-tone weathermen on television.

That thought depressed me but it vanished quickly as I found the hand I'd raised, hoping to arrest one of the passing escaped convicts, clasped by Mopsa who was lightly kissing the top of my head.

'I'm not late,' she said. 'But I thought you would be. A boy's privilege.'

I tried to get up from the table, scraping back my chair on the stone floor with a noise unpleasantly recalling the end of lessons at school. My attempt to embrace Mopsa left me awkwardly clutching at a fold of her loose, cocoa-coloured dress while she sat down calmly smiling, adjusting a row of thin, blue-glass bracelets on her bare arm. Besides, I suddenly noticed, our table had been overshadowed by a bulky presence: a white-bearded man with fat fingers splayed over Mopsa's shoulder and a grinning, frog-like face, as creased and almost as dingy as his planter's suit.

'Mopsa, my darling, you must have a drink,' he said possessively.

'We'd love one, Rory,' she responded, with a glance towards me.

'A Pernod,' I said, willing him to disappear.

'No,' he replied. 'We don't serve Pernod – can't stand the stuff. Have a Campari.'

'I'd like a bitter-lemon,' Mopsa said.

'Then so would I,' I said curtly, not looking up.

'Come and see what's cooking,' he told Mopsa, as slowly he withdrew his hand and shuffled away.

'Who,' I had to ask, though impatient to start talking of other things, 'is King Leer? And don't tell me he's sweet really.'

'Rory owns the place – and he is a marvellous cook. You mustn't mind him.'

'I shan't. And I know what I'm having for my main course – doigts du patron flambés'.

Unfortunately, there wasn't a cleaver in sight when we got into the kitchen and watched Rory among his copper saucepans – a candidate for assault and *batterie de cuisine* – posing for some Colour Magazine feature I hoped would never appear.

'Ecoute, Mopsa,' I began, as soon as we were seated again. At least a carafe of promised 'rough' red wine had by then reached the table and I could put aside the dreadfully soppy pith-and-fizz I'd only ordered in temper. Rory's red wine turned out to be oddly good; perhaps I ought to have trusted Mopsa's judgment after all, as usually I did.

'J'ai quelque chose de très grande importance à te dire.'

'I'm with you so far,' she said. 'But can the rest be in English? I don't want to miss it.'

It took me a moment reflecting that 'importance' must be feminine, mustn't it, before I could respond. And then when I looked across at her she seemed a little tense even while she smiled and shook her always strangely pale, almost colourless hair, to adjust its ringlets around her pointed face.

'Ah,' I said appreciatively, longing to start a formal address: 'Madame' or 'Très belle Princesse'. Instead, I toasted her silently as I drank some more wine.

'I haven't told anyone else, but the thing is – ' I paused, then rushed on. 'The thing is, I've decided to leave school.'

It might have been what the waiter was waiting for, banging down the pottery platters with Mopsa's sea-food salad and for me two avocado halves ruined by a rash of pink shrimps which I had specifically not ordered.

'I'm glad,' she said, lightly. 'That's super news.'

'You don't seem very surprised.' Or interested, I suddenly felt like adding, seeing how enthusiastically she crunched and dug into her heaped-up plate.

'Should I be? It seems tremendously sensible. I can't think they had anything more to teach you, and didn't you tell me ages ago that "d" was silent in boarding school?'

'Maybe.' I wanted more pondered thought on my step. 'But I've still got to break it to Philip, and even Mother might make a fuss. They'll wonder what I'll do.'

'And what will you do?'

'I don't know. I could go abroad, I suppose – ' Like old Philip once did, I thought ruefully.

'Oughtn't you to go to a university?' She glanced up at me, concerned. 'Wasn't your avocado ripe?'

'No. Yes,' I replied. 'Actually there's a difference between crevette and vinaigrette, but it doesn't matter – now. My ecology means save shrimps as well as whales. As for education, I don't feel like any more education; I've been educated. Now I want a change.'

'You'll have to do something, Nicko. Have you any ideas?'

'Plenty. I'm full of ideas, but they aren't for anything as tedious as a career.'

'What *do* you want?'

'To be happy, of course. Don't you?'

'Obviously. Very much so.' She shot a smile like a kiss towards me. 'I'm trying hard.'

'Moi aussi.'

I returned her smile. I never feel I've quite mastered this convention. It seems such a conscious grimacing: the social semaphoring of emotions which shouldn't need overt display. Only with Mopsa did I manage it at all instinctively. I wanted to signal back that I shared her target. Get happiness, I might have snapped in some *film noir,* as if it was somebody to be gunned down.

She caught at my wrist gently, as though checking my pulse. Solemnly I laid my hand over hers.

'I plight thee my troth,' I intoned.

Now she laughed. 'Actually, Nicko, I had something to tell you. I haven't told anyone else yet.'

'A girlish secret?'

'Naturally.' I felt her fingers under mine shift and tauten. 'It's to do with happiness – mine, I mean. I'm going to marry Simon Sinclair.'

'What?'

I ought to have been on my feet shouting, the table overturned and the whole restaurant frozen into apprehensive silence. Nothing seemed to happen, except that I clutched my wine glass and went on sitting there, feeling quite sick.

'Marry him? You can't mean it. You haven't even slept with him. For God's sake, how bourgeois – bourgeoise – can you possibly get?'

'I should have thought I'd answered that. And, if you must know, your information's out of date, since last night.'

'Mopsa, you're mad. One night with that Slazenger's advertisement and you're going to marry him? Oh, come on. Sleep with him, till he doesn't know his backhand from his forehand, if you like. Go and live with him, if you must. I don't care.'

'Thanks.'

'No, Mopsa, you can't do this. Look at your parents – they're married all right.'

I was determined to save her from disappearing down some pseudo-Gothic aisle in a cloud of lace and confetti, leaning on Sinclair's smug, muscled arm, to the fate of a cake decorated with silver-paper racquets.

'You must be mad,' I said again. 'Where would you get married? Lillywhites?'

'You're being rather foul,' she said. 'Don't be envious; I didn't expect that.'

'Envious? God, I'm not envious – just shocked.'

I looked up and saw how hard her face had grown: hard and alien, as if carved out of shell, calm yet quite unyielding. I meant mine to harden too and my eyes to blaze, striking sparks off the cameo surface of her features.

'It's so trite and hackneyed and stupid. And utterly unlike you.'

'Are you sure?' she asked coolly.

If I were Renaissance prince, I'd have had her haled before me as soon as I heard the news. Perhaps I'd have threatened her with torture. Briefly, she'd defy me, and that defiance would give the final excitement to our confrontation as cousins – and more than cousins. I could see Mopsa almost swamped by some velvety, heavily patterned gown, at first proud, then sinking slowly, shaken by sobs, to fold around my knees – shown to advantage in tights – and confessing that the person she really loved was me.

'We could go away together,' I said. 'Let's do that, Mopsa. We've never been abroad, and I'm free. It'll give you time to think.'

'About what?'

'This ghastly marriage idea, of course – his idea, I bet.'

'You bet wrong. We happen to be in love, which I suppose is hackneyed. And last night – well, this morning – I proposed to him.'

'He would accept; I can see that. He would. He's just the sort of person who would want to be married. He probably needs a wife. That's it – a wife in every court. And you'd give up your life to be dragged around dreary sea-side resorts, watching while he practises his stupid service or something. You'd have to do all the packing too, I expect. And probably wash his filthy clothes – as well as having hundreds of children born with gold bracelets and soppy, shoulder-length hair. I mean it, Mopsa.'

'Maybe it's what I want. I'm more conventional than you ever cared to recognise.'

'I don't believe it.'

'We're not soul-mates, you know. Only cousins.'

'Not even that, from the way you're behaving. Mopsa, please. It's a fatal thing to do. We'd never see each other.'

'It's my life, isn't it? Sorry to have shocked you. For the rest, that's up to you.'

'You really want to tie yourself legally to someone you'll be sick of in about two years? What on earth for?'

'Obviously, you wouldn't understand. It's pointless to go on.'

'No, it's not,' I groaned. 'I care for you, Mopsa, can't you understand that? And now I'll have no one.'

'Get someone. I thought you were the focus of attention wherever you went. And anyway didn't you tell me last Christmas there was some coffee-coloured tart who fancied you in the supermarket at Spenn?'

'I'm talking about something serious.'

'So am I. But we're talking two different languages. Now please shut up about Simon and me.'

I longed to lay my head on the table and moan aloud until they sent for a doctor. My weakness was no joke. It really was a physical dissolution which I thought of as literally losing heart. I had lost Mopsa, and I welcomed the possibility of losing consciousness. The future was blank, but that frightened me far less than my abrupt sense that the past had been a blank. For Mopsa, it had been a game, at best. I had never properly been there: not the living, feeling being I knew myself to be – that I had often enough asserted I was. Now it was as though she had extinguished me, even while I struggled. Shut up I was indeed: compressed as if into a box, with the lid firmly closed and sealed. From a distance I could hear her telling Sinclair what fun it had all been, charming, rather touching ... And inside that box I was impotent, being carried away from them, growing gradually unable to struggle any longer; and soon I knew I should cease to exist. That feeling was what I was fighting – vainly – as I sat kicking my suitcase to death in sunny summer-evening Spenn. The soft grey leather of it wouldn't resist; it just lay there flabbily, not making a sound yet obstinately surviving my attack.

It had spilt most of its guts in the shape of my clothes, and after a while there would be nothing to do but pick them up and put them away. I thought again of Mopsa and of what I had prophesied. She was doomed to packing and unpacking in endless hotel rooms, handling Sinclair's shirts, his shorts – himself for all I cared – and she wanted it to be like that.

'Why not? I always meant to marry someone,' she had said to me finally before we left the wretched restaurant. I made no reply. I was still too confused to put my hand on the right cutting weapon – and growing afraid that in fact my armoury lacked it.

Outside, in the street, her face had looked as hard as ever, petrified, aloof, untouchable and undamageable by me. I suddenly realised she was the perfect offspring of Margot and Hugh: such a wonderfully well-polished simulacrum of a human being that I had been deceived. In turn, I would be hard and unyielding, though I knew my stiffness was all on the surface. She had only to let her bare arm brush mine and I'd crack open as sweetly as the top of a crême brulée.

But she held herself very much away from me. We had walked aimlessly a few yards, faced each other, juxtaposed yet as lacking in contact as two chessmen. Why, I wondered now, hadn't I hooked a finger under one of her glass bracelets, launched a last appeal, or knelt in the street so that she had at least to pause? Instead, I found myself swept along at her pace, marching silently, as if to the scaffold signalled by the rising concrete gibbet of a bus stop.

'I'm going back to the office,' she said, stopping to join the straggling cluster of the queue without glancing at me.

It wasn't the best setting for drama or a speech. The extras around looked of poor quality, faded indifferent, and – despite the fact that two were Arabs – left out too long in the sun.

'Thanks for lunch,' I muttered feebly.

She shrugged, and her sulkiness made me angry. I saw a bus approaching. She would take it, I guessed, if only to leave me, and I still searched for the word that might halt the traffic, bring her round, literally, and set us on an island site – one where amber lights flashed warnings to keep clear.

'Goodbye,' Mopsa said. 'Let's meet when you recover.'

I pushed forward as she moved to step on the bus.

'Listen,' I began.

'Are you or are you not getting on this bus?' I heard a man – educated, by the sound, at Harrods – demanding loudly behind me. I ought to have jumped on to it then, punched the bell and shouted, 'Selfridges, and drive like hell.' Near-castration from his rolled umbrella flying out at an angle made me dodge when he leapt for the platform as the bus pulled away. From behind I saw only a blue, pin-striped back and horribly florid fair hair. It should have been Simon Sinclair. And he should have slipped.

Sitting on my bed, I distinctly watched him miss his footing and fall painfully into the gutter. A touch of something red that wasn't blood was visible beside him, a carnation from his button-hole or perhaps a silk handkerchief from his breast-pocket, looking incongruous amid the dusty trash of discarded tickets and other litter accumulated at the kerb. I might bend ostentatiously to retrieve it, leaving him to scramble slowly and stiffly to his feet, bruised, dazed and now dusty himself from rolling in the road.

It didn't help a great deal. It was difficult to know what would, as I surveyed the deepening custard-coloured walls of the flimsy room: like living in an empty ice-cream carton since Philip had brightened it up so hastily that fat flecks of yellow paint spotted the windows, hardened now and resistant to being scraped away with a fingernail.

For something to do, I got up with exaggerated energy and peeled off my slightly tacky shirt and then my trousers.

Stripped for action; but there wasn't any action. Besides, something heavy and incongruous remained about shoes and socks, so I took them off as well. Aerial, if not positively Ariel, and certainly elemental was what I felt I should become, but for once it seemed it wouldn't work.

I remained very much earth-bound, unexcited, as I ran my hands over my torso, making a celestial body-check, as if in search of sprouting wings. My hands paused, poised, over my crotch – but that was too vulgar, too lonely, too obviously a *recherche* of *temps perdu* in Brixton yesterday (if it was only yesterday). I braced myself by a snap of the elastic rim of my underpants. Equipped only with them and my large watch – non-digital, non-trendy though it deliberately was – I could have stepped from outer space to destroy Spenn, even though little of it was visible except television masts rising stiffly against its crooked chimney pots.

The very curve of its high street would straighten out under the first impact of the ray I directed at it. Bottle-glass melted in the panes of the antique shops full of tea-pots and the cafés full of copper hunting-horns. In an instant the puce and gold capitals and cursive on the bow-fronted facade of *AMANDA for Chocolates* had blistered and dissolved. Amanda herself, just smilingly packing an ounce of something expensive in a pound of puce and gold paper for two grateful tourists, would go more slowly: first her finger holding out the looped package turned as grey as her hair, then it and the package crumpled into powder on the counter. The visitors fled screaming towards a parked car long since buckled into a twisted heap of scrap. I spared the supermarket, on account of its yoghurt more than for Sadie, its dubiously coloured teenage tart, who would giggle and rattle her beaded hair as she totted up my tower of cartons. There was panic in the near-Palladian bank where I had often had to listen to homilies from the self-consciously youthful, squash-playing manager: privilege of an account … your age … not questioning of course your mother's wisdom. Six gilt buttons off one of his fearful, Melton cloth waistcoats were all that would be found – apart from an indestructible onyx desk-set, ideal for his grave – amid the charred bricks I surveyed, murmuring sardonically, with overtones of the morgue, 'return to drawer.'

A sense of mission accomplished invested me as I put on a

motto-less white tee shirt and cream jeans, and ran weight-lessly downstairs. Philip's absence gave me a chance to check up in his dusty den on his existence as curé de campagne, English-style. Even the sunlight, with real motes in it, filtering through the faded cretonne curtains, looked and seemed somehow to smell English. The sherry decanter on its brass tray was an advertisement in itself. What would Maigret have made of that? Something to do with the Protestant rite? A confession of weakness, or declaration of being above temptation, in a household unable to offer the police a vermouth or even a glass of local white wine?

Shoving the *Radio Times* off a rush-plaited stool, I sat down with the slim clues from the mantelpiece, where Philip propped papers amid the souvenirs of his travels: rows of glass animals, a Japanese doll, and some pink and yellow china spoons that might have come from China. I wanted Philip to have some sort of secret life, and Sadie kept hinting, with a wriggle of her skinny, sand-coloured body that he was mad about skinny teenage girls sexy and silly like herself ('nobody could conceivably be as silly as you,' I'd told her, fighting off her advances in a field near the river, but she just went on giggling and wriggling). Boys certainly didn't interest him. I felt convinced of that only too well; and of course I had long ago realised that any scribbled note of Philip's with a name and a time on it must refer to no rendez-vous with a parishioner but to a horse.

This afternoon there wasn't even that. A bill for repairing his motor bike, two advertisements for summer jackets in crease-resistant, clerical-grey drablon and a blurred, cyclo-styled invitation to join the fandango at the Youth Club's impending 'Spennish Evening' seemed to tell all, until I spotted the gigantic green ink semi-capitals which spelt Mother. It was a postcard of Chiswick Flyover with a Portu-guese stamp, but I felt glad just to see it. Come to that, I wouldn't have minded seeing Mother herself, manifested in the grotty room, accompanied though she doubtless would have been by some ageing 'Darling Boy' of a lover. It seemed too long since I had talked to her, and nothing could be deduced from the message to Philip except that Matilda (underlined three times) was tedious beyond something, while somebody – looked like Stephen – was unexpectedly angelic.

I hoped I never had to sit through the film, but the thought of Mother's plummy tones describing life off the set made me smile, though I wanted to be sad and think of Mopsa. Somewhere in Portugal she was making 'Lady of England', all about a twelfth-century royal battle-axe-cum-frump who helped to darken the Dark Ages before disappearing from history. In Mother's film, I knew, Matilda would come on like Florence Nightingale crossed with Queen Elizabeth I, since it was backed by the strongly feminist Boadicea ('Drive Men out of Britain') Group. 'Boa-constrictor,' Mother had dubbed it. 'But, darling, I couldn't care less. I'd play Henry VIII in a film backed by the Vatican.'

As I sat there, balancing her card on my knees, I reflected that she would too – and she'd be pretty good. Perhaps she wasn't so good at being a mother if one meant it in a conventional maternal sense, all smother love. She had audibly sighed with relief at the speed I grew up. Not to be tiresome was what she had asked, only gradually realising that I was much more: better-looking and far better company than the sad-fag actors she usually took and converted into lovers. Just for this afternoon – evening, by now – I longed almost guiltily for her to be less admiring, less amused, less convinced of my cool attitude to things.

It was a bit late to relapse into being a tiny child, but I drew up my knees and clasped my hands tightly round them, shutting my eyes as I did so. I felt myself suddenly become a ball of desperate misery. It was dark. I had gone blind. A poor blind boy, alone in the world, a beggar-boy, a waif, whose sharp knees and thin arms increased his poignant appeal as he rocked himself in a trance of grief, on an outcrop of stone beside the cold sea-shore of some Northern coast where the only sound was the icy slap of the remorseless, incoming tide.

I nearly overbalanced at a touch on my knee. I looked up startled. Mother's card fell to the floor.

'Hullo, old chap,' Philip was saying. 'I didn't expect you so soon. Are you all right?'

'Perfect.' I got up awkwardly, feeling rather stiff. 'Perfect.'

'It's awfully hot in here. Been very hot the last few days.'

I watched him drift like a grey dirigible, softly but inevitably, towards the decanter, longing to halt him with a cry of 'it's poisoned!' How puzzled his shiny pink features would be as they turned, with dawning horror, towards me. Mrs Rainbow did it: secretly hated your influence over Rainbow, always detested me, typical housekeeper syndrome, malice accumulating over the years, like her pension.

'Shall we have a spot of sherry,' he said.

3

Each morning I woke to relentless sunshine, beaming round the room as if operated by a tipsy lighthouse keeper, when it ought to have been raining – was raining, pouring, as far as my mental state was concerned. 'Sunlight can damage your health,' I would mutter, twisting the sheet into a tight toga-cum-burnous effect and quite enjoying the contrast of my slim, increasingly tanned arm against the white cotton: as appetising as biscuit and vanilla cream. I was now almost Sadie-coloured, and I felt it must have come from rolling around with her on the river bank on the numerous afternoons she took off ('My uncle give me French leave,' she tittered. 'No,' I replied sternly, 'he didn't. That's not the idiom. And no,' yet more sternly. 'Leave my crotch alone.')

I had chalked 'L'avenir?' on the bedroom door, like something I had to learn by heart. Of course, even the door didn't fit properly, and as I lay there I would hear it rattling cheerfully while Philip literally jogged along to the bath-room, usually whistling or singing some snatch of pop-song so archaic that it seemed to derive, I thought, from the days not of radio but of the crystal set.

'Is it really "There'll be *blue*birds over the white cliffs of Dover"?' I had to ask, after having previously made him blush by enquiring one morning at breakfast about what I'd heard sung of the activities of something called the 'love-bug': 'The love-bug will bite you if you don't look out, If the love-bug bites you, you'll sing and you'll shout'.

'During the war, you know,' Philip mumbled. 'Lots of silly

songs like that, and it's jolly hard not to be stuck with them. I hadn't really thought about the words. I just like the tunes.'

'So I hear,' I said smartly, as he fell into a humming mood over the marmalade. The odd thing was that Philip – I had ruefully to recognise – possessed an instinctively tuneful voice. A squeak or a bellow ought to have issued from such naturally blubber-like lips, faintly mauve tinted, incongruously small in the crumpled expanse of his face: Mr Sun-man, all right, grinning inanely, from the back of some over-coloured cereal packet, always rising and never setting. I couldn't quite forgive that musical gift, especially when wasted on such improbable goals as to find a little nest, away out in the West

> "And let the rest
> Of the world go by."

At school I never minded not being in the choir, or not too much anyway, since the opportunities for acolytes during the services were actually greater; it was more effective to give visual force to the old cliché of being seen and not heard. Still, I had myself been absurdly moved by the soaring total purity of voice of some otherwise smutty, only too solid, stolid boy treble, temporarily transformed on a Sunday into an alien ethereal being as he grew rapt, listening to his own tones.

Certainly I theoretically raised the musical standards of Philip's establishment, as well as got in a satiric jab (too subtle for him to notice) when I descended the stairs solemnly singing, 'And in my vest shall I see God.' Yet I knew I wasn't entirely in tune, and Philip's bright morning smile did not hide his awareness too. I dreaded the day I came down to find him fumbling, mumbling and pinker than ever, but effortlessly whistling the correct notes.

That would at least break the routine of our breakfasts together, passing the plates and exchanging enquiries – or rather, my answering tepidly Philip's absent ones – until I could have shrieked with frustration. Is this life, I longed to yell, as I stared at the sticky spoon with its enamelled heraldic crest of Bognor Regis which protruded from the pottery hive of the marmalade pot, its lid topped by a clumsily modelled bee.

'My favourite meal,' Philip remarked nearly every morning, usually before inserting a further piece of flabby white bread in the mildly corroded pop-up toaster. 'What about you, old boy? More toast?'

'Man does not live by toast alone,' I finally retorted, helping myself from the Ryvita packet.

'True, true.' He smiled and put up a hand to one of his few remaining, positively silvery curls, as if to reassure himself it had not blown away in the night. 'Want the paper, Nicky?'

'I suppose Sung Eucharist won the 2.45, did it, by a short head from Vicar's Folly and Curate's Egg in the Church Plate?'

The toaster pinged complacently. Presumably it would go on pinging until someone tore the plug from the socket or hacked at the flex with explosive results. The incident might not make *The Times* but it would undoubtedly be on the front page of next week's *Bucks Bugle,* displacing police puzzlement over death of ex-mayor's sister-in-law in luxury bungalow bathroom: 'Boy hero saves godfather at blazing breakfast table ... Godson's prompt action a miracle declares greying Rev. Philip Kerr, 51, still dazed by domestic drama.' I could expect a rotten photograph, of course, judging by most of the smudged daguerreotypes posing as likenesses in the local paper. Still, that bloody toaster would never ping again, and Philip would be reduced to Ryvita.

Yet all over England toasters would go on being switched on, down the years, until the ping of doom. Technology would soon offer the friendly talking toaster (British Rail style): 'Good morning, today's toast is available in two sizes, businessman's special, big, extra crunchy, and slim-style, lightly done, for the lady of the house.' And, oh God, my future might consist of coming down daily to eat in some nook adjoining a spotless pitch-pine kitchen where a porcelain wife matching the striped blue-and-white breakfast china was, with sickening vivacity, preparing for school a pair of even more vivacious children, one of each sex and suggestive down to contour of a salt-and-pepper set.

And that would be if I was, as people say, lucky. She would probably be called Caroline, the children Justin, Jon or even Jason, and Candida or Annabel ... maybe Zoe. I'd never feel I'd begotten them, however much people admired their looks, anymore than I'd begotten the two cars standing outside on the curve of gravel we called the drive. It would mean nothing to me that Zoe, or whoever, was brilliant at maths while the boy was mad about cars. It wouldn't really be me a rather lanky, unloveable, faintly aggressive youth, fair like his mother, approached asking, 'Dad, could I borrow yours tonight – if I clean it on Sunday?' I might die, but surely never come to that.

'Mother, mother,' I wordlessly called across the litter of Philip's table.

She ought to have sent me a postcard, whereas all I had received was one from Dennis (typically in an envelope, thank goodness) which I'd thrust into the back pocket of my jeans and – symbolically, no doubt – let get crushed as I rolled around fighting off Sadie's crude assaults. His neat italic hand might look prim, though what he conveyed was the very opposite. But an awkward weekend at his parents' house near Brighton was not an answer to anything for me. ('No, Major Rickard, I don't play golf – my dead father did though, rather well. Yes, Mrs Rickard, I'm sure it would be nice if Dennis settled down and got married'.) And no, Dennis, I should not like to go to France again. I can't be bothered to explain why: just not. I decline to 'remember Auxerre', though actually I think it was there one rainy morning as we retreated into the hotel for our macs that I blurted out by mistake to Madame at the desk, 'il pleure.' She thought that truly a touch of the poetic. Dennis, characteristically, was annoyed.

How, I longed to ask someone – not Dennis (only complicate things), not Mother (too tactless), so perhaps ce gros monsieur Philip – does one grow up, grow old. But that wasn't quite my question. What I wanted to know was: how do you go *on?* Go on over the years doing things like cutting your toenails until the merciful day you can't any longer reach or see them? I felt fairly sure I'd be dead before then.

Beastly shock for Caroline to find me crumpled up in the garage – no, the garden shed – beside the shiny new motor-mower or possibly floating in the swimming-pool, only a few days after we had had it cleaned out. She could tell the Coroner in a tremulously brave, black-edged voice that we had no marital problems, no financial ones, children virtually off our hands, looking forward to many more years of happiness (gulp) together ... Many more years of that bloody blue-

and-white breakfast china which I'd often longed to throw out since it obviously never wore out, rarely chipped and appeared unbreakable. Of opening the linen cupboard and never failing to find a fresh stack of ironed shirts and clean socks (the children never failed to give them to me for my birthday), opening my desk on Sundays to find my cheque book and pay the gas bill, the water rate (extra for our hoses) and look through a few travel brochures for our summer holiday (Corfu, as usual).

But suicidal though that routine might make me, it would be – in the end – being driven to the walnut dressing-table drawer yet once more, seizing its silly moulded metal tassel of a handle and taking out the nail scissors that triggered my action: pausing, with my left foot already propped up, to real-ise that I was on the point of starting a second mile of nail clip-pings. No wonder it was there that I stopped, and quit, leav-ing Caroline and the Coroner equally baffled over motive.

Philip, I estimated, must be well into his third mile, and he showed no signs of stopping. In a jiffy, as he would remark, he would get up and carry the breakfast things through to the kitchen before the hag Rainbow arrived to 'do' for us. Perhaps she – donning the armour of a dingy nylon overall on which the splashy daisies and marigolds had long ago wilted to washed-out blurs of yellow and orange, and settling to drown crockery and crusts of toast in two inches of warm water – was the person who really held the secret of survival. She looked indestructible all right: as unchanging over the years I'd known her as a cartoon character. Still, I was hardly going to ask her for elucidation – not that she'd have given me it (or anything else). I didn't like to think of her living at all: sleeping beside, even – ghastly thought – with, Rainbow, climbing out of a rubbish-dump bed and putting on some fearful Coke tin-like corset and once more stumping into sullen life on her squat little legs.

Philip, and Rainbow too, and the population of Spenn, just got up and went on, day after day, never asking why they found themselves sitting on the side of the bed pulling on their stockings or socks (Philip's always grey and long and hairy, regardless of the time of year), squeezing out the last half wriggle of toothpaste, making a note to buy another tube as if guaranteed something to plan for (and the comfort of knowing that as long as you had teeth you were needed by somebody – the toothpaste manufacturers), fitting up their bodies daily and volunteering for active service which never came. What, I longed to know, gave them the staying power to keep their seats on the un-merry-go-round which bore them through their jobs, their visits to the pubs or the shops, taking children on board, waving regularly to passing neighbours, dipping and rising to inane music as they bent to tend now their beds of sweet-peas and now their pools coupons? Tomorrow was always the inducement, I suppose: better weather then, more money then, and the very fact that there was a tomorrow around the other side of the carousel – only, when you got there it turned out to be the same old places and faces, to the sound of the same old music.

I liked to think that I would bring the whole thing to a violent halt, jamming on some lever that sent everyone tumbling off those grotesque wooden animals, so solid, secure and unyielding, and smashing everything to smithereens (whatever they were) in a jumble of greasy machinery, bits of tatty roundabout and fragments of possessions spread out like the débris of an air crash.

If I took an inventory of Philip's claims on life while he nursed the remains of his too-large breakfast cup of tea, it made a pathetic list, a pauper wardrobe in its sparseness. The races, his motorbike, church services, doing good in Spenn – where the nearest thing to a derelict was the drunken cripple who occasionally helped out by spilling tacks all over the floor at the ironmonger's in the high street, and where in a peculiar mixture of sherry and sympathy Philip advertised his willingness on Wednesday and Friday evenings to see young people – usually girls with problems (much to Mrs Rainbow's disapproval). At the bottom of the sad pile of interests and aspirations, lay, I suspected, a folded, never-used or avowed *tendresse* for Mother, born perhaps out of some romantic feeling for the ex-wife of his best friend.

This morning, not tomorrow or the day after, I had resolved I must talk to Philip. He would help me. Perhaps it was with Mother that I should begin, though it was about myself I wanted to speak. I really meant to – I felt too miserable not to burst out in the short time remaining before Mrs Rainbow clattered at the door – but the sight of Philip's meaty pink wrist protruding from a flapping cuff from which the button had broken off, leaving, held by a cotton thread, a useless segment of mother-of-pearl, abruptly increased my despair. It would have to be another day. Then without warning and yet as if rehearsed, he began.

'I've been wondering, Nicky. I'm always delighted to have you, you know that, but it's awfully boring for you here. Hardly any young people of your sort around. It's bound to be dull, I'm afraid, all through the summer.'

'I amuse myself,' I said, unprepared, with automatic defensiveness which already seemed an error as I heard myself uttering the words.

'Still, it's lonely. And I'm not much company for you, old chap. So – ' He hesitated. 'So I wondered what your plans might be. For the holidays, I mean. Going to see much of Mopsa?'

'We leave for Trebizond on Tuesday. Would we did. But am I in your way? Has the vicar complained? Or hag Rainbow? She's annoyed I won't let her enter my bedroom?'

'Not at all,' he said heartily. 'As long as it suits you here. But I've never felt Spenn was quite your – your scene. You're usually off pretty quick.'

I bit back that I had nowhere to go. Suddenly I didn't want to confide in Philip; my instinct had been right, and now I felt both humiliated and angry. He misread the expression which, despite myself, must have trickled onto my face.

'I'm not prying, Nicky. I know you like to lead your own life.'

'Lead, kindly life.'

'What?'

'A joke – I think.'

'I see. Well, I ought to be getting a move on. You take your time. And of course stay here as long as you like – it's no bother to me.'

He put down his cup and got to his feet.

'I might want to bother you, Philip.'

'You won't,' he said, laughing as he misheard or misunderstood.

For a terrible moment I thought I was actually going to burst into tears. The arrival of Mrs Rainbow, coming in like tongs falling on a tin tray, checked me.

'Lovely morning again, Mrs R.,' Philip sang out in near-descant.

'It won't last,' she sniffed, starting to attack the breakfast-table. I got up and moved away, grabbing my denim jacket from a chair before she could contaminate it by proximity.

'Super day for a funeral,' I said. 'Not a cloud over the crematorium, so far.'

I hadn't time to run boyishly full-tilt into her as she turned with a tray of piled crockery ('Lawks, Master Nicholas,' you wouldn't hear her comfortably exclaim. 'No use crying over spilt milk. Never you mind. I'll be baking this morning, and you know how you love my deep apple pies.')

Slamming the front door, I set off for the supermarket. It was tucked well away down a side street, near the Laundro-mat, so that driving through Spenn you saw only the gleam of antique shops and tea shops, interspersed by half-lowered awnings over windows where embalmed in a stately way stood a coffee-roaster and a few ginger-jars, like the double-fronted establishment of 'Cherry and Sons, High Class Groceries and Provisions.' Inside, even deaf and daft Mr Cherry had arranged the shop on self-service principles, though he liked to accompany customers ceremonially on their rounds before taking his place, rather flustered, at the till, which under his arthritic hands usually jammed as he pressed the first price.

Very different was the shabby but always busy 'Nuros-wamy Nu Shop' where Sadie chattered and banged away at the checkout as if playing the piano in a honky-tonk somewhere between Basra and Bombay. Various fat, mous-tached, middle-aged Asians in very white shirt-sleeves stood around and constantly gave harsh orders to each other to lug bulging sacks in and out of the shop. All of them, according to Sadie, were her cousins, except the eldest, Jack, who was her uncle. I suppose she'd already slept with them all – judg-ing by their indifference to her – but Jack was her boss and still went to bed with her (she said) at the back of the shop.

'Anyway, it would be horribly uncomfortable,' I'd told her. 'And you're such a bloody little liar.'

She had giggled as usual. 'It's great, man. I'll show you – come on. You just settle on to those sacks. I'll show you.'

'For Christ's sake, stop it.'

Two yoghurt cartons had rolled to the floor as on that occasion I'd tried to protect myself. Nobody in the shop seemed very interested. When I want rape, I thought, I'll call for it – but at present Sadie made a change. And as long as I resisted her (as I certainly meant to) she must want me. I was one of the few males in Spenn she hadn't had.

'What about the Vicar?' I had asked before I knew her well.

'Poo, he tried but he's too old for me. One evening late he come into the shop and guess, man, where he put his hand.'

'On your shoulder?'

'I don't keep my shoulder up my skirt.'

'You don't keep much hidden up your skirt. He probably wanted to help you adjust your dress before leaving – teach you some English manners.'

'I learn from Len. You know the blond fella at the butcher's? He's fantastic, man – best lover I ever had. For his age. And he's smashing, really handsome – maybe more handsome than you.'

'If you mean the pimply, anaemic lout who cycles around in a bloodstained apron, your eyes must be as dim as your brain. Now stop this soppy chatter and add up five yoghurts and three packets of crisps – if you can.'

'See you at the disco tonight?'

'I've a proper date, in London – dinner, candlelight, sophistication. Not your thing.'

'Who needs candlelight?' she had hooted after me as I virtually swept out triumphantly with my purchases and my total lie.

In a bitter way, it was funny to think of Mopsa herself as no more real to me now than had been that particular evening. I could almost believe she had never sat opposite me in a restaurant, that I hadn't moved some horrible arrangement of frozen rose-buds to see her eyes better as she smiled across the fan of floppy menu or left me her lighter to play with while she went to the lavatory.

Spenn high street was as over-animated as if being filmed for some typical TV series, 'What hope our Heritage?' presented by a silly-ass actor in a polo-necked pullover and blazer, combining suggestions of cricket-pitch and show-jumping; without seeing, you knew he was wearing hush

puppies. Too much arc light sun was flaring on the roofs of busy little cars pulling up and driving off in a hectic shoppers' rally, inspired, I hoped, by rumours that food-rationing and nuclear holocaust both threatened Spenn.

In front of the church I noticed the announcement of a special service to welcome the arrival at Spenn Common of the latest missiles – something Philip had carefully not mentioned to me. ('Vouchsafe, O Lord, to bless these humble instruments of merely human endeavour and so guide them by Thy grace that they bring peace to those nations of the world that survive them, as we earnestly desire, trusting in Thy infinite goodness. Amen'.) A few tattered volumes priced at 10p were fading in the tray outside 'The Book-Nook', its door flanked by two potted fuchsias and not yet propped open; it was hardly worth pinching what looked like the collected works of Maurice Hewlett, but tourists sometimes paused over the tray for bargains. I stopped only long enough to scribble on the flyleaf of one of them, 'To E. M. Forster with all my love, Maurice'.

Coming smartly out of 'Amanda for Chocolates' was the tall, gingery-whiskered figure of Callum MacGregor, for once unaccompanied by his equally tall and gingery friend Angus.

'Well, laddie,' he greeted me gruffly, putting a hand on my shoulder in a gesture which might almost have passed for brisk and semi-military, as though arresting or enlisting me. 'You're a stranger in Spenn.'

'I wish I were. How's Angus?'

'On a wee trip North, to see his family, so I'm a grass widow. And yourself?'

'I'm on the run.'

'Is that so? Perhaps you'd all the more enjoy a mint humbug then. Take one.' He held out the striped paper bag, but I shook my head. 'Who are you on the run from, laddie?'

'Oh, women – and things.'

'Women?' He gave the word a long whistling vowel of suspicion, looking grave and interested. 'That's very bad. Keep running. I could have warned you of that. You're bound to attract them but you've no call to go gratifying them. Still, this isn't the place to be discussing the matter. Why not drop into the restaurant this evening for a light snack and a strong word of advice?'

He half-turned towards the sausage-shaped sign, 'Whoppers', projecting from the dark-brown facade at the end of the street, where the shops petered out. Over his shoulder I could see a newspaper placard: 'Schoolboy's heart given to man of 60.'

'I can't promise, Callum,' I said. 'I've a lot on. But thanks.'

He nodded curtly and strode away, very much again Pipe-Major MacGregor, of whatever Highland regiment it had been, marching with a swing that called for the kilt, skirl of martial music, and even a regimental mascot. Several middle-aged women in tweeds, emerging from Cherry's with crammed shopping baskets in their gloved hands, greeted him as 'Major'. And I knew that both he and Angus, who had been in the same battalion, were deeply respected in their regular pub in Spenn, not least for drinking so abstemiously and sitting there so silently, each solemnly chewing on a briarwood pipe while they sipped their half-pints. To Spenn they were just partners, hardworking ones: their restaurant itself forbiddingly respectable, scrubbed and plain in furniture and fare. Only to my mind there was something suggestive about the name they had given it. But then perhaps only I had experienced the sharpness of Callum's glance crossing with Angus's the afternoon I went with Philip to the church fête in shorts.

Behind the high street lay Spenn *inférieur* – in every sense. There were still plenty of cars but a lot less tweed and tweedy voices, and in place of a faint tang of coffee in the air was the scent of aerosol. The fire station was about the smartest building. Peach-coloured net curtains askew across the windows of the Chinese Take-Away quite failed to convey oriental mystery, any more than did the menu made out of the sail of a green plastic junk that hung suspended in front of the curtains. Outside the Laundromat gathered mothers and small children – something rarely seen in the high street. At its entrance bloomed the only sign of flowers: some dyed thistles in an ugly jug, marking it off from the stairs up to the one-eyed dump of an oculist.

Opposite was the bland brick façade of the Public Library, a single-storey building, on wet days more full of prams than books. I had been in it only once recently, to ask loudly if they would reserve for my reverend godfather *Vet at the Vatican*

('Sorry. We never reserve fiction'). I approached the Nuros-wamy from that angle, avoiding the shady side of the street where the rustic-style Police Station dozed in a deserted way suggesting it was permanently closed. 'Never pass a Fuzz shop, man,' Sadie had once warned me. 'They bring bad luck.' And, it emerged, a policeman in Peshawar had first chased her and then raped her after one of her earliest thefts – of a silver bangle she still wore: 'He just forgot,' she explained.

'Listen,' I told Sadie, who was wriggling and jiggling at her till. 'It's your lucky day. I might be able to meet you at lunchtime. Usual place by the river – and you can bring something from here for us to eat.'

By the time she actually arrived I was dopey from the sun, crumpled mentally as well as physically. The river bank was not only boring but extremely uncomfortable. Its Pre-Raphaelite vegetation increasingly smelled in the heat. One or two fat flies buzzed about hopefully, as if wondering whether at any minute the Lady of Shalott's corpse might come floating by. I had spent most of the morning pulling off and putting on again my tee shirt, and I'd got it on once more when Sadie crept up and threw her thin, wiry arms round me: a real snake in the grass.

'What keeps you going?' I asked earnestly, turning to look at the pink and red beads glittering in her teased-out crinkled hair-do, and her eyes sliding around like beads under high-arched eyebrows. 'And don't say sex.'

'How come?' she said pouting big brown lips, kneeling beside me as she unwrapped from foil some pungent bright yellow bread – it looked like.

I kissed her curry-scented mouth, without having meant to. I just needed some human contact – something – and I felt quite glad to find her body subsiding softly alongside mine.

'Sadie St John Kitts,' I murmured. 'What an improbable name.'

'My mum chose Sadie,' she said proudly. 'It's a name from a book.'

About her father I had already heard. I couldn't recall if he was a Jamaican who worked in Pakistan, or vice-versa, but she claimed he was knocked down and killed, when she was only six, by an ambulance-driver hurrying home to his evening meal.

'If he'd rung that bell, man, my father be alive today.'

'Not necessarily,' I answered. 'Besides, the driver wasn't on duty, was he? It would have been wrong to sound the bell.'

Now I gently let my fingers follow her unnervingly fragile almost slippery, barely-clad shape as if trying to give it some meaning, while she stared fixedly into my face.

'So,' I said. 'You exist. Tell me why. Tell me what you feel. Tell me what you want to do with your life.'

'I feel good.' And she put out her hand to touch my thigh in a gesture much more subtle than usual. 'You certainly got blue eyes,' she said. 'Bluer than Len's.'

'Of course,' I said impatiently. 'Sapphire crossed with emerald – they give me the power to pierce your skinny little heart. Why should it go on beating? What's the point of you? I mean it. I want to know.'

'Love me.'

'That's not an answer.'

'It's my answer – so there.'

'Oh, come on, Sadie,' I said. 'Even you can't want to spend the rest of your life at the check-out of a supermarket in this dreary little town. God knows how you got here anyway – and don't tell me. How are you going to get out? That, as somebody once remarked, is the question.'

'You come on yourself,' she said, grimacing at me and pushing her hot exploring hand between my tee shirt and the waistband of my jeans. 'Then I tell you.'

I rolled away from her, half-excited but half-apprehensive about how sustained my excitement was, and absorbed in my own sensations: the skin of my hand darker now than hers, and the slight twill of my rucked-up olive tee shirt magnified, it seemed, by the glaring sunlight. I shut my eyes, as though by blotting out the actual Sadie, awkwardly wriggling, bony yet warm and determined against me, I would experience a sense of her reality so overwhelming that I'd be utterly taken over by it and oblivious to everything else.

I wanted to think of her naked: a coffee-coloured flower opening at my will, elusively flower-scented, perhaps wearing a flower in her unwound hair, released from its bead-decorated bootlace-effect as our bodies merged and melted until all consciousness was gone.

Distantly, but not too distantly, I could hear the traffic on the main road. Lorry drivers perched high up in the cabs of their pedantically labelled 'long vehicles' would have a good view of us young lovers rolling around on the sunlit river bank and would still be thinking of us randily when they got home, stripped and had a wash. Even those tweed-clad Spennite ladies who trotted their laden Minis like ponies along the winding tracks back to glossy cottage lairs, where retired husbands waited to stack the deep-freeze, might catch a glimpse of us, involuntarily smile then be inexplicably angry when Tom or Tony took his usual age in limping out to help unload the car.

Once or twice I had idly wondered if my mission lay among them. Had I wasted in some seedy Fun Arcade off the Charing Cross Road, amid popping light bulbs and rigged rifle games, time which might better have been spent playing it very straight in cretonne lounges, sipping pale ale out of a silver tankard and being thanked for having helped over planting the tulips? But I loathed pale ale, and the role was bound to be unrewarding – not least financially. By the time they realised what appealed to them about me, alerted possibly by a busybody friend, it would be necessary to withdraw; I wouldn't even get the tankard as a memento.

'Hey, you asleep or something?' Sadie hissed at my ear.

'Yes, I am. Asleep and dreaming of you naked beside the Nile.'

'Dreaming's no use, man. You wake up and start loving me. Or I'm off.'

'I thought,' I said, shifting round reluctantly, 'you were making love to me.'

She was sitting up, morosely nibbling a piece of the yellow, crumbly substance. 'That tart of yours in London – I feel sorry for her. She got someone as well as you? You ain't much use to a girl.'

'That so-called tart happens to be my fiancée. And please don't worry about our sex life – it's not conducted in the open air but it's fine, thank you very much.'

'You know what I think?'

'No idea. Do you think? Can you?'

'You're not engaged. You haven't got a girl in London at all, I bet. Len says you're the old curate's boy-friend; that's why you stay there.'

'Len can sod off. Philip's virtually my uncle – and we don't all go to bed with our uncles. Anyway, he's not like that. You know perfectly well Philip's far more perverse. He fancies silly girls like you.'

'Where's your mother?'

'Do you mean at this minute? I think she's probably in Portugal.'

'Why she there?'

'She is making a film, if you must know. But I fail to see the relevance.'

'She a film star, then?'

'Of course.'

'What her name?'

'Oh, Bette Davis.'

'I think I heard of her, man. She's famous.'

'Certainly.'

Abruptly she collapsed weightlessly on top of me, brushing at my cheek in a beguiling way and then taking gentle hold of my ears. I had to smile up at her grinning pointed face amid the dangling, liquorice-like strands of hair which tickled me as she bent closer.

'I want to be in films,' she whispered, almost shyly. 'Your mother help me?'

'How could she possibly help you? You need talent and luck – things like that. And what on earth do you want to be in films for? It's a ghastly life most of the time.'

'That's what I want,' she said stubbornly.

'Yes,' I said meditatively. 'I can see you – not in films but on television. You'd be in one of those moronic quiz shows: too dim of course to know what happened in 1066 ("was it the discovery of America?") but just about gifted enough to keep the scoreboard. Yes, I can see your giggle coming in useful.'

She didn't reply: just lay there, sulkily sucking what I first thought must be her thumb but then realised was that yellow substance adhering to my chest. Sprawling more in than out of the piece of flowered cotton that served as her dress, she perfectly illustrated the phrase 'a bit of skirt.'

'Do stop nibbling that bloody stuff,' I said. 'Or at least give me some. Is that all the lunch you brought us? You ought to have nicked half the shop.'

'What you want – bacon and eggs?'

'I wouldn't mind an ice-cream.'

'Go get one, then. I'm not your slave.'

'Well, you ought to be. Ministering to my needs, and so on. It's filthy hot and prickly here, as well as smelly. You don't feel the heat. That shows you're a slave.' And I ringed quite tightly one of her ankles, as she scrabbled with her free foot at my fingers. 'It's the career for you. My slave. I might take you with me on my travels.'

'Where you going?'

'Who knows? But somewhere, believe me. *N'importe où.*'

She was silent, while I went on examining the almost gazelle-like form of her foot and ankle. It would be easier to break a bone in that fragile leg than love her, or make love to her. How could anything about her mean anything to me? Come to that, I probably meant nothing to her – or certainly wouldn't once she had had me. Even if our bodies did manage to get together for a few minutes' writhing and release, it would scarcely differ from me burrowing and pressing myself into some convenient grassy hollow on the bank. More pointless, really, since it would suggest feelings we didn't have, an intimacy we could never share. How often that Old Testament euphemism 'he knew her' had annoyed me: knowing someone was about the last thing the heroes of those exploits ever did.

'Bet you something,' Sadie said.

I murmured lazily, far away on my travels. On the last of the old-style liners I was a teenage croupier (I'd seen a newspaper advertisement offering training, exotic postings, intriguing prospects ...), with a smooth white tuxedo and a small black moustache. It would be an advantage – wouldn't it? – speaking French. My tapering, ringless hands on the green baize or gathering in the cash with a long-handled ivory rake would in themselves convey sophistication as well as competence. Nobody guessed my age or my origins, still less my sexual tastes; but I added new allure to the appeal of gambling. Enigmatic, calm and beautiful, I enshrined the deity of chance.

'Bet you,' Sadie was still grumbling.

'What?'

'Bet you got no mother. And if you have she ain't in films.'

'You're the liar. Not me. She is alive – I trust – and she is making a film. But I bet your father isn't dead. I bet he wasn't run over in Limpopoland, or wherever. I bet he lives in Liverpool with his drunken Irish mistress and ten little grubby bastards.'

'Don't you say things against my Dad.'

'But it's to his credit. Can't you understand? Keeping a good distance between himself and Spenn – living his own life – no responsibility for you. Very sensible.'

'He don't live in Liverpool. He's dead. And you're a liar.' She scrambled to her feet. 'I'm off now.'

I didn't want her to go, or at least not until I was ready to release her. 'I might be free this evening,' I said. 'I could take you to a film, if there's anything not too abysmal on.'

She shook her head. 'I've a date with Len at the disco.'

'Put him off. Sadie,' I shouted as she moved away. 'Sadie St John Kitts! You have been ordered to come to the cinema with me. It's your last chance. No more loving by me if you don't obey.'

She turned, only to gesture rudely and then start running along the river bank. Pan and Syrinx I know it ought to have been, but I just felt too hot and tired to bother. Besides, racing and shouting after her would probably lead only to some characteristic Spenn-like incident such as encountering the bank manager in shirt-sleeves taking a lunch time stroll with his foolish, obsequious retriever, which would join in the chase, or having stones thrown at me by a couple of schoolboys whose stupid fishing rods and jam jars I had upset.

Typically, it was in Spenn that I had once been driven away from 'The Book-Nook' by its apoplectic owner, a bald man with popping eyes, far too vast a moustache and a matching stomach, an obvious case of dyslexia. 'I was only browsing,' I'd explained, after he'd accused me of moving several leather-bound volumes on to the 'All at 50p' shelf. 'Well, browse off,' was his parting witticism. At the time I had meant to go back and rescue the wretched fuchsias chained to his doorway, but they would have been too heavy to carry and I suppose Philip would have insisted I return them before the police came plodding round: 'We have reason to believe you are in possession of stolen plants.'

It was odd about my bad luck in Spenn, even in trivial things. I remembered for some reason the occasion I had spotted a pair of quite nice bottle-green jeans hanging folded on a rail outside the only possible clothes shop. Just as I held them up against my waist they unfolded to reveal I was clutching a skirt. I stuffed it back before anyone noticed and managed to drift away calmly, but I was left absurdly ruffled, angry with myself.

Sadie was a bore, I decided. She would have to go from my life, as would quite a lot of people. I had to travel lightly, unencumbered, to settle the question of the future I'd chalked on my door; I understood that now.

Plans must be made. No more hesitation. It was to myself I must look, of course, to make things happen. I would have to turn off the downpour in my heart ('... *comme il pleut dans la rue*') and start soaring into a cloudless sky hand-tinted to my own choice.

Now I felt I really was in tune as I rose, trilling triumphantly, seeing myself as I sang, pure, ethereal, clad in a brilliant blue singlet, piped with white, moulded so closely to my torso that it might have been painted on. All Spenn fell away before me, and I descended on it, passed beyond it, firm in my ringing declaration of faith: 'And in my vest shall I be God.'

4

'Oh, they all shoot up so quickly nowadays,' I could hear a woman's voice declaring brightly, as the door of Philip's den opened and he came bumbling out, escorting a little blonde woman in a geranium trouser suit.

Runner beans or children, I wondered, waiting for the next remark to be about either early staking-out or the influence of TV. As I lounged there, I felt like drawling, 'Okay, this is a shoot-up.' And in fact the scarlet woman gave a tiny cry on discovering me suddenly looming darkly in front of her.

'How silly of me. Of course, it's your nephew. Richard,

isn't it? I'm Eve Fullerton-Jones. Your uncle has been incredibly helpful and I mustn't keep him a moment longer.'

'Nicholas,' said Philip, smiling nervously and too much, 'is – is rather on his own. And actually he's – '

'Nicholas, of course. So stupid of me to forget, but you're quite grown up now.'

'Quite,' I said.

'Bless you,' she remarked vaguely, gesticulating with a crozier-like red parasol. I half expected Philip to go down on his knees, which was where she seemed metaphorically to have him already. 'I should run. Some delightful people are coming over from Amersham for dinner, and I'm not sure what we're giving them. Doesn't that sound awful? Look, you simply must come sometime and see us, if you're at a loose end. I expect you adore tennis. My brood do.'

'I hate amateur tennis,' I said, not bothering to look at Philip who hovered silently and uneasily, an alpaca balloon on the verge of slipping his moorings.

'Ah, you'd be too good for us, I can tell. Not to worry. The boys are almost as mad about croquet this year. It gets quite hectic; I have to laugh. But you can always cool off in the pool afterwards.'

'It's very good of you,' Philip said, after a pause. 'Isn't it, Nicky? He loves swimming.'

'And you were such a sportsman yourself, I know. Perhaps we could tempt you to join us, at least for lunch.'

'He loves lunch,' I said.

She laughed merrily, pushing up her face towards Philip's as if asking him to admire the rows of pearly peas in a scarlet pod which were not merely teeth but the apparatus of a miniature musical-box. There was something of my aunt Margot's ageing sleekness in her beaky little face, unlined, undisturbed except for the crispy noodles of streaky blonde hair which lay all around it, some of them daringly touched with black.

'Well, that's a date. Don't forget. We'll be in touch before we go off to France in September. Now I really must love you and leave you.'

I let Philip take her to the door, watching her strut nautically over the shiny linoleum as if buffeted by the wind along some upper deck, prattling and laughing up at his ghostly grey bulk as it bounced beside her. 'So terribly kind … ,' I heard her knife-hard tones. 'Quite relieved my mind.' There was a last laugh at the doorway: 'My punk hairstyle … really, that's too sweet of you.' She put up the parasol and stumped off across the baked uneven ground, while at the open door Philip lingered, obscuring the flow of the strong evening sunlight.

A wistful, perhaps apprehensive smile was on his face, pinker even than usual, as he virtually tiptoed back, somewhat deflated, to the foot of the stairs where I ominously waited.

'What did she want you to do?' I asked. 'Consecrate her croquet lawn or organise total immersion of infants in the swimming pool?'

'She came for some advice, Nicky. Of course I can't reveal the problem, and you mustn't be unkind. She was trying to be nice to you.'

'She fancies you. Oh yes she does. Wake up. That's why she was trying – trying – to be what you call nice to me.'

'I didn't think you were very nice to her,' he said, stung. 'She was only – '

'Trying to be nice. For God's sake, don't say it again. I haven't the faintest intention of going near her place, and I very much doubt if she'll ask me.'

'Still,' he said, teetering awkwardly before, like a balloon giving birth, he drew a great streamer of cream silk handkerchief from his pocket and mopped his plump neck, 'you are rather at a loose end at the moment, aren't you? And they own that very nice house, the white one, not far from the common.'

'Oh, goody. It should be the first casualty of the nuclear attack. Or have they got an absolutely divine underground shelter? By the way, you never told me about blessing the missiles.'

'You don't take much interest in church affairs. And it's not exactly a blessing. The vicar felt we ought to give the community a lead. Of course, it's a thorny matter. Everyone's entitled to their own opinion.'

'We must do the best we can.'

'That's it, old chap.' He sounded relieved and began to retreat towards his den. I gripped the knob of the staircase so tautly that it might have twisted and spun in my hand, spinning with it Philip's thin slice of house as smoothly as one of those toy weather-houses which secretly I always wanted to possess (even live in, I think, when I was very small).

'Philip,' I called. For a moment I thought he hadn't heard. Then he paused and came back. Did he look apprehensive or puzzled? Or just vacant? Anyway, there he was: obedient, over-large, over-familiar in features and yet remote, more like my butler than my godfather. I tried to conjure up some recollection of our being close emotionally – or even physically Had Philip ever kissed me when I was a child? I seemed to recall one clumsy dry embrace after my father's funeral: a gingerly touch, as though anything more vigorous might cause me to detonate. How he perked up, became almost indecently cheerful, when he realised I would display no open grief. And much more warmly and instinctively had he taken Mother's arm, turning her quite bridal despite the dripping black garments hung about her.

Mother, no doubt, was the unconscious recipient of those presents which he bought me from then onwards, especially on my birthday on 6 December ('please say name-day, Philip,' I had once instructed him, during an intense Russian phase, when Mother had to call me Kolya). She was about as likely as I was to want rows of plastic model cavaliers and roundheads which arrived one year, complete with a coloured booklet about the Civil War. 'They're rather dear,' she had bravely announced, balancing a cavalier on top of the crowded drinks cabinet. 'Do you mean expensive?' I asked. 'Well, poor sweet Philip does try,' she sighed. 'And boys aren't easy, you know, darling. At least he hasn't sent you a cricket bat.' Probably in the back of the kitchen cupboard in some flat long vacated by us would still be the chemistry set of another year; I had hardly used it apart from concocting a drink out of copper sulphate crystals that Mother's then lover was nearly persuaded to sample as blue curaçao.

The presents might have meant almost anything or nothing, but, I could now see, they aptly symbolised Philip. From him emanated a fuzzy brightness – a halo slipped down over his eyes – which ringed him off from people and made it hard for him to distinguish individuals through the unfocused friendly haze he projected. Not even the idiosyncrasy of

Mother had penetrated it, I guessed; she must have hovered slightly out of his myopic mental vision, and gone on hovering there agreeably while nothing happened. He couldn't quite stir himself to step closer. Without enquiring about what I had once feared, I realised that Mother never would have married him. Besides, he would never have asked her.

A small boy was a bit of a handful for Philip, especially one who quickly grew tired of knocking a ball about, but he'd been very gentle when I'd gashed my knee badly on his barren waste-ground substitute for a garden. Briefly I had come into focus: a boy with a bleeding knee, a problem with an everyday straight-forward solution of bandages and manly comfort. Much easier for him in the days when I ran in with that sort of accident than as I now appeared, grown up, grown invulnerable – always supposing he had noticed the change.

If I reached out and drew him closer to me by his clerical-grey lapels, drawing him as caressingly as Sadie had taken my ears, he would be astonished, embarrassed. I must be joking again. And no charge or message would pass along my arms, however violently I shook him, to convey that I might welcome awareness of my existence. At least as much as bloody little Mrs Fullerton-Jones I could do with something: if not exactly advice then concern, interest – for God's sake, something.

'What is it, Nicky?' Philip was asking, with near-impatience. 'I've a choir-practice at half-past six.'

Cancel it, I ought to have riposted. Cancel everything such as it is in your life, and listen to me. *J'insiste* – more, *J'accuse.* You are guilty, Philip, of the unforgivable crime of indifference.

'That bag of golf clubs in my room,' I found myself saying. 'Did they belong to my father?'

'Are there some clubs in your room? I'm sorry. I hadn't realised. Sling them out, if you like.'

'It was a question, not a complaint.'

'Well, I suppose they're bound to be mine, though I can't be sure. Yes, they must be. I wouldn't have any of your father's. I haven't played for ages. It was not really my game, you know. Let Mrs Rainbow have them; she'll find a home for them, never fear.'

'You'd better fear when she serves up mashie niblick cutlets soaked in gutta-percha sauce.'

'Now, now,' he laughed, somewhat relieved, walking away. 'She's no great shakes as a cook, but her heart's in the right place.'

I suppose I might have tripped dramatically on the staircase, torn a ligament and my jeans and brought him out again from his burrow. But for that to be effective I needed the crash of thunder, either from an orchestra or the weather – and perhaps also a stained-glass oriel window at the turn of the stairs, luridly lit as he bent over me while I sprawled in agony; and at last he understood me. Instead, I thumped and banged my way up, shaking the frail, fretwork banisters which could so easily give way – certainly would give way in a horror film – as one reeled back from the lop-sided gallery of photographs of Philip revealed by a flash of lightning in their full grotesqueness. I paused to gaze at one of him parading a scull, beside the College barge, Hilary Term, 1950, and there were distinct signs of mould creeping from the grey mount on to the photograph; already a piece of the hand-painted College crest had flaked away, though some time would elapse before the mould penetrated to Philip's beaming face, instantly identifiable with his face today.

It was more shocking than 'The Picture of Dorian Gray'. Not even mould would alter it, I suppose. Philip was simply preserved in the religious-flavoured beefy aspic of his own good-natured sterility. His face told it all. Nothing had affected him probably since the age of ten. He had played games, gone round the world, been ordained. Some cups, caps and photographs, a clutch of tourist curios and a few dog-collars attached to parachute-like pieces of grey cloth documented as much.

I looked at the photograph of him swathed in an enormous striped scarf and pullover, and thought that you could make a museum out of the clothes Philip must have worn and discarded in his half-century of existence. Probably the clothes would tell you more than Philip could. He'd cheerfully talked to lots of people, listened, smiled or nodded gravely, sipped a sherry and knocked back some beer, looked at the racing results, turned on the television, and then to bed, by himself, as usual. Nothing had impacted; deflected him, touched him or made any difference to him. Perhaps he had never actually been in bed – gone to bed – with another person. Nature's eunuch, in whose eyes we were all denatured, depersonalised: castrated to the level of being amorphous chaps, regardless of sex, without balls but with hearts in the right place, doing our best. Somehow I just couldn't see Philip and the teenage girls anywhere but at choir-practice.

I wondered if Mrs Fullerton-Jones had sensed a challenge as she settled her pseudo-punk hair on leaving and elicited some boyish-clumsy compliment from Philip. Her problem was probably Mr Fullerton-Jones. He had to be a broker, if he wasn't a Tory MP, or both. When not making disgusting physical demands on her, he was playing around with the Finnish au pair. Whatever happened, she felt she must keep the home going (keep the house, anyway), if only for the children's sake. The word might eventually prompt a return confidence from Philip: 'I never quite know where I am with Rich—er, Nicholas.' She would be glad to hear it, though outwardly sympathetic. As a mother herself, become by piquant role-reversal a mother-confessor, she could impart a confidence: 'It's largely a matter of age.' A burst of noisy splashing from the pool might prompt her to add a neat jab of pride plus psychology: 'And isn't he an only child?'

As a matter of fact, we can't be sure – though I wouldn't expect Philip to say so. My father might have begotten any number of children. If he'd lived longer that girl in Nottingham would surely have had a child, though I preferred to think of an unknown brother or sister somewhere in the world (golfers travelled, after all): *mon semblable* perhaps ... Was Baudelaire an only child? Dennis would be very annoyed I had forgotten, but then I was beginning, half-regretfully, to forget not so much Baudelaire as Dennis.

Anyway, Philip looked quite unscathed the next morning when I went rather sleepily down the equally unscathed staircase. I had slept horribly, untypically heavily. From some clammy dream of travelling with Philip on a long, oppressive train journey, where he constantly climbed out of the carriage to try and discover our destination, I had been woken by a fierce shaft of sunlight like a torch flashed in my eyes.

'Postcard for you,' he sang out ebulliently as if choir-practice was still on.

I groped towards the table, perhaps exaggerating a bit, while Philip laughed. Suddenly I too felt cheerful. Mother, I thought, staring in a gummy stupor at the reproduction of the 'Critian Boy', slowly turning it over to see a Greek stamp and the at first meaningless message signed 'Julian'. I groaned savagely.

'Are you all right, Nicky?'

'Bloody cheek, writing to me. No, I am not all right. I don't want postcards from him, least of all of rotten Greek nudes – looks hideous anyway. Bloody, bawdy Julian!'

'A schoolfriend?' Philip asked idly, getting up and folding the paper.

'Shades of Brixton,' Julian had written in painfully clear script, 'but alas he's made of marble. Guess why you came to mind. Hope we'll keep in touch – sorry! XXX. Julian (amico di Caravaggio).'

'And so we're off any moment,' Philip was saying. 'As soon as Bert Rainbow arrives.'

'Who is off where?' I asked wearily, stretching for the Ryvita packet. I didn't yet feel strong enough to go and make some coffee. Philip, of course, had tea for breakfast.

'Windsor. Bert and I are making a day of it, popping over for the racing.' And he mumbled something cryptic that sounded like 'Loudmouth Nursery Stakes', suggestive of red-faced men reduced to rompers and bawling in the sun.

'Well, keep hag Rainbow hence who's foe to man.'

'I've given her the day off,' he said gleefully, too absorbed to demur. 'Ah, there's the bell.'

He left me brooding malevolently over the disappointment of that postcard. I suppose Julian had wormed my address out of Dennis (a black mark for him, or mark of his dwindling interest in me?) The 'Critian Boy' stared out, sightless, severely mutilated and unmistakably stupid, as well as pug-ugly. Nobody need go as far as Athens to encounter him. Every school in England had at least half-a-dozen, with exactly that sullen-mouthed expression of uneasy inner vacuity as though compelled in class to ponder the nature of a quadrilateral triangle. ('But, sir, how can there be? Is Gonville trying to take the piss, sir? Oh, *sir*, I was only asking …') Did purblind Julian imply that I resembled him?

'Cup of tea, Bert?'

Philip threw the door open as effusively as if announcing the arrival of the Archbishop of Canterbury. Rainbow limped in, older, more wizened than I remembered – almost a dwarf, a dwarf in a khaki shirt and cut-down green tweed suit – with his carroty hair as thick as ever, though now flecked with grey. He had dreadfully dainty pointed feet and elfish pointed ears.

'Had mine,' Rainbow replied, adding after a pause during which he scrutinised me suspiciously, 'thanks.'

Philip attempted to dissipate the cloud of rapidly accumulating dislike with puffs and squirts of bonhomie, signalling that we knew each other, my being on holiday, the fine weather, the going today on hard ground, while all the time patting his pockets and adding to his bulky gear in a way which made me aware that I was dressed in only a pair of jeans.

Rainbow's rancid little mouth worked as if he was chewing tobacco. Looking at him I thought instinctively of spittoons and sawdust on a taproom floor; I could almost detect the smell of saddles and horse-dung.

'Off are we?' he said curtly, as Philip solemnly began to don a luminescent orange stole.

'Indeed, indeed.' Philip looked quite flustered, though he kept on smiling. 'So sorry to take so long. I ought to be better organised by now.'

Not for the first time I wondered if, absurd though it seemed, Rainbow had some hold over Philip. He appeared to take a sour pleasure in showing me at least that he had Philip in his pocket – and I couldn't think of many more unsavoury places. Rainbow might ride pillion, but it was his grip of Philip's shoulder that guided where they went, even perhaps what they did.

'No crash helmet?' I asked hopefully of Rainbow after Philip had bustled out of the room, murmuring a farewell which blended with something about the petrol gauge. He gave me a glance as virulent as a stream of tobacco juice in the face. A moment or two later I saw from the window his pixie figure grown the more sinister by the great globular metallic swelling of his head. He hopped up nimbly behind Philip, and with a shattering, unexpectantly flamboyant gunning of the engine they drove off.

Could Philip have a secret life as banal as owing Rainbow money? Betting debts or something actually crooked? The race-course is meant to be a vision of silks and green turf smooth as a bath-mat down which pound the hooves of glistening, sinewy thoroughbreds, but one look at Rainbow tarnished that image – and probably he'd be only too pleased to lead someone as innocent as Philip into the seamier aspects: the grime, if not crime, beneath the silk.

I didn't have the energy at present to start investigating, and Philip's absence prompted me to devote my day rather to doing nothing. I carried a cup of coffee upstairs, arranged the curtains to keep out the sun, stripped and lay down on my bed.

It was quiet, restful but dull. Once I heard the telephone shrilling away, and I let it ring. I pondered on whether to read a book – strong indication that I didn't want to – and then decided to play the cassette Mother brought me back after touring as Gertrude (of course) in some *Hamlet* that visited Russia. 'How could I be that creepy slob's *mother?*' she had asked indignantly throughout rehearsals and probably throughout the tour, referring not to the Prince but to the leading actor. 'Darling, I don't think he ever had a mother; he's the offspring of a profile and a press-cutting agency.'

The cassette had come wrapped in an oily, oddly smelly morsel of Russian wrapping paper which I'd carefully preserved, since Mother had inscribed on it, 'Gertrude's present to her *real* son.' I didn't mind that it had begun as an official gift to her. Wild, melodic and gutturally incomprehensible songs streamed from it, but it seemed to bring Mother speaking at the bedside, despite its surreal, crudely-misprinted label of 'Polk-music of Uzbekistan.' A white rose and two maidens were in it somewhere, she felt sure. 'There usually are, darling, in that sort of musical bortsch.'

I smiled dreamily, drifting towards and every so often returning from sleep. Rural Spenn receded, only to be brought back in a sudden cataclysm of noise. A lorry had arrived, I saw when I got up briefly and was tipping broken paving stones on to the scrubby ground below the bedroom window: a rockery we hadn't ordered or the materials for a do-it-yourself fall-out shelter.

The next sound was the door bell pealing. I must have fallen asleep, and there was a sense of evening in the room, as well as of somebody standing outside determined not to take their finger off the bell. That suggested a good cause. 'The vicar asked me to call ...': a coffee-morning for kleptomaniacs or something for the missions or the missiles. Very well. They should be rewarded beyond their deserts, as I draped myself lightly in a sheet, by a superior version of house-boy crossed with young Lawrence of Arabia: 'The imam is out. The ayatollah is not at home.'

What was standing where the doorstep would be outside a normal house was enough to make me forget my own appearance. For a few seconds I wasn't absolutely sure of the sex, despite the green headscarf sprinkled with horses' heads. A tall, very thin girl it was, wearing buff jeans, high boots, a shapeless top and dark glasses. Even without brandishing a weapon, she looked ready to hijack something.

'The curate – Mr Kerr,' she said aggressively. 'I've called to see him.'

'Are you expected?' I responded with deliberate, delaying over-suavity.

'Am I what?'

The aggression cloaked a certain nervousness, I realised, realising also from her flat accent that she was local.

'Isn't it Wednesdays,' she went on, 'when he sees people? I want to see him. He knows me.'

Under her stare I hitched up the sheet and shifted my bare feet which were beginning to prickle from contact with the bristles of the doormat.

'He's had to go to Windsor.' 'Castle' I ought perhaps to have added, though I doubted if she would be impressed. 'I don't know when he'll be back. Very late, I should think.'

'You live here, then?'

'I'm staying – for a holiday.'

'Funny place to come for a holiday. Have you been ill or something?'

'Just having a siesta.'

As she relaxed, her curiosity seemed worse than her aggression. For the first time she gave a pert grin, tossing her head back to reveal long straw-coloured hair that rippled down her spine. Without the deep eyeless pools of the sunglasses and constricting headscarf she might be quite pretty. And despite her height and the sub-combat clothes, she was definitely very young indeed.

Nodding at me, she went on, 'You look like you were rehearsing for the Nativity Play. I'm in the choir myself. I haven't seen you around. Staying down here long, are you?'

'My plans are vague. I'm in a good deal of demand,' I added kindly.

'Is that so? Well, don't let me keep you.' Her tone hardened. 'And you tell Mr Kerr that Lesley called and I'll be calling again. It's Lesley with a "y". He'll know the name.'

Awkwardly she took a step back, obviously unsure how to retreat now she had, with her chin thrust forward, delivered her message. She moved to the side of the house and I looked for a waiting jeep or a pony tethered there; but it was only an old-fashioned, very schoolgirlish bicycle on which she wobbled resolutely away, not glancing round.

'Lesley called,' I rehearsed in the hall. 'Lesley left a message. Oh, by the way, Lesley came with a problem but we managed to solve it together. Of course, I'm bound to respect her confidence, Philip. It's a personal matter. Young people can have problems, and often it's hard for an older person to be on quite the same wave-length.'

The words hung a bit limply. Philip seemed in fact to have set up his own secret radio station, with no shortage of recipients. I was the one who had failed to tune in properly. How much shrewder Sadie's gossipy chatter was proving than any of my assumptions. It was galling to realise it, and faintly demeaning. As I went back to my room, the photographs on the staircase appeared not only beaming but positively leering, with a mocking air of having fooled me and eluded me.

In turn, I ought to find some way, if not of fooling Philip, at least of surprising him and catching him out. In the end I settled to begin at breakfast, and take him unawares as I introduced the Lesley visit with a touch of boyish bewilderment and concern for his reputation.

'By the way,' I opened, interrupting his euphoric account of the racing and Rainbow's stable tip for some literal dark horse at fearful odds, 'a certain Lesley – Lesley with a "y" – called yesterday and seemed very fed up you weren't in. She made quite a thing of wanting you to know she'd called. And that she would again.'

It was all less pondered than I'd intended, and a good deal less subtle. Something had jolted me the previous evening. I wasn't quite so sure of how to tie Philip up with the gossamer threads I had envisaged; there hadn't somehow been time to spin them, for one thing. And I was strangely apprehensive, unusually so, at having had a glimpse of the puzzling complexity of human relations for which I wasn't properly prepared.

Bored and hungry, I had telephoned Callum and gone, after all, to see him: a visit I had never meant to make, especially while Angus was away. I was in no mood for teasing or fighting off what might well be ferocious advances, but I felt distinctly sulky at his dour response and delayed, morosely delivered invitation to a meal. We sat decorously all evening, separated by an expanse of well-scrubbed table on which Callum had laid out a sparse still-life of uncooked food that made *crudités* sound a gourmet's dream.

After a while he started speaking of his childhood in Banff and idyllic days with his grandmother away from the coast, describing her method of making black puddings: swirling round the pig's just shed warm blood with her fingers to extract the veins. I wouldn't be eating ham or pork again, I decided; and even Callum's onions began slightly to nauseate me. He gave me a tot – a tiny tot – of whisky and took one himself. When he pulled out his pipe I felt I ought to match him, but instead I lightly enquired about Angus's return.

He took a long time to reply, sucking at his pipe and tapping it before rousing himself to say, 'I'm no so sure he is returning.'

After another pause he told me a letter had come from Angus, rambling on about the age they were both reaching ('Aye, he's right enough there,' he commented), the need to reconsider things – perhaps make a break – each be free to go his own way.

'Is it his family?' I asked, bewildered.

He shook his head. 'No, he's no-one left but a widowed sister, living by herself in Kildrummy.'

It might have been tempting to make some silly joke about the place but he laid down his pipe abruptly and put a hand over his eyes.

'I can't understand it, Callum,' I said at last, to break the prolonged silence. When eventually he raised his face I was horrified to see trickling across its battered, ravine-like features a tear. With one hairy hand he brushed it away and then reached out and convulsively squeezed my hand – squeezing and then carefully releasing it.

'It's very simple,' he said hoarsely. 'He's found someone else, laddie.'

Can you be sure, I wanted to ask. And even if it is true, you must fight back. It may be only a temporary infatuation. These things happen, I could assure him. He ought to go up to Scotland and talk to Angus, insist on meeting whoever it was (probably some uncouth, freckled, raw-boned boy reminding Angus of himself forty years ago). But somehow I hadn't the courage to try and comfort his misery. I knew it wouldn't shift. I realised he longed to be by himself – I was no solution, not even for a night – and I too wanted to leave.

Walking back to Philip's, I had felt still shaken by the bleakness exuding from Callum. Sad though I might feel for him (all the more recollecting his earlier contented assumption of mere grass widowhood), I felt far more disturbed by implications beyond him. So much love and trust, I supposed, which time was meant to be deepening just vanished on receipt of a letter. Parting from Mopsa had made me miserable, but increasingly I recognised that time would anyway have parted us or reduced our relationship to a level where it no longer mattered whether or not we met. To be as old and bereft as Callum was very different. I didn't want a future like that, but I wondered how you avoided it. And by going on loving – as he did – you suffered more. I had always thought myself good at commanding people and that I should continue commanding as I grew up. Now I felt less certain, about everything.

It was chill in Spenn high street though not yet entirely dark. There was a ghostly, misleading grandeur about the portico of the bank by night; and the sterile caverns of the antique shops, full of silver tea sets nobody could want or afford, shone out attractively, lit by cunningly-placed oil lamps wired for electricity. Only a few people stumbling from the Queen's Head, the pub on the corner, briefly suggested life as they called good-nights to each other and went their separate ways. One of them, a heavily-built man in a blur of shirt sleeves, lurched into me and shouted jovially, 'Watch your bloody step, mate,' before disappearing chuckling down a side road.

The narrow slice of Philip's yellow ugly house looked as flimsy and insubstantial as if carved from stale cheese. No light showed in it as I crept near, though why I was creeping I couldn't tell. It was quite silent and seemed empty – but then so it might with Philip there. I had shut the front door without locking it: Philip believed a clergyman should never lock his house, which intensely irritated the vicar whose wife's jewellery was Victorian and valuable. Creeping up the shadowy staircase, I passed Philip's room and reached my own.

'Lesley,' I repeated at the breakfast table, tilting my chair and putting my hands together in a headmasterly steeple. 'Have you any explanation to offer about Lesley?'

I expected anything except Philip's burst – snort, almost – of laughter. 'Simply that she's an extremely silly girl,' he said. 'She had no right whatsoever to come here and try and bully you. She's a pain in the – the – the choir, and everywhere else.'

'She strongly hinted she had a personal problem for you to deal with. It was Wednesday, after all.'

'Her problem is an inflated ego, or worse. She's a sex-maniac in my view. I suppose she'll be complaining next that I've molested her – or whatever the term is.'

'Philip!' I was so disconcerted that my chair tilted back to the floor with a bang. 'I'm a minor myself,' I said with mock reproach. 'And you are a clergyman.'

'It doesn't prevent me stating that Lesley Coombe is a pest: a very conceited and cheap piece of goods as my dear sainted mother might have put it. Also, she hasn't the foggiest idea of even tonic sol-fa, despite her pathetic airs and graces. As for you, old chap, I didn't mean to shock you. It's just that that girl gets my goat.'

'Isn't the phrase rather suggestive? Nobody has ever cared to explain it to me. Anyway, she seemed quite pretty – I couldn't tell yesterday under the gear and dark glasses.'

'If you go for albino giraffes. No, that is uncharitable. And Mrs Coombe, I admit, is a very nice woman. I see no reason why the sins of Lesley should be visited on her mother. A handsome woman too, for her age. Of course if you and the daughter want to go out together, that's entirely your affair. It might help her a lot, and I'm sure it would help me.'

I had to laugh, and Philip quickly joined in. 'Not even to

oblige you,' I said. 'But I never realised a curate was in such demand. You must be part of the revival of Christianity I read about.'

'Well,' he said, flushing though still smiling. 'It's being unmarried, I suppose. And, after all, the vicar is older – considerably older. But I fear it's a hazard for the clergy – and of course on occasion it can be flattering, even fun, you know.'

'All is explained, Philip. You're coming down like a wolf on the fold. May I please have the marmalade?'

'I'm so sorry. Incidentally, we ought to try and finish breakfast a bit earlier. Mrs Rainbow likes to wash up as soon as she arrives. It's nice to have a jabber, but I've the morning before me and what you call my fold to visit and so on.'

'Who's the lucky girl or woman?'

'Now, that's not fair,' he cried, but he didn't seem totally displeased. 'And as it happens, poor Cherry from the high street, you know, is in hospital. I really ought to go and see him, if only he didn't think a visit from me meant he was dying.'

'The shop always looks embalmed,' I said absently. I was rather pre-occupied accustoming myself to the extra sheen and bounce on Philip. He embodied breakfast-food vitality with suggestions of advertising toothpaste and shampoo. Even his stray silver curls had a special springy vitality this morning, as if new-sprouted manifestations of inner exuberance. Perhaps it was just that he had won a huge sum at the races. Or was it having an affair with Mrs Coombe?

'Ah, Mrs R.,' he called out cheerfully. Her disapproving rat's snout had poked round the door with unusual quietness. 'Good morning, good morning. Just finishing, aren't we, Nicky? And it looks like another lovely day, doesn't it?'

'They say Mr Cherry's very poorly,' she whined, coming into the room and frowning at us both.

'Well, he's in hospital but just for a check-up, I think – nothing too serious. I might pop over and see him this morning. Give him our love and best wishes.'

'Visiting hours are only in the afternoon.'

'Aha, but that's where I claim the privilege of my cloth, you see.'

'Mrs Cherry says it's his insides. They haven't been right for years; he's always suffered from wind, and she thought nothing of it. Bert's the same. And now if Cherry's taken, it'll show what comes of putting things off, I say.'

She wrinkled up her face at Philip's boisterous laugh, relentlessly clashing plates and saucers until I had to move away from the table.

Philip continued to stand there, oblivious, beaming. 'Life goes on, you know,' he said. 'We must always remember that, mustn't we?'

Mrs Rainbow paused to push her gimcrack spectacles into position while clutching the marmalade spoon from which gradually dripped a blob glinting in the sunlight before it fell on the tablecloth.

'Don't say you're going to love us and leave us,' I said to Philip.

'Where there's life there's hope. In for lunch as usual, Mrs R.'

5

As soon as I woke I detected a difference. No tipsy shafts of sunshine this morning but a stifling feeling as if the air was full of feathers, and a dankness in the room as though it had been left out all night.

I felt rather the same, and so did my clothes. No sound came from any part of the house, but as I paused at the head of the stairs I thought I heard the sibilant whisper of rain beginning. Standing there was oddly like being on a high diving-board; the longer I hesitated the harder it seemed to descend. And now I could see the shapes of one or two envelopes lying on the hall mat. I ran down and picked them up.

There was something like the electricity bill for Philip, a card poetically advertising the services of a new plumber in Spenn ('Summer foresight foils Winter's worst') and a letter for me from Mother, forwarded from St John's Wood in handwriting that I mistook at first for Mopsa's but in fact was

Margot's. As I moved across the hall towards Philip and breakfast, I was abruptly conscious of a sickly smell pervading the atmosphere: a strong reek of sherry that seemed to be coming from his den.

I hesitated: poised between going to investigate and going into the dining-room. I didn't want to call out, for some reason, and when eventually I pushed open the dining-room door I found the table laid for breakfast as usual but no sign of Philip. The room struck damp, and the breakfast things had a forlorn, untouched look. I put down the post, then picked up Mother's envelope again, faintly puzzled and distracted. He might have overslept, but that was untypical. And he had presumably been in last night; it was the Wednesday after his Windsor jaunt, and he had declared he was prepared that evening for anything, even Lesley Coombe's arrival.

Inside Mother's envelope was only a plain card, scribbled all over and up the sides. 'Darling Boy, I feel so guilty,' I read, still not totally concentrating. *'Ought* to have written long ago. Exhausted by meddlesome Matilda role, but hopeful will soon be finished shooting and dream of being banal, snatch few days for bathing at Estoril, maybe have sweet Stephen (*too* muddling he's Stephen – Steve – in real life as well) along. Would you join us? He's not only dishy – trust Mum – but full of old-fashioned virtues like domesticity and devotion, I *think.* And not dull! Had to prise him away on set from ghastly GIRL (well, a change for once). Fondest love and hope all fine – have you gone stay Philip? Nobly sent him card. Best to Mopsa and any other conquests. A thousand kisses. The *older* wonder-woman, alias your loving Mother.'

I turned back to the beginning for a postscript creeping along the upper edge: 'Shall wire Margot if Estoril plan settled. Hugh loan you cash your fare etc. I will repay!'

Now it had arrived, I found I was strangely unstirred, not least by the prospect of joining her and this Stephen person – and I doubted if he would be overjoyed to meet me. I was getting too old to have my place in such a holiday ménage: far too old to be sent to bed after coffee, and too old not to feel myself alien in a trio drifting along some southern waterfront in the soft after-dinner dusk. All the same, I realised I should, however reluctantly, soon be doing just that. And in many ways, leaving Spenn would be the ideal solution – a change. Nobody kept me; or wanted me. Then there would be Mother, abroad, the bathing, and perhaps we could conspire to get rid of Steve – straight-nosed Steve, I dubbed him, with round blue eyes, broad shoulders, and a white towelling, monogramed dressing-gown, auditioning in his own mind as the definitive Henry V.

'Philip,' I called as loudly as I felt able, as I crossed the hall. 'Hallo.'

There was no reply. By the time I reached the door, the smell seemed so horribly pervasive that I thought I might almost faint. The door was ajar. 'Philip,' I called again, waiting and hoping desperately for some answer.

Suddenly, it seemed ridiculous to go on standing outside the room trembling, fearing some awful revelation when the whole scene could so easily dissolve into laughter as Philip bounded breathlessly down the stairs or burst into the house from some eccentric expedition. But I knew I had to stop waiting. Each moment passing made me more tense. I grabbed the handle and thrust open the door.

The upturned sole of his shoe was so close that I almost stumbled on it, before I drew back. He had fallen heavily forward, rucking up the carpet and smashing the sherry decanter, whose stopper had rolled to rest beside the grey expanse of one hairy sock exposed by his fall. I dragged my eyes from what I could see of his discoloured foreshortened face, a purplish-yellow mottled marble, cold and swollen, bruised and glaring. The room looked in disarray. Papers seemed scattered all over it; a window was wide open, and most of the mantelpiece ornaments lay amid fragments of glass on the floor around the body.

My stomach heaved, and I had to get out of the sights and smell of the room. I went out and sat down on the bottom stair, listening to the tearing sound of my irregular breaths, keeping my head bowed so that I shouldn't be able to see anything beyond my tightly clenched knees and my now slightly fading multi-coloured sneakers – plimsolls – that Dennis had once fondly laced on for me. It seemed long ago.

I was shivering so much that I thought I must be shaking the staircase and with it the whole fragile edifice of Philip's house. He was dead, I knew, but it meant nothing to say it. I was devoid of feeling: quite empty. Only, I had to stay calm; that was the important thing. I knew nothing about doctors in Spenn. It was the police, surely, that I must telephone – especially when I thought of the disarray in the room and my sight of Philip's angry, appalled eye upturned palely in that livid expanse of flesh. I couldn't recollect if there had been blood. All I kept seeing was his head, twisted sideways on the threadbare carpet, bloated in a beached fishy manner, and – deadest of all – the flabby protuberance of his ear, looking like some convoluted, outmoded mechanism, incongruously large and useless.

It seemed essential not to think or speculate, just act. First, I had to check my shivering fit. I must be coherent on the telephone, not nervous, panicky or melodramatic. And I must telephone before Mrs Rainbow arrived. What happened after that, I couldn't foresee. It didn't matter to the same extent. Anyway, it would be out of my hands.

I felt ashamed that, when I finally got to my feet, I couldn't raise my eyes from the ground as I shuffled over to the telephone that stood outside the den. Even as I picked it up, a bout of feverish shaking came on me again. I put it down. 'I prefer the bally thing in the hall,' I could remember Philip once saying robustly in answer to some expostulation of mine. 'Makes people who ring realise you've had to come and get it. And if you live alone there's jolly well nobody to overhear you.'

At the second attempt I succeeded quite calmly, though I could feel the dryness in my mouth, so that I was hoarse before I began to speak. Then it was like speaking words in a language one had learnt the sound of but not the meaning. I grew more stilted at the response of the slow, deep countrified voice at the other end, asking for my address, repeating with maddening, questioning assonance, 'Mr Kerr the curate, is it?' until I felt hysterically involved in an idiotic game of happy families. 'It's his godson,' I could hear the voice explaining slowly, while I gazed down at the police station number ringed and ringed in red by Philip, perhaps idly one day, in the front of the local telephone directory.

'Very well, sir,' the voice said at last. 'Please touch nothing and just wait. We'll be with you as soon as we can.'

'Thank you very much,' I said, with a sense almost of

having obtained the plumber or ordered something from a shop.

All I had to do was wait, and now I felt nervously that I had undertaken a great responsibility: issued an invitation and must face the consequences. Supposing Philip wasn't really dead, or that the whole thing was an illusion or a monstrous hoax? Without moving from my place by the telephone, I peered round the door sufficiently to see the leather tip of his solid black shoe, and inhaled a fresh whiff of that sweet sherry aroma which made me gag.

I walked back to the bottom of the stairs, walking carefully so as to make no sound, and waited. My mind ceased to function. I was merely someone standing, waiting for the police and feeling obscurely that it was raining outside. It would be wet weather for them.

The ring of the bell made me start – it was so sudden and sustained. I hadn't heard a car, so perhaps it was only the milkman choosing by chance this morning to be paid: a nice irony I tried to think, but the effort was clumsy.

When I opened the door there was a police car I could see, half blocked by two uniformed men who flanked a shortish man in a navy trenchcoat and waterproof hat.

'Detective Inspector Grice,' he said rapidly, with a mirthless flash of teeth, snapping out and returning to his wallet something that might just as well have been a credit card. 'Sorry to disturb you, sonny, but we've had an urgent call from the curate. May we step in and see him? I'm afraid a body has been discovered on these premises.'

'Of course it has,' I began, with a petulance that made all three of them look oddly at me. 'It's Mr Kerr who's dead, I think.' I went on more quietly, gesturing them in and indicating the den. 'I'm his godson and I telephoned just now.'

'Hiscock,' said Grice sharply, taking off his quite dry hat and unbuttoning his coat. 'You reported the curate rang about finding his godson's body.'

'Horder took the call, sir. I only reported what he told me.'

'Horder,' said Grice, turning to the other tall policeman. Both of them looked very young, healthy and solid behind big droopy dark moustaches, in effect more vintage 1910 than trendy. Hengist and Horsa, I thought; and it was as if my mind was starting gradually to de-ice.

'Sir?' Horder remained as solid as before, and Grice seemed to detect as much.

'I'll go into that aspect later,' he said in a would-be ominous manner, marred slightly by a whistling over some of the consonants. 'Where is Sergeant Parrott?' he added brusquely, as if dropping his minor complaint for a major one.

'Telephoning for an ambulance, sir, before joining you.'

'And Doctor Metcalfe? He should have been informed immediately.'

'Sergeant's doing that, sir,' the other one answered slowly, with a comfortable burr in his voice similar to the voice on the telephone. I had already lost track of which was which, and it didn't seem to matter.

'Well, let's cut the cackle,' Grice said. He turned on me as he spoke. I saw how tanned he was – his tan set off by his slicked-back black hair and the gleam of his teeth and the luminous white of his shirt-front down which hung a knitted strip of crimson tie, matched by the handkerchief in his breastpocket. 'You discovered the body? I assume you touched nothing? Please be good enough to take us to it.'

I led the way but stood aside when we were at the door of the den. The smell seemed even stronger and more sickly-sweet than before.

'The answer is Yes,' I said, 'to both questions. He's in here.'

'And you identify this as your godfather?'

'I do.' It had a horribly inapt echo of the wedding service.

Grice pointed vaguely across the hall. 'Sit yourself down in another room somewhere within call, sonny. We'd like to talk to you later. And you leave answering the bell to us.' He paused in the doorway. 'You've no cause to worry now we're here,' he said in a professionally soothing tone.

I went into the dinning-room and propped myself up at the table, staring blankly at the breakfast china. If I had had a moment's euphoria, prompted perhaps by some sort of relief, it had certainly fled. I felt utterly exhausted. Although I wasn't hungry, I leant over and crumbled a slice of Ryvita on to a plate. The pottery bee on the marmalade pot seemed clumsier than ever, and somehow pathetic in its clumsiness, its inability to deceive.

Waiting made it impossible to concentrate, and anyway I

was sinking under the weight of so many confused impressions, half-listening, too, to steps and voices in the hall, wondering what at this moment was actually happening. Once I thought a doorbell rang. Now I ought to have been able to summon Maigret to my side, arriving in the *petite auto noire de la P.J.,* sighing a bit but conducting an investigation which stirred memories of his own boyhood while he questioned me. Maigret never had a child: one of his secret regrets. Yet, or for that very reason, he always shows great sympathy for the young. I could have confided everything to him.

Even socially I felt confused, I became aware, as the door started to open and I heard outside a fruity voice in mid-sentence saying firmly 'doubtless a contributory factor ... ,' and then some response by Grice before he entered the room with another man. Somehow I was expecting the doctor and stood up, only to realise that the doctor, if it was he, must be leaving and that Grice's companion was presumably Sergeant Parrott.

Grice seemed pleased by my accidental mark of respect, but I sat down hastily before he could tell me to do so. We took our places round the breakfast table, and I wondered if I ought to be offering cups of tea. Or was it too early for that? The memory of Philip ushering in Rainbow on the morning of their Windsor expedition came to me and momentarily made me, I felt guiltily, smile.

'I'm afraid this has been a very nasty shock for you, sonny,' Grice said. 'There can be no doubt about Mr Kerr's death. We must express our sincere condolences.'

'Thank you,' I said in as neutral a tone as I could, mentally rebuking him for the absurd form of address but not quite knowing how to stop him using it.

He had taken off his trenchcoat, revealing a charcoal-grey suit, as well as an expanse of white shirt-cuff with miniature barrel-shaped gold cuff-links. 'Impeccable,' I heard him murmuring to his image in the mirror before he left home, though the effect was strangely like a uniform; and even his patent-leather hair might have passed for a cap. He had a ballroom-dancing dapperness tinged with some suggestion of the petty officer. I could see him adroitly executing, if such a thing existed, a naval two-step.

'Now,' he said, 'I hope you feel up to helping us. I have a number of questions to ask you and Sergeant Parrott here will be taking down your particulars.'

We had shrieked with laughter over the phrase in the lowest form at my prep school but I had never heard it since.

I glanced without much interest at Sergeant Parrott who looked built in the same mould as Hiscock and Horder, not so hefty but with a rather similar style moustache, though a good deal less walrus-like, and blond not dark. He seemed younger than Grice and somehow much simpler. There was something of animal muzzle about his rather blunt face, snub nose and wide brown eyes. He met my glance in a shy but not unfriendly way, before clearing a space on the table and flattening down the pages of his notebook.

'Your full name is?' Grice asked with painstaking articulation which I found it hard not to echo.

'Nicholas Gonville. Well, my full name, if you want it, is Nicholas Taylor Gonville. Taylor was my mother's maiden name.'

'I see.' He made it sound rather incriminating. 'And your age?'

'I'll be seventeen in December.'

'So you're sixteen and a half? I put you a bit younger in my own mind. Ah, well. How are you related to the late Mr Kerr, sonny?'

'I'm not,' I said, annoyed, hoping he grasped the double nature of my rebuttal. 'He was just my godfather – a friend of our family, my father's friend really.'

'Where is your father at present?'

'My father? He's dead – I'm afraid,' I added stupidly. 'He died some years ago.'

'I'm sorry to hear that,' Grice said solemnly. 'What about your mother?'

'She's in Portugal.'

'On holiday is she?'

'No, she's filming – she's an actress. Norah Naylor is her name.'

'I thought you said her maiden name was Taylor?'

'It is – was. But she changed it for professional reasons. Alliteration makes it sound better. It's more memorable.'

'H'm. And whereabouts is she in Portugal?'

'I don't know. I heard from her this morning but she doesn't say. She's rather vague like that. This is the card I had.'

'May I see it?'

I hesitated, and he noticed my hesitation. 'Don't worry if it's a little personal,' he said, with a gleam of teeth. They were too regular to be real. 'All sorts of communications come the way of the police. Don't they, Skip?' Parrott nodded without much conviction, I thought.

'But how can it be relevant?' I asked. 'To Philip's death, I mean. Mr Kerr's death. It only came this morning.'

'Tell us about this morning, then,' he said as though humouring me.

I kept hold of the card as I spoke, feeling I was describing events which had happened years ago or simply never happened as far as I was concerned.

'By the way,' Grice interrupted when I described coming downstairs as usual and first noticing the smell of sherry. 'Do you normally wear a watch?'

'Yes,' I said, surprised.

'You're not wearing one now.'

'Oh.' I looked down, genuinely disconcerted, at my wrist, where against the sunburnt skin there appeared a distinct whiteish outline. 'I must have forgotten to put it on. I suppose it's upstairs.'

'In that case Hiscock or Horder is bound to see it.'

'They're searching the house?'

'They are conducting a routine investigation,' he conceded. 'But please go on. I'd like to get as good a picture as possible of what you did, though obviously' – he just bared the teeth – 'you won't be able to give us times.'

I stared at him aghast, and then at Parrott whose fair, slightly curly head was bent over his notebook. 'Look,' I said, 'is there some insinuation in that? Do you imagine I'm making it all up, or what? I got up and got dressed exactly as I've been doing here every morning since I arrived. It must've been about eight o'clock. The post was lying on the mat.'

'Just go on describing what you did when you came down. That will be most helpful.'

He crossed his legs carefully as he spoke. I ought to have guessed about the crimson socks neatly matching the tie and handkerchief, but Inspector Grice was turning into something more hateful than diverting. We seemed very far from the relaxed world of Maigret, and I began to feel desperate and angry. Soon they'd be telling me that Mrs Rainbow knew there was bad blood between Philip and me: often enough heard our terrible quarrels while she cleared up at breakfast. I wanted to shout that of course I'd rushed downstairs and lured Philip into his den, and then hit him over the head with the sherry decanter – or perhaps they thought I'd put poison in it days ago.

My eyes actually clouded with tears. It was like being back at school: the same sense of being pre-judged, of not carrying conviction even while one described facts as they had occurred and one's voice rising, despite every effort, in the hostile atmosphere. Grice appeared indifferent to my struggle – perhaps not fully aware of it – and increasingly un-interested in what I was saying. I determined to control my voice and my emotions, and take on a narrator-like detachment.

'Thank you,' he said gravely when I finished. 'Quite an ordeal for you, I'm sure. The shock of finding your godfather and then having to ring us, and describe it all. I appreciate your telling me about your fit of nerves – very understandable. By the way, why did you phone the police?'

'I couldn't think what else to do. It seemed as if there'd been some sort of struggle. Philip looked – looked dead.'

'Of course. Did you think about a doctor?'

'A doctor? I don't know one down here. Philip never had any doctor that I'd ever heard of. The police were the first thing that came to mind.'

'I see. You don't live here, I take it. Just staying, was that it, for the summer holidays?'

'Well, for part of them. It wasn't fixed. I'm at a boarding school – have been, anyway. Every so often out of term I come down here, or stay in London, go abroad, or something.'

'Very nice too,' he said. 'Makes a change, going abroad. Mrs Grice and I are only recently back from Benidorm. Ever been there?'

'I'm afraid not. I know France quite well.'

'Gay Paree and all that.' He paused. 'If you're not too up-set I'd like to ask you about yesterday, and when you saw Mr

Kerr last – before this morning, of course. Just a second. Come in,' he called, though I had heard no knock.

I expected almost anything except Mrs Rainbow bearing a tray of teapot and cups (Philip's best non-breakfast set) and looking, for her, quite clean and animated. Her overall was patterned with wisteria, and I wondered if amid the scrag-ends of hair there wasn't a mauve plastic bow.

'Thought you'd welcome some refreshment, Inspector,' she said, preening herself as she put it down. 'Pardon the intrusion. I didn't realise you and the Sergeant weren't alone. I just brought the two cups.'

'This is very kind, Mrs Rainbow,' Grice said. 'If we're not in your way. And if we might have a third cup, for our young friend here.'

'I don't drink tea,' I said. 'At least, not for breakfast.'

'Breakfast,' she sniffed. 'It's long gone breakfast-time. What a morning it's been. A shocking thing to happen in Spenn; I can't recall anything like it all the years we've lived here. I feel quite sick to think about it. They've taken him away, poor old gentleman. Always so cheerful, and now this. A clergyman too – that makes it worse. You must be sorry for yourself,' she said to me accusingly, producing a plate of biscuits.

'Thank you. I am.'

'If I were you,' Grice said to me, 'I'd have something, sonny.'

'There's some Coke in the fridge,' I said.

'What that does your guts I don't like to think,' Mrs Rainbow said.

'Oh, for God's sake,' I said. 'I'll have a large gin and tonic.'

Parrott looked up, startled, with a perplexed, doggy expression, as if I'd trodden by mistake on his tail.

'Could you add to your kindness and bring the lad a Coke?' Grice said to Mrs Rainbow. 'They're his guts after all.'

I'd never seen her leave a room and return so promptly, though she brought no glass, only the tin.

'Lovely drop of tea, isn't it, Skip?' Grice said with emphasis, raising his cup as she left again. 'Now, would you just think back to yesterday. Saw your godfather as usual at breakfast, I expect?'

'Yes. But I didn't see him again. I was out most of the

morning. I suppose he was too. In the afternoon I came back, went up to my bedroom – and just dozed. I didn't feel very hungry at supper-time so I came down and only had a yoghurt. I expect Philip had something on a tray in the den – his study – and watched cricket on television.'

'That was quite normal, was it?'

'Watching cricket on television?'

'Your not meeting in the evening.'

'Fairly. And of course Wednesday evening was one of his times for seeing parishioners. I kept out of the way.'

Grice laughed tersely. 'Can't say I blame you. Now, while you were up in your bedroom dozing, did you hear any particular noises? Did the bell go at all?'

'It may have done once or twice. I can't be sure. And I was playing my radio, so I probably wouldn't have noticed.'

'Get up at all before you went down to supper? Oh, and I suppose you wouldn't know when you did consume that yoghurt?'

'I got up to pee, I think about six o'clock. It must've been around half-past seven – or a bit later – when I came down to the kitchen.'

'As you went to the toilet, you might perhaps have looked out of the window. But, if you did, you saw no one arriving or leaving?'

'Not that I'm aware of. I'm sorry. There may have been, and it just didn't register.'

'You're sure you didn't see a girl outside?'

There seemed to be a quickening of atmosphere in the torpid, rather shabby room. I tried to think, while watching, as if lightly drugged, the now teeming rain outside. Grice and Parrott, who had raised his head, waited. Suddenly Parrott broke a biscuit in half with a crack that made me start, and Grice veered rapidly round on him, though without speaking.

'I suppose I might have done. If I did, I'd have thought she was only one of Philip's visitors – parishioners. I'm sorry but I can't be certain; I was fairly dozy.'

Grice got up, adjusting his trousers and straightening his tie. 'You've been most co-operative and you must be feeling very tired. We shouldn't keep you any longer. But two last questions, if I may. Of course, you didn't live here, I realise, so perhaps you can't answer. But who would, as far as you know, let in Mr Kerr's parishioners on these visits?'

'Mrs Rainbow. She stayed on for that – anyway until about half-past six.'

'Thank you,' he said earnestly. Parrott remained hunched over his notebook. I wasn't sure whether to move or not, waiting until he had stopped questioning me before I put some questions to him.

'We must think,' he said, 'what to do about you, mustn't we?'

'I'm quite all right,' I said. 'I feel fine, really, though I'd like to hear what's happening – what happened to Philip, I mean. I'm not a child. I'd rather know the facts. But you said you wanted to ask me two questions.'

'Oh, yes. About your own movements last night. This isn't a very large house. When you came downstairs to eat, I expect you'd have heard if the television was on in the study. Was it?'

I thought hard. 'I'm sure I didn't hear it. That's all I can say.'

'And the study door – was that definitely shut?'

'I'm not sure. Yes, it must have been'.

'Good,' he said. 'Now, let's see how we can fix you up.'

'I don't need fixing up.'

'Don't you?' He looked relieved as I stood up to mark my declaration. I was about to start questioning him, but he went straight on. 'Stay with Mrs Rainbow could you perhaps, or have you got an auntie living in these parts?'

'I've got an aunt in London, if that's what you mean. But I don't want to stay with anyone – least of all the Rainbows, and they'd hardly want me.'

'I'd rather you didn't leave this area,' he said, 'while our enquiries are going on. Certain formalities are likely to arise. Besides, you'll want to be at the funeral, won't you?'

'The funeral?' I said blankly, suddenly afraid I was going to begin trembling once more. 'I hadn't thought about the funeral.'

'Quite natural,' he said. 'It's all been so very sudden for you. The vicar will be making arrangements after he's been in touch with the next of kin. Skip, I think we'll give him another ring: he'd be glad, I'm sure, to put up Mr Kerr's godson in all the circumstances. Sonny, you'd best go and pack your bag.'

'I don't want to stay with the vicar.' I no longer cared if my voice sounded desperate. I meant to be mutinous. The whole misery of the morning, far from fading, had deepened, just when I felt on the point of escaping and getting away on my own. 'He's a silly old fool, with a ghastly wife. Anyway, he loathes me. And I'm an atheist.'

There was a pause. Parrott was now standing, and Grice gave him a look I found difficult to interpret but I sensed their growing embarrassment. I wanted them to feel the encumbrance I threatened to become. Then, before either of them could speak, I said, 'I don't mind staying here. Isn't that the answer? I wouldn't be afraid. And I'd be on the spot.'

'It's out of the question,' Grice said, tightening his tie until the knot grew minute. 'From every point of view. I have to tell you that your godfather met his death in highly suspicious circumstances. A post mortem is being carried out and foul play has to be seriously borne in mind.'

'Perhaps you think I'd tamper with the evidence, Inspector?'

'The matter is of the greatest gravity,' he replied. 'It would not be right least of all to leave a lad of your age alone here. I must ask you to go and pack, while we ring the vicar.'

'Oh, fuck the vicar,' I said, slamming the door as I walked out, too angrily frustrated to care that I'd been reduced to such a banal retort.

I hurried upstairs, half hoping to encounter Hengist and Horsa on their knees with magnifying glasses and attendant bloodhound. Perhaps they were interrogating Mrs Rainbow. Obtaining her 'dabs' would be easy enough even for them: just press her grubby fingers on to any clean surface. I looked suspiciously round my room to see if it bore traces of recent search. Untampered with, apparently, lay my watch on the rickety table by the bed. Nobody had yet ticketed it 'Exhibit A'. It lay as I had left it – idiotically overlooked it on getting up – unless a microscopic bug had cunningly been inserted in it, placed there by Horder, *mettons,* after Hiscock had prised open the back with the penknife awarded to them at the Police Sports for coming first in the three-legged race. Did my clothes show signs of having been mauled by Hiscock, while

Horder had laboriously hunted for clues by examining the dusty bag of golf-clubs, leaving his own enormous thumb-print on it? I dragged from under the bed my smart grey suitcase which seemed to slide out suspiciously quickly, disturbing no fluff as it came. As I flung my clothes and books into it, I thought how baffling it would have been for the Horder-Hiscock team to enter the room and find none of the anticipated evidence of youth: no pop-star posters, no strewn dirty socks or Sci-Fi paperbacks – not even chewing-gum. If they picked up *Fleurs du Mal* I expect they quickly put it down again, seeing it was foreign; only *The Tale of Genji* probably sounded like it might be some fashionably fey modern story for children and adults about a rabbit in a top-hat who stood for Parliament or finally appeared at the Palladium.

Clasping my radio under one arm, I started along the corridor, passing Philip's room and then remembering my toothbrush was in the bathroom, stuck in a mug alongside his at the side of the washbasin. It wasn't worth stopping for (let the vicar produce a miraculous toothbrush, I thought savagely); either that, or I seemed absurdly reluctant to encounter the toothbrush which had been Philip's. And I had been prepared, positively looked forward, to being alone in the house.

I entered the bathroom and picked up my toothbrush. There was Philip's, with an almost episcopal magenta handle, quite new-looking and quite ordinary. It failed to cause me any revulsion – any emotion at all. I would leave it for Detective-Inspector Grice to send to 'Forensic', or whatever, and thus learn – if he was lucky – that after each meal Philip cleaned his teeth.

They were his own teeth, I felt sure, unlike Grice's, which were on display in the hall, where it seemed that my departure rated a full police turn-out. Outside the den, across the closed door of which there appeared to be stretched some tape, stood Hiscock and Horder, eyeing me as warily as if my suitcase was loaded with bombs.

'Now, sonny.' Grice stepped forward, looking far more affable than before. Behind him Parrott hovered, still shy, though he too, in a slightly depressed, deprecating way, smiled at me. They might have been my hosts, speeding me off amid mutual gratitude and relief after a country weekend.

'Please don't go on calling me that, Inspector,' I said coolly, delighted to give dignity to the public farewell scene. At least at the vicarage one thing would be spared me.

'Right,' he said, in an offhand tone. 'Now, there's a change of plan. Sergeant Parrott and Mrs Parrott have kindly offered to accommodate you for a day or two, so we needn't trouble the vicar. It's very good of them, and the Sergeant can drive you there straight away.'

'You'd certainly know where to find me to assist in your enquiries. No, it is awfully kind, but I can't really—'

'I spoke to my wife.' Parrott's voice was agreeably resoant, countrified but not slow, and much firmer than I was prepared for. 'She'd like it. She said it would be company for her.'

'Well ...' I felt chez Parrott might prove more socially awkward even than the vicar's.

'Lucky to have such an invitation, to my mind,' said Grice, obviously longing to add something like 'stuck-up young sod.' And I did have to stop deliberating, stop anticipating garrulous Mrs Parrott combined with the Sergeant's heavy-footed constant surveillance.

'Super,' I said, inanely. 'Thanks very much. It's most kind of your wife – and you: just for a night or two, of course.'

6

In the car I was conscious of Parrott glancing every so often at me uneasily. My presence seemed to distract him from driving – or perhaps it was the filthy weather which made him drive so badly: hunched up and peering ahead timidly as we approached bends obscured by drenched, high, waving hedgerows along the narrow road. If he slowed down much more, we might as well start walking – or just stop.

The forced intimacy of the small car didn't exactly help. Though I had duly slung my suitcase on the back seat as he indicated, I had had a moment's impulse to follow it and let him become in every sense my chauffeur. But Grice was watching from the front door, taking care not to get wet, and the gesture might even have rebounded ironically with overtones of convict status.

'We live a good way out of Spenn,' Parrott had said apologetically, as he swung the car awkwardly in the opposite direction to the high street. 'Just a cottage, you know – nothing much – at Trencham Croke.'

'I abominate Spenn,' I replied conversationally, shifting slightly to allow him more room to reach for the gear lever without touching me. His hands looked rather big: of the sort conventionally thought competent (perhaps woodwork was his hobby?), a shade more tawny than his face and quite thickly covered with small blond hairs. There was something not unpleasantly paw-like about them.

Sleepily in the gathering fug of the car, I thought of journeys along French roads with Dennis in his, navigating and declining to be instructed at the same time. 'Please watch for the direction Angers sign, Nick. Do you know what the inhabitants of Angers are called?' 'Easy ... *anges,* obviously; though I bet you wouldn't guess it to look at them. Anyway, Dennis, what goes on in a *"Foyer Jeunes Travailleurs"?* – one was advertised at Orléans – and there's an organisation called *"Femmes chefs d'entreprise"* of Touraine who would disapprove of your *entreprise.'* He had to grin a little, if only because he felt flattered, as well as probably rather drowsy as we drove on in the late afternoon, both thinking about the evening and where we should stop. He preferred to ask for single rooms, and I too preferred it. It made everything more amusing – even at times more risky – and gave me anyway some necessary privacy. I liked inspecting our two rooms and their outlook, arranging who would call for whom, and debating with myself what shirt to wear at dinner.

At Angers, in a stuffy hotel with thick carpet on its twisting corridors and stairs, I terrified him one evening by knocking on his door and coming in naked: 'If somebody had seen you, you little fool ... For God's sake take my dressing-gown when you go back. What an incredibly childish thing to do.' All the next day Dennis had 'kept me in' in the car, and it had begun to rain in a gentle, half-hearted way; I tired of listening to him on tapestries and who David d'Angers was and what du Bellay had written, and I failed to notice which was the fork for Le Mans. Communication broke down. It would have been so simple to stretch my arm along the back of the driving-seat and by that action re-establish contact. But I did nothing, sitting there immobile. He watched the road with exaggerated concentration. Dinner that evening was studied-ly formal; we spoke chiefly through the waiter and afterwards Dennis said he was tired and would go to bed early. Half an hour later I went up to his room and knocked on the door. He looked out gloomily, at his most Kafkaesque. I put my hands very lightly on his dressing-gowned shoulders, and rather reluctantly he drew me into the room. 'I forgive you,' I said, kissing him.

From contemplating the rain streaming over the wind-screen I glanced, without moving my head, towards Parrott. The silence wasn't oppressive; but it seemed to point to our total lack of *rapport*. He might well be regretting whatever had moved him to suggest putting me up – or had Grice made the suggestion? I couldn't think what to say to him – well, I could, but not in any suitable conversational manner: anything I speculated about life in a cottage for a few days at Trencham Croke would or would not very shortly be proved true. It would be an experience; brief and however dull, it must be different from travelling with Dennis, on holiday with Mother, staying with Margot ... or with Philip. At least Parrott didn't say anything about what had hap-pened. Nor did he ask me about myself or what I was going to become. And, after all, Mrs Parrott could scarcely be more loathsome than Mrs Rainbow, surrounded though she might be by smelly little Parrotts (I hadn't thought of that) and awful livestock: possibly an evil-tempered goat and two mongrel dogs, one large and silly, the other small, old, mangy and aggressive with strangers.

'I can't help wondering.' Parrott met my glance with a bashful look, accentuated by his droopy moustache, before resuming worried scrutiny of the road. He sounded earnest but uncertain whether to continue. I tried to appear encour-aging. If he felt he had kidnapped me, or merely been landed with me, I must show I wasn't always alarming. Indeed, when at ease I could behave extremely well, act rather graciously to his wife and show a muted interest – or conceal repugnance, anyway – when confronted by the tangled *tableau* of his animals and children. 'Have you got a mac?'

'Have I got a what?'

His profile seemed to go rather pink. 'A mackintosh. You're going to get soaked if this continues. It's a good yard or two to the house from where I can park.'

I looked down at my bare arms cradling the radio. 'I've got a denim jacket. Damn and blast. It's hanging in the hall at Philip's, my godfather's.'

'I'll bring it back this evening. What's it like?'

'You'll easily spot it. It's brown. Oh, and I think my "I love paedophilia" badge is on it.'

'Right.' He showed no sign of having heard properly. With a jerk, the car stopped. 'Well, this is it. Do you mind hopping out here?'

We appeared to be nowhere. Hopping was the verb for negotiating the ruts and puddles and the shaggy, dripping hedge against which he had parked. I could see some trees on the verge and then the wooden gate of a small pair of red-brick, red-tiled houses, standing a few feet back from the road. He seized my suitcase, and I followed him, running breathlessly up the short brick path, dodging one or two fallen gladioli, towards an already open front door.

Mrs Parrott was rather formidable-looking, tall and plump, with a lot of dark hair and a hefty chin. She shook hands as I quickly introduced myself – before Parrott could make a mess of it.

'This really is most kind of you, Mrs Parrott,' I said. 'I must be an awful nuisance.'

'You're not,' she said, unsmiling. 'Terrible weather, isn't it?'

Parrott deposited my suitcase on the red-tiled floor of the hall, and the three of us stood there. I felt like the baton in a relay race.

'Now, you be away, Bob,' Mrs Parrott said. 'I've put Mr Gonville in the back room. We're less shut-in that side,' she told me.

'I'll be home when I can,' he said. 'With what's happened, you know – I can't say when.'

'Thanks so much for driving me, Sergeant,' I said, aware

that my voice sounded rather thin and flute-like after the low, solemn tones they shared. Mrs Parrott spoke in an unhurried way, with a marked Northern accent.

She left me to carry my suitcase and led the way up the narrow stairs. From the back, in her dark green dress or overall, she conveyed a quality not only of the matronly but of matron in the hospital sense. I might have arrived for a serious operation, so gravely and silently did she escort me along the polished landing, to open the door on a blue-painted room.

'You get the morning sun in here,' she said, moving to the window and pushing yet further back the blue-and-white checked curtains. 'And you've the garden, and that's the Croke beyond.'

I walked over to join her, ready to murmur appreciatively about the blaze of colour or the view. I wasn't prepared for the massed, variegated greenery below: a vegetable garden densely planted and plotted, it seemed, down to the last inch, and closed off by a few fruit trees from damp fields stretching away into the distance.

'What is the Croke?' I asked politely, noticing the blue china donkey on the window-sill, its paniers stuck with garden flowers and a sprig – I thought – of mint.

'Of course, you're not local, are you?' she said. 'It's the river hereabouts – more a stream, I'd call it, though it does widen further on and they say you can bathe in it. Now, I'll leave you to unpack. It's gone one o'clock.' She sounded quite disturbed. 'You must be famished, but I expect you'd like to be left on your own for a while, so I'll bring you up a bite to eat. You've everything you want, I hope. The bathroom and so on is just next door.'

She adjusted the fringed white counterpane as she passed the bed, though it appeared to need no adjusting.

'It's all very nice,' I said. It came out more tremulously than I had intended. As soon as she left I thought I would throw myself on the bed, not forgetting, all the same, first to fold back the counterpane. Misery and weariness had suddenly engulfed me. I was waiting only for her to go, but at the doorway she paused, as if with a final message that had to be delivered.

'I'm very sorry for your loss.'

She said it so simply that I could do nothing but nod in reply, nodding in fact to the door she had quietly closed behind her. For a few moments I stood there, unrelaxed, listening for the sounds of the house, staring at the white, rather forbidding slice of bed which took on an almost bier-like inviolateness. I was still standing there when I heard a tap – more, a rap – at the door. There was no response to my 'come in'. I went to open it, and lying outside was a tray of thick-cut sandwiches, two bananas and a cup of very milky coffee.

Siege provisions, superior prison diet: yet I couldn't remain for ever barricaded in my cell, though I paced out its extent, went again to the window and saw the rain had lessened, examined the clumsily-coloured, framed view identified as 'Whitby Bay' which hung over the bed, then turned up the corner of a sandwich to find it was ham. I was hungrier than I had realised, and it was aromatic, unplastic ham, tasting as if cured by being suspended in some faintly smoky farmhouse kitchen – delicious, until I remembered Callum MacGregor's dear old grandmother massacring a pig, with a bowl at hand ready to catch the warm blood (something I must have missed in the TV advertisements for fine country fare).

Still, I munched on, squatting on the floor beside the tray. The thought of Callum prompted thoughts vaguely of other people, of things I ought to be doing, like getting Mother told of Philip's death. Every time I came round to that fact, it was not so much like a blur as an enormous obstacle. I could not see beyond it. And then there was Grice and his investigation, and Sergeant Parrott, and my presence in the household of which this bedroom was a part.

Increasingly it was hard to keep a grip on my own individuality. I lay half-collapsed against the familiar bulk of my suitcase while the sky gradually cleared and watery afternoon light explored the dustless corners of the sparsely-furnished but spruce room. The fawn and blue knitted rug might have been nailed to the floor, so straight did it lie. The dark wood of the chest-of-drawers looked to have grown waxy from years of polishing; inside I should discover a scented muslin bag and very clean sheets of folded paper lining each drawer. Nobody, probably, had sprawled in this room before. It wasn't easy to think of anything untidy happening in it – least of all of anyone doing anything in the bed except sleeping alone and as straight as though bandaged within its narrow confines.

It all had its effect on me. Perhaps I was feeling too inert to rebel against the atmosphere, but I found it soothing – rather like, I suppose, being in hospital – even if it seemed monotonous. For a day or two I could play at being a casualty. Anyway I was probably still in shock. Further shocks might lie ahead. It seemed the best treatment to lie there, not disturbing the intense silence by playing the radio otherwise than softly; I twiddled and tuned, avoiding every scream and beat of pop, until I encountered some eighteenth-century-sounding music as wavering and muted as the light, tinkling out as if from a slightly rusty musical-box.

I was much calmer when at last I left the room, though I left it a little reluctantly. Already it was subtly marked as mine. My shirts, socks and underpants were in the vaguely fragrant drawers, lined in fact with newspaper, discoloured but rustlingly crisp and clean. Across the bed were draped my discarded tee shirt and jeans, and I paid homage to my environment by wearing grey trousers and a lemon-yellow, long-sleeved voile shirt. The not very adequate mirror of the cabinet in the otherwise surprisingly trendy chrome and sea-green bathroom had at least confirmed my sense of looking *fils de famille,* with a slightly Sunday air. In these clothes I could better have dealt with Inspector Grice. I might almost be the eldest of the Parrott children, coming down for church or drinks with a neighbour – supposing such things existed in their life-style.

I carried my tray with a certain amount of deliberate noise, clattering like a social leper, alerting whoever awaited me downstairs to my approach. The house remained absolutely quiet and still; very much leaving me to discover it: reminding me of some game of the kind I had always disliked at children's parties. Perhaps the Parrott family were all out – which gave me an opportunity to learn more about the way they lived. I set down the tray in the hall with a challenging rattle and followed the strip of floral patterned runner to the doorway into which it led.

Seated alone in a mushroom-coloured easy chair in what was clearly the sitting-room, with tea laid out and some pink knitting in her lap, was Mrs Parrott. My arrival seemed neither to disturb nor fluster her, though she quickly put aside the knitting and handed me a plate. It might have been a regular afternoon ritual for us both, as I took my place in another of the deep, buff chairs and helped myself unthinkingly to the scones, cream and obviously home-made jam.

'I expect you like your tea strong,' she said. 'Bob does.'

She held the cup ready and for a moment I was tempted to agree. It must be an aspect of the routine into which I was being absorbed, as familiar as the untrodden-looking mushroom carpet, the set of lustre jugs on the low mantelpiece and the needlework screen of a bounding stag in the fireplace.

'Actually,' I said, asserting myself, 'I'm not mad about tea, I'm afraid.'

'Would you like a glass of wine instead?'

'Well, that's very kind.' I found I was stammering, unprepared for the sophisticated alternative and mentally adding a cellar to the dimensions of their establishment.

'The old gentleman next door – Mr Latimer – he's always fond of a glass when he drops in.' She got up. I felt I too ought to rise, though it was genuinely difficult from the depths of the huge chair. 'I've parsnip or elderberry,' she said. 'Which is it to be?'

I hesitated. 'I don't think I've ever tasted either – I'm afraid. Perhaps whichever ...'

'Parsnip, I'd say,' she said firmly, before I could finish.

I sat there while she went to fetch it, though I was longing to get up and examine what appeared to be their wedding photograph, propped up in a corner beside a basket-shaped bowl of candytuft. Somehow the room told me there was no dog, mangy or otherwise – and possibly no children. I felt pleased to have been so wrong. What I didn't find easy to guess was how old the Parrotts were; but they could be of an age, if they married very young, to have been the parents of me.

It became almost an indecent thought, as I looked at Mrs Parrott and took from her the glass of pale liquid: indecent or at any rate disloyal. But it did not go away.

I made an appreciative noise over the wine – by no means insincerely. It was not bad, once you forgot the connotations of parsnip. She poured herself another cup of tea and cut into a sponge-cake, which I refused.

'We're not big eaters,' she said. 'Leastways not at supper time. But you must speak up if there's not enough. There's few things worse than an empty stomach.'

'I don't feel I'm going to starve, somehow.'

'That's as maybe. Where I come from we've a saying: other folk's food and other folk's houses mean a rumbling belly and a cold backside.'

I laughed instinctively, and she gave me a shy smile, almost a grin, that turned her strangely girlish, despite her heavy face and projecting jaw. Her large dark eyes, blacker and bolder than her husband's, were rather beautiful and perhaps also a little sad.

'Have you lived here long?' I asked, thinking how for all her unconscious stateliness there was a touch of gypsy in her appearance.

'Nine years,' she answered promptly. 'Since we were first married. And that wasn't long after we met. On a bird-watching holiday Bob was, in the West Riding – my part of the world. Coming south was a wrench for me, I don't mind telling you. Yorkshire born and bred my family always has been. My father's still alive,' she added proudly. 'And he's seventy-seven next birthday: lives alone and looks after himself wonderfully.'

I made no reply, just sitting there, settling down in a pleasantly sluggish way in the comfortably over-furnished room but aware that beyond it and its small windows with their snug, tree-enclosed view problems as big as boulders were rolling up. Unknown to Mrs Parrott, resuming her knitting and pleasantly lost in telling me of her sisters, Marion, Angela and Elspeth ('I'm the youngest by a long chalk') and their young families, the house from where I sat seemed almost under threat, ringed as dangerously as if by tanks by the forces of the world outside.

'Such a lovely baby as she is I never saw,' she was saying. 'I'm her godmother and they've christened her Edna, after me.'

I hadn't thought of it before: I might have been called Philip. But I couldn't see myself so. The name had only one connotation for me, and I wondered what – if anything – Grice was discovering. Did anyone yet know how Philip died, or did that wait for an inquest? And what were they unearthing about Philip's life, while he remained – his body remained – unburied, on some ghastly sluiced-down white slab where that fishy, bloated appearance I could not forget would only have increased?

'I must be thinking of our supper. Maybe Bob'll be back soon and you'd like to walk along to the pub with him, now it's cleared up, for a jug of beer. You're looking a bit peaky. A breath of fresh air would do you good.'

She began slowly to gather the tea things. With an effort I tried to shake off my lethargy.

'What I ought to do, if I may,' I said, 'is make a telephone call, to my aunt in London. To let her know where I am – what's happened.'

'You be doing that, and I'll be getting on in the kitchen. You've the phone here.'

Looking shiny and unused, it stood on a low glass-topped table with one or two books beside it. I knelt there, dialling the number I always thought of as Mopsa's, though as I listened to the ringing at the other end I visualised the scarlet and gold Pagoda-phone object that fitted in with Margot's drawing-room décor. While I waited, I glanced curiously at one of the plastic-bound public library books: *Princess in Pawn,* by the author of *Sullied Ermine, Daughter of Spain, A Crown to Win,* etc., etc. Rather similar seemed another book, *Baltic Falcon:* 'A rich tapestry woven of love and ambition in sixteenth-century strife-torn Riga ...' It was quite surprising that something slimmer, called *The Yellow Wagtail,* turned out to be an entirely factual bird-book, probably the Parrotts' own property.

Margot's cool hard tones poured down the telephone like so much vocal nail-varnish: almost as incongruous in the room where I knelt as a broken bottle of gin.

'Lovely to hear you, my dear boy. We're just back from Venice. Are you having fun down there with Philip? ... Oh, no. How dreadful.' Now somebody might have spilt the nail varnish all over her silk upholstery. 'When did it happen? What an awful thing for you. They are sure, are they? I can't hear very well on this terrible line.'

' ... And try and let Mother know.'

'Norah? Of course. I'll ring her agent; she's bound to know where they are. It *is* wretched for you, my poor boy – such a shock: so suddenly too. Oh, how annoying – horrible – for you. I *am* sorry. Had he been ill?'

The corpse, as it had become, was certainly awkward, precipitated without warning on to the centre of the Chinese carpet; I could feel her anxiety to have it shifted as soon as decently possible.

'Mopsa's in Greece with, er, Simon, but you must come and stay straightaway ... The funeral? Of course. But you don't know about an inquest? Shouldn't Hugh speak to someone at Scotland Yard? Or I suppose he could come down if it's really vital ...'

'I'd rather he didn't – truly, Margot. Thanks, but I can cope.'

'I'm sure you can, my dear boy. Still, I feel we ought to do something. We hardly knew Philip, but perhaps we could send flowers. Are you in a hotel or what? I expect the neighbours are making a fuss of you – they certainly should. There's so much more sympathy in those small places, isn't there, than in London ... Oh, good. That's a relief. And they *are* on the phone? I didn't quite catch the name ... Oh, how amusing: easy to remember, anyway. I hope they've been sweet to you.'

I glanced across at the ineffectively-tinted wedding photograph which showed Bob with fair, ruffled hair looking almost soppily innocent and naked, despite his police constable's uniform, standing proudly at attention beside a bride nearly as tall as he, who glowered out darkly as she gripped his arm with one large hand, appearing ill-at-ease in a long veil and shiny, somewhat too short white dress which revealed boat-like white shoes. (I suddenly realised I had never seen a photograph of my own parents' wedding.) They looked happy to be united and yet unsure of each other, and even more of the camera's scrutiny.

'Are you still there?' Margot was demanding, her voice a shade less controlled than usual. 'You will keep us in touch, won't you, my dear boy? If Hugh can do anything ... And of course I'll ring Norah's Barney Bunkup tomorrow, without fail.'

'Her name's Burnham, as a matter of fact.'

'Yes, darling, I know.' She sounded quite mournful. 'It's only my little joke. Now, don't worry about it all, and I hope we'll see you very soon. I do feel for you down there on your own, with the funeral and the police if there's a dreadful inquest. But I'm sure Norah'll fly back at once when she hears. Then you can go off together.'

'Yes,' I said.

'My dear boy, do try to put it behind you. It must be an awful shock, but these things happen.'

'Even in the best families. Anyway, I'm fine – I think. I'd better ring off. Sorry to have disturbed you.'

Bob's voice out in the hall was the first indication I had that he was back, and Mrs Parrott must have come out to meet him. Now Margot seemed reluctant to stop talking, and Mother's return and Mopsa's absence and poor Philip's family – did he have any family? – relentlessly came and went in an almost tearful way, as though she felt she must not release me without sprinkling some conversational talcum powder over the incident.

As I listened, half to her and half to the voices in the hall, I idly turned a page or two of *Baltic Falcon:* 'Wanda's slim breasts heaved under the thin satin ...' It seemed as if Sadie had slipped into sixteenth-century Riga. 'The amber cross at her throat gleamed dully. Stanislas noticed how well it matched the fire of the eyes she raised to his, lit by a pride of race that nothing could quench.' Wanda-Edna Parrott would probably soon feel the first touch of his lips against hers, more chiselled than her husband's, I should think, while hands slimmer than his urgently sought in her costume sixteenth-century Riga's equivalent of the zip.

'Yes, yes, of course I will,' I told the telephone, none too coherently. 'Thanks so much, Margot. I feel much better. I shan't worry. I shall sleep well. Yes, I know ... No, fine, really. Love to you too.'

'Mr Gonville has just been speaking to his aunt in London,' Mrs Parrott explained as I opened the door, though I felt she must already have given this explanation.

'Please,' I said, 'I'd much rather be called Nicholas.'

'Well.' She looked gravely judicial, and it was clear while we waited that the decision would be hers alone. 'If you're staying it does seem more friendly to be on Christian name terms. I'm Edna.'

I sensed that in her eyes it would be a breach of decorum or etiquette to say that I already knew. We both waited, almost formally, for my host to contribute. He seemed changed – perhaps partly the effect of being in shirt-sleeves – less awkward and inevitably less on duty.

'My name's Robert – Bob,' he said cheerfully, though not without a faint flush. 'By the way, I picked up your jacket. At least, I suppose it's yours.'

As I took it and thanked him, I found myself folding it over my arm to conceal the badge. It must be that I wanted to avoid shocking Edna.

'What's been happening?' I asked, more sharply than I meant to, suppressing the urge to ask who had been arrested (Mrs Rainbow handcuffed, confined in a cell at Spenn ... Rainbow failing to give her any alibi). 'Oh,' while Bob was gathering himself to answer. 'I must pay for my phone-call, Mrs Par— Edna.'

'Time enough for that,' she said. 'Now, Bob.'

'I think the funeral's to be on Monday,' he said. 'We've traced a cousin of Mr Kerr's, a lady on holiday in Devon. She's the next of kin and she's coming to Spenn for the funeral.'

'Mr Latimer's Jim would run Nicholas over for it, I'm sure,' Edna (though I wasn't yet used to it) said. 'Why not have a word with him, if he's in the garden, when you go down to the pub? Mr Latimer's son has got his own van,' she said to me. 'He runs a business round here, shampooing people's carpets and all that. Makes a tidy penny at it, but he's a good lad.'

'About Philip,' I said, as though restoring the meeting to order. 'What actually happened? Do you know how his death occurred?'

'Give me a minute to wash and change,' Bob said pleasantly, moving towards the stairs.

'Nicholas might be glad to walk down to the pub with you, Bob, mightn't you?' She watched him disappear. 'Yes, he likes to change when he gets home. It's easier in the village too, somehow. Or that's what he feels. Now, I've nothing much for supper but bacon-and-egg pie and cold potatoes and salad. Still, there's plenty of bread and cheese. I don't know if that's enough for you. My nephews and nieces aren't greedy, I must say, but they've good healthy appetites. It's only right at your age.'

95

'Well, I often have just a yoghurt for a meal, thanks.'

'The things in those little cartons, are they? There can't be much in one of them. They'll never put flesh on your bones, believe me.'

'Perhaps he doesn't want to get fat like us,' Bob called out from the landing.

'Fat?' She looked up quite indignantly. 'Don't be so daft. Nobody's the worse for a square meal. And if you've filled out, Bob Parrott, it's because you've been properly looked after since you married, so I trust you're not complaining of that.'

'I'm not complaining of anything,' he said, bounding down the stairs, virtually barking, and transformed into Rover the retriever going for a walk. He was wearing a pale fawn knitted cardigan inset with patches of rust-coloured suede, and it only increased his animal-like appearance. He looked so healthy and washed and happy, and so much younger than I felt I could ever have been. He gave Edna a playful kiss which she put up a hand not very seriously to ward off. A sudden spark of jealousy, or something sourly like it, flashed on and off in my mind, so rapidly that I stood there bewildered by the sensation. It was as if she at least had detected my reaction; or perhaps she simply felt the scene was too clumsily intimate for a stranger to witness.

'I'll get you a jug for the beer,' she said, 'and we'll eat when you're back.'

In a strangely sulky mood – like an owner resisting the tugging on the leash of his eager, frisky pet – I let him lead the way out of the house. He told me Mr Latimer usually stood and smoked a pipe in his garden at about this time of the evening, but I was pleased to see no sign of him. I was less pleased when Bob made me wait outside the pub ('I wasn't going to be served alcohol over the counter,' I muttered), an ugly modern building in no style, ludicrously called The Old Wheatsheaf. Trencham Croke seemed barely a village: just a few red brick cottages of urban appearance little softened by straggling hollyhocks in unkempt gardens, a sub-post office that looked to have been closed, behind its calico blind, since the death of Edward VII, the concrete Wheatsheaf and a giant drum of cable abandoned beside a ditch, possibly explaining why the local telephone line was so bad. Somehow

I couldn't see Trencham Croke getting on to next year's 'Visit Britain' calendar.

While I lounged outside the pub – not for long because Bob emerged speedily enough – two girls in jeans strolled by giggling, not even noticing me, and Trencham Croke's token punk-rocker-hell's angel drew up on his scooter, took off his death's head helmet, ruffled his spiky blue-green hair, scowled around and then rather nervously pushed open the pub door, just as Bob came out.

'Evening, Mr Parrott,' he said, falling back respectfully. 'Nice now, isn't it?'

'Hallo, Terry,' Bob said. 'How's your mother?'

'Getting about again, thanks.'

'Some bastard driving too fast to London nearly killed his mother,' Bob told me angrily as we walked away. 'Knocked her over and never bothered to stop – and in broad daylight.'

'Is London part of the offence?'

'How do you mean?' He halted, holding the jug in front of him, looking at me in a puzzled way.

I stared back into his brown eyes, under the faintly crinkled forehead, thinking that now he might almost be a giant toy lion, blond, big but soft, standing on his back legs and clasping the jug in those slightly furry front paws, on one of which shone the broad gold band of a wedding ring. Only now, in the uncertain evening sunlight which seemed turning everything tawny, even his open-necked white shirt, did I realise the attraction he exuded – and how unconscious he was of it.

Why we were on the brink of quarrelling I no more understood than why I had stopped at this tree-lined roadside, in the midst of nowhere, pierced by a feeling of utter loneliness. Who was Bob anyway? 'Be a good creature,' I wanted to say. 'Carry your master home, tuck him up and then you could sleep at the foot of the bed.' It was in the blue-painted room with the narrow white bed where I saw us.

'I couldn't understand what London had to do with it,' I said feebly, after a long pause. 'Oh, it doesn't matter. I'm more concerned with my godfather than Terry's mother. And he is dead, don't forget. And I've had a fairly hellish day. And—' I ought to have had another reason ready but no coherent thought would come. I just stood there disorientated.

'I know,' he said, moving closer to me but then seeming

uneasy at the proximity. 'It must have been tough for you; I do know that. I'm sorry. Let's go back, shall we, or Edna will start wondering what's happened to us.'

'Can we talk over supper?'

'If you like,' he said gruffly, yet gently.

'You will tell me what you – the police – know, won't you? About Philip, I mean. I've a right to know. Do get it into your head that I'm not a child. I am not in need of care or protection. I probably know a great deal more about life, frankly, than you do. You won't shock me, but I might shock you. So there.'

'I'm an ordinary bloke,' he said slowly. 'Look, let's start walking back. Life down here is pretty quiet, I grant you. Something like Mr Kerr's death is out of the ordinary as far as we're concerned. It's not been a normal day for me either – not in any way. And it's not my case – it's the Boss's, Mr Grice's. I do what he tells me, but he doesn't have to discuss his theories with me.'

'I thought that was just what the police did do. Don't you retire to a pub or café and mull it over, swap clues and eliminate suspects?'

'That's not Mr Grice's way of proceeding. He's not one for much chat, not at any time.'

'I suppose he wants to catch the criminal himself – always assuming there was one, of course. How did Philip die? That must be a fact, not a theory.'

'There'll be an inquest next week, I can say that. Probably on Thursday. Then the Coroner may give a verdict. I'm afraid you'll have to be a witness; and the Boss wants to see you tomorrow. I expect he'll tell you a bit more then.'

'You obviously won't,' I said rudely. But he looked so hurt, shaking his head slightly as if he'd been punched, that I felt quite sorry to be tormenting him, anxious and confused though I was. 'Not fair,' his doggy brown eyes seemed to be saying, while he remained silent. I wondered if Grice bullied him, snapped at him with those gleaming false teeth, shoved him aside socially with talk of Benidorm with Mrs Grice. (Somehow I couldn't see the Parrotts ever going abroad for their holidays.)

'One thing you can tell me,' I said as we reached the gate. I felt oddly pleased to see the cottage; it was commonplace, if not positively ugly, but already familiar. It meant Edna, laying the table, setting out the meal, preparing to scold us mildly for delay. Perhaps there was even natural wisdom in Bob's reluctance about talking over supper. I foresaw that altogether talking wouldn't be much required, and that seemed both calming and consoling.

'Was it Grice's idea,' I went on, 'that you took me in – sort of unofficial surveillance-cum-custody? Anyway, I bet it's much nicer than Spenn police station, being here.'

'It was mine,' he said proudly. 'Edna agreed. And there's no surveillance intended. I'm sorry if you feel that.'

'I don't really. It was a silly remark. Actually I'm grateful. And I'm glad it was your own idea. That makes a difference. I'm grateful to you both – truly.'

'Well.' He looked embarrassed and then brightened. 'Ah, good evening, Mr Latimer. Fine now, isn't it, after that nasty start.'

'Good evening, Sergeant.'

In bow-tie and waistcoat, complacently smoothing strands of straight silver hair over his pink scalp, Mr Latimer stood in his porch like God Almighty surveying his garden as good and puffing away at a short pipe. If he hadn't been in a bank or a solicitor's office, he must have been the games-master at some particularly dim school. I stuck a whistle in his mouth and added baggy shorts. Of course. Mr Latimer must be a retired referee, his park now only a minute portion of turf with merely flowers to control. A glance at his garden suggested that he had it – almost literally – taped, so obediently did everything seem in bloom and in place.

'A young friend staying with us just for a few days,' Bob was explaining, with an air of seeking to obtain for my presence Mr Latimer's approval (something I rather suspected might not be forthcoming).

'Yes,' I said, bowing distantly, the youthful prince, incognito, in exile, and half-pleased, half-sorry to be so conventionally well dressed when I might have worn a tee shirt with a special 'Drop dead' message for the over-seventies. 'I'm an orphan of events, I'm afraid, but Bob and Edna are being very kind to me. I expect Edna's waiting for us, Bob,' I added, with a graceful air of nephew-like familiarity, *touché* for the 'young friend' epithet. 'I'm ravenous, and you must be too. It's been quite a day.'

Leaving Mr Latimer to put that in his pipe and smoke it, I

did a Bob-style bound towards the front door. He had to follow – at heel, I thought. With a slightly febrile feeling of forcing myself on in a role I didn't know very well, I called, but not too loudly, 'We're back.'

7

'Wixton Reservoir?' I found myself saying dubiously. 'Well, I don't mind. I've never done any bird-watching before, I'm afraid.'

I seemed to have spent the weekend telling them what I hadn't done before: from pulling up leeks to humping bricks and helping Bob build the verandah he had planned outside the kitchen.

Any minute now, as the three of us sat sedately in the sitting-room, each with a plate of late-night snack on a tray in front of us, Edna would surely turn and have me stretch out my arms so that she could wind her wool on, if not positively around, me. How tame I had become through their instinctive policy of simply presuming I must be; disarmed, even charmed, by sensing that I was welcome, somehow wanted.

Edna had put away her pink knitting. It was replaced by something that looked very complicated, with different yarns and changes of pattern that required her to keep studying an illustrated magazine on the arm of her chair: a Fair Isle winter pullover for Bob, I guessed, glancing across, as if measuring him, hunched in a short-sleeved, chocolate-brown shirt, with a notebook propped on one broad raised knee and a pile of other notebooks lying beside his snack. I thought of how I had first become conscious of him, taking notes on the space cleared on Philip's breakfast-table. Now he appeared absorbed, much more suitably, in writing up the case-history of nothing more dramatic probably than the greater spotted foulard's mating habits or the more dubious behaviour of wanker's night-jar.

'May I look?' I asked unkindly, realising that little drawings accompanied his notes and wondering not too seriously at the same time if I might encounter some clue about the case of Philip amid the bird-babble and chiff-chaff.

'Help yourself.'

Each notebook was neatly labelled and dated: Dungeness/ Sandwich Bay, Summer 1978; Redcar, June 1976; Staines/ Wixton, Spring 1980 ... Bob's handwriting was big and careful, as painfully clear as facsimile handwriting in a book, but his drawings were unexpectedly professional, even though the wretched birds scarcely emerged from the barbed wire entanglement of surrounding arrows indicating on them peculiar things like 'pale superciliary'. Nothing very personal seemed to be recorded. 'Heavy rain. Cycled home for tea' was about the most revealing, apart from 'Edna with me', when he first spotted a sooty shearwater.

'Is there actually a bird called the lesser stint?' I asked. 'It sounds like a schoolmaster handing out prep.'

'I think,' he said slowly, without raising his head, 'it's called the little stint. It's a type of sandpiper. You won't see it around here.'

'Oh, really.'

'It'd mean an early breakfast, Nicholas,' Edna said gravely after a pause. 'If you are going to Wixton. And just sandwiches for lunch, though you should be back by tea-time. Bob would like it, I'm sure, but you're to please yourself.'

'That's not always as easy as it sounds.'

She went on with her knitting, unperturbed. I felt she would do so even if I yelled that there was an anaconda coiled among the wool. But how would she react to a hand – my hand, say – on her knee? Or supposing I suddenly flung my head on to her ample enough lap and sobbed out my fear of the funeral, the inquest, the future altogether? Perhaps I was longing for her just to embrace me, almost stifle me with such intense, unreasoning affection that I ceased to be adult and sank back into a pre-pubertal cocoon created by her strong arms.

'What's Mrs Grice like?' I asked, abruptly it might seem to them.

'Very young, isn't she, Bob?' Edna said. 'Not that I know her, except by sight.'

'Very pretty, too. And always dressed smartly.'

'Like her husband,' I said. 'Are there smartly dressed Grice children?'

'No, there aren't,' Bob said shortly.

'Only been married a year or two, haven't they? She always looks such a little thing to me and rather washed-out – I shouldn't think she was very strong.'

Grice would want his wife pretty but weak, I quite saw that, as well as much younger than he was. A woman like Edna would not have suited him; mentally and physically she was far too robust. Mrs Grice probably wilted in the kitchen and never stepped into a kitchen garden. She spent her days pre-occupied with her clothes and hair, exercised a pet poodle perhaps, made-up and changed her dress before Grice came home to pour her a cream sherry and expatiate on his clever hunches of the day. I wondered what he'd given her so far on the Philip case.

Gunmetal-grey had been the colour of his knitted silk tie on the previous morning, when he interviewed me at Spenn police station. It was just a shade darker than his suit, toning in most tastefully, though the crisp breast-pocket handkerchief was merely white (difficult, probably, to match the exact colour of the tie). Did his wife apply the last delicate touches before he left? I doubted it. Even if she wasn't too indolent, he was likely to prefer to do them for himself, to be sure they were done effectively.

For some reason unexplained Hiscock (or Horder), not Bob, sat with him, allowing him to begin as I took the upright wooden chair opposite he had indicated.

'Everything hunky-dory at the Sergeant's?'

'Yes,' I said tersely, determined to reveal nothing. 'Not too bad.'

'I should think not.'

There was hardly a gleam of teeth, and as much animation as if he was a gas inspector and I the meter he was compelled to read. All right: it suited me, as off we cantered over the barren ground of Philip's parishioners and whether I knew any of them.

'Never met them at all? They never called when you were there?'

'Well, I never saw them.'

'Didn't a lady called Mrs Fullerton-Jones come one evening recently when you were there?'

'I'd forgotten about her. Yes. Actually, she was just leaving when I got in. Still, ghastly though she may be, she's hardly my idea of a suspect.'

'A suspect for what, might I ask?'

'Theft, murder – whatever happened. And what did? I think I really ought to be told.'

'That will be a matter for the inquest. You never encountered other visitors? You don't recall answering the door one day when your uncle – godfather – was or appeared to be out?'

'Oh, the day Lesley something arrived.' I couldn't help smiling at the recollection. 'When Philip had gone to the races.'

'A Miss Lesley Coombe.' Grice gesticulated at the stolid policeman beside him, as though by that setting in motion an incongruously bass interior tape-recorder. 'It was a Wednesday when I went to see Mr Kerr. A boy in a towel opened the door. He said Mr Kerr was not at home. I did not know if he was lying. I did not like his manner. I was very upset and wanted to see Mr Kerr urgently.'

At another Grice gesture Hiscock (or Horder) halted.

'Did Mr Kerr ever mention Miss Coombe to you?' Grice asked.

'Yes, he did.' I found myself picking up the strange rhythm of this session. 'I told him the next morning she'd called, and he said she was a pest.'

'Did he say why?'

'Well, for one thing, she couldn't sing in tune – in the choir. Oh, and I suppose she literally pestered him, as a sort of teenage sex-maniac.'

'You seem very poised for your age, so perhaps you won't mind my asking if it might have been the other way round?'

'With Philip pestering her, you mean?'

'Exactly.'

'I suppose it might have been, but I doubt it somehow. I think he just thought her a pest.'

'You are probably aware that middle-aged men do often – er, fancy young girls.'

'Don't girls also often get crushes on older men?'

'I should like to turn to the Wednesday afternoon – it was an afternoon, wasn't it? – when Lesley Coombe called.' He paused and looked levelly at me across the table. 'You, it seems, were wearing a towel. You wouldn't happen to remember what she was wearing?'

'Trousers, dark glasses – and a headscarf, I think. I wasn't wearing a towel; it was a sheet.'

'Can you describe the scarf in more detail?'

'It was green or greenish, and patterned in some awful sporty way. Perhaps it had horses' heads on it – something like that.'

'Turning to the day before yesterday, also a Wednesday. You are with me?'

'Yes.'

'You neither saw nor heard anyone arrive in the early evening for Mr Kerr?'

'I thought I told you that yesterday. I don't think I heard anything; I'm not absolutely sure.'

'Would it surprise you to learn that a girl, wearing trousers, dark glasses and a headscarf came to the house?'

'Why should it? If she did, she did.'

'You, however, did not see her?'

I paused, thinking hard. 'Perhaps I did see someone like that riding away on a bicycle.'

'Not walking?'

'I vaguely recall a bicycle.'

'Only vaguely?'

'I'd been half-asleep; I told you; I got up—'

'Around six o'clock, I believe you stated to us yesterday. And now you feel you have some recollection of seeing a figure cycling away – someone seen from the back, I take it?'

'Yes. The more I think about it, the more sure I am. It just meant nothing at the time.'

'Continuing to think carefully, as I ask you to do, could you describe this figure? Was it, for instance, obviously male or female?'

'That's not very easy. I suppose the headscarf made me think female, but it might have been a man. It was certainly wearing trousers.'

'And the colour of the headscarf?'

Grice had dropped his neutral tone and snapped the question triumphantly at me as if trapping my wrists in handcuffs.

'I see it as a sort of yellow,' I said slowly.

'Thank you.' He glanced down at his tie, re-aligned it slightly and then gave a perking-up pinch to his handkerchief. I felt somebody ought to have been ready to take his photograph. He exposed his teeth. Snarl please.

'I think I may tell you this much.' It was the way he spoke to his wife, I suspected, when things were going well. 'Your evidence is useful corroboration of that given by Mrs Rainbow. On the evening in question, shortly before six o'clock, as far as can be established, she admitted a girl in trousers wearing sun glasses and a yellow headscarf of a kind often worn at sporting events, who asked for Mr Kerr. She conducted the girl to Mr Kerr's study and then, as she customarily did at that time, left for her own home.'

'I see,' I said earnestly.

'It is likely, you understand, that that girl was the last person to see your godfather alive.'

'What happened next? Mayn't I know a little more?'

'All in due course. The case as such is merely at a preliminary stage, and my own mind is open on a number of aspects.'

He had looked across at me quite amiably as he spoke. I seemed to have become a blend of Mrs Grice and cub-reporter ('Do you have a lead, Inspector?' *Police keep open mind on curate's mystery death.* In an exclusive interview yesterday Inspector Grice, dapper, tanned 42-year-old rising star of Spenn's police constellation, revealed ...).

'How old is Grice anyway?' I asked Bob.

'The Boss?' He seemed disconcerted by the question.

'You'll dream about him if you go on,' Edna said comfortably. 'Better to forget it all, I'd say. If you do settle for Wixton, Bob, I could pack a Mars bar each with your sandwiches. And you'd have to wear something warm, Nicholas. It will be quite damp over there first thing, I'm sure.'

'I've got a green and black shaggy sweater – or would that make me look dangerously like a caterpillar?'

'Get on with you,' Edna said. 'The birds aren't daft.'

'Best not to wear anything bright,' Bob added, glancing up rather anxiously at our exchange.

He still seemed faintly anxious the next morning, as we wobbled off like a pair of cyclists in a silent film into the surprisingly chill atmosphere before the sun rose, and what there was of Trencham Croke slept in the knowledge it was Sunday. I was the one who ought to have been anxious. I was riding Edna's old-fashioned bicycle, with a shopping basket on its handlebars and a strange fan-like contraption of green string shielding the spokes of the rear wheel. My shaggy sweater was hidden under a dusty-greyish parka Bob had lent me (bloodstained too, I thought at first glance, but it was only the remains of some vermilion paint he had once used when helping Mr Latimer brighten up the bay-window of his lounge). With a haversack weighting down my left shoulder, I felt the sole recruit in Bob's army: the one volunteer to follow him in the Wixton Reservoir campaign – or perhaps, as we cycled on without speaking through a colourless, coldly luminous no-man's land, we had become the only survivors of an overnight nuclear holocaust annihilating all Spenn. Everything was as dead as Philip; but now there would be no ordeal by funeral or inquest.

Nightly I should go to bed a little before Bob and Edna did, entering that blue-painted room that seemed to require pyjamas and some sort of fawn dressing-gown, trailing its cord, hung on a hook behind the door. Had I come to kiss them both goodnight before going upstairs? Climbing into my narrow bed I would feel reassured hearing them, as I had, unhurriedly locking up, switching off lights, barricading the household against the forces outside, and I would lie there tingling in the darkness, almost as if it were Christmas Eve and Bob would soon come creeping in with a sack of presents. The days I would loiter away, half-hindering Edna as she worked round the house or in the kitchen, fetching her some parsley, reaching up to a cupboard for an elusive jelly-mould or the largest, seldom-used pan for damson jam making. Eventually I might begin my own bird-watching note-books, but Edna and Bob in their habitat would prove to have edged out the birds as the subject of my study.

On the compact, gleaming toy-like bicycle under him, Bob's bulky, muffled figure looked even bulkier, though he glided smoothly on beside me, a frail, desperate stick insect, struggling to keep up, pushing and pedalling away absurdly at the unyielding iron-framed rocking-horse – it seemed – on which I was perched.

'Let's swap on the way back,' I was ready to say, when I got a chance to say anything.

I was secretly sulky with Bob. He had talked to me about

anything except the case, and obviously he didn't want to discuss Grice. I knew exactly where he intended to plant an extra bed of spring cabbage next month and how much he would like to be allowed to extend his garden into the scrubby field beyond. Yesterday I had certainly learnt the dimensions of the proposed verandah, even if I hadn't listened carefully as my hands grew roughened as I helped align bricks and waited for an opportunity to speak. I knew Philip's funeral was tomorrow, and that not Bob but Mr Latimer's son, Jim, would run me over to Spenn for it in the van he used for his carpet-shampooing business. The inquest was fixed for Thursday. Bob had finally told me that.

'Wixton.' Bob turned his head and virtually mimed the word at me. 'We're here.'

'It looks more like a motor-rally.'

I could see no reservoir, only a rough lay-by carved out of sandy earth and filled with cars and a few motor-cycles, even some bicycles, though nothing resembling Edna's antique.

'Nobody would want to steal it,' I said, dismounting, 'unless for a transport museum.'

Bob was folding up his bicycle and chaining it to a parked caravan labelled JOC in bright yellow letters.

'You looked so funny on it,' he said, 'but I didn't like to laugh. No, I'm sorry; it's nice you agreed to come.'

'As I've probably ruptured myself on the bloody thing, it certainly was nice of me. But what is this? I thought we'd come to watch birds – not check drivers' licences.'

'Popular place the reservoir at this time of year. It's a good wet-land complex. The migrants are getting ready to leave.'

'I don't blame them.'

'You could join that,' Bob said, pointing to the caravan. 'If you find you're really interested.'

'Join it?'

'The Junior Ornithological Club. Anyone under eighteen can be a member.'

'It doesn't sound very exclusive. Would I get to wear a badge or something?'

'It was only an idea. Now, there's a longish walk ahead, and we've got to go quietly.'

'Yes, Sergeant.'

'Sorry; it wasn't meant to be an order.'

He moved away, head bent and obviously hurt, absorbed apparently in adjusting the binocular case hanging on his chest. Subdued, awkward, even angry with myself, I followed. He doesn't know how to handle me, I thought, feeling a little less moody as I became conscious of my *double-entendre*. Nor I him – that was, more surprisingly, the trouble. A day spent playing gardener's boy and builder's mate hadn't advanced things at all. Though surely I had played to the point where Dennis would hardly have recognised me. I was much more at ease with Edna, and she with me. Instinctively, she liked me, though perhaps nothing overt would ever convey it.

It was too pointedly true, as I tramped along behind Bob, avoiding the brambles, that I didn't know where I was with him. Occasionally we encountered other silent figures, a group setting up a grass screen around a tripod-mounted camera, some anorak-clad men who gestured in a friendly way to Bob and paid no attention to me. Suddenly I saw – without much interest – the wide expanse of the reservoir, with indeed the dark shapes of birds dotted over it like bread on the waters. Bob stopped. His back told me nothing. But I sensed he hadn't entirely adopted me, perhaps couldn't decide if he altogether liked me. This was something deeper than the circumstances of my seeming to nag him over Philip's death, for wasn't that in a way my duty? It was as if I was only with Bob on approval. And I certainly wasn't used to that.

With people in the category of that grotesque Julian, or even in the far more complex case of Dennis, I prided myself I always knew how to behave. Behaving was one of my great strengths. After initial, understandable faltering, I thought I'd behaved rather well when interviewed by Grice. Though I dreaded the funeral, I was sure I should behave well at it. Probably, if I stayed long enough with Bob and Edna, my behaviour would bend pompous Mr Latimer to my scarcely exigent will. It wasn't quite clear what I would help him over – perhaps watering of his regimented garden – but I ought in time to drift into being a nice lad, a nice-looking lad too, well-spoken, thoughtful, interested in his Alpine plants, grown from cuttings taken doubtless on his annual holidays in Switzerland.

'Better lie down,' Bob said abruptly.

'Why?' I felt like asking languidly. 'Are we under fire from enemy ducks?'

But I collapsed obediently in the still damp grass, trying to avoid crushing my haversack of Mars bar and marmite and cheese sandwiches. Bob had got his binoculars out and was solemnly scrutinising water and sky. 'If you move a bit closer,' he said, still fixedly scanning.

'I see birds,' I said helpfully.

'You ought to be able to spot some varieties of duck with your naked eye. Can you see the ones with tufted heads? You see it best in silhouette. It's most noticeable on the drakes, but they've all got it. Well, they're tufted ducks; pretty common really.'

'Ah.' I meant it to sound not snide, but interested, moving yet closer until our parka sleeves lightly brushed each other. 'Bob, are we going to see a sooty shearwater?'

He laughed, without taking the binoculars from his eyes. 'They're not so common, and I've never heard of one inland. Why d'you ask?'

'Oh, I like the name. And didn't you see one once with Edna?'

'Only time I ever have; it was at Redcar. But there's nothing very thrilling about shearwaters. Tell you what we ought to see, if we're lucky, and that's some terns. They gather around here before they migrate, and they're easy to spot. You can't miss the cut of their wings. Anyway, have a squint through the glasses.'

I felt some Order was being conferred on me as I lowered my head to receive the loop of the unexpectedly substantial binoculars – or perhaps it was symbolic of my meekly accepting Bob's yoke. Our faces had come very close, and he was looking at me quite naturally, unembarrassed, and concerned only that I got the strap round my neck without its twisting.

'You can adjust the eye-pieces separately, don't forget.'

'God, they're heavy—' Much heavier than Philip's was the intrusive thought I mentally brushed away.

'Prop your arm up,' Bob said. 'Like this.' He took my elbow firmly and planted it against a tuft of grass. 'How's that? You ought to have a good field of vision. Now, some birds are just settling at the edge of the water. Describe what you notice about them.'

'They merely look like birds to me: black birds, literally.'

'Come on. You can't be focusing properly. You can see if they're ducks or geese, or something different. Look at their bills.'

'They've run up enormous – oh, all right. Their bills seem much narrower.'

'Correct. Go on describing what you see.'

'Bob, you really ought to have been a school teacher.'

'I wouldn't have minded being if I'd had the education. Anyway, let's see how good your observation is. Or perhaps you haven't got very good eyesight; do you wear glasses for reading?'

'Of course I don't,' I said. 'My eyes are perfect.' I lowered the binoculars far enough to be able to look at him severely over them. Even Sadie hadn't missed the intense sapphire of my eyes. Patiently and also fondly (I detected), he gazed back, his doggy gaze a little strained, but this morning – despite his padded bulk and his silly woolly cap – he wasn't any longer my pet animal; more likely, I was becoming his. It was as though in transferring the binoculars he had carried out some ritual hand-over, of something between crown and *toga virilis,* passing from senior to junior, from father to son.

A son. That was it; and only my dazed state of sub-shock had prevented me perceiving it clearly before. Now I had a sudden intuition that Bob and Edna desperately wanted children but for some reason were unable to have them. That blue-painted room of mine was not intended to be a guest-room but a nursery. My hands grasping the binoculars trembled at the awareness of its implications. Munching over what I had detected, I should even eat my marmite sandwiches with a different feeling.

'Narrow, sweeping wings,' I virtually carolled, as my vision cleared. 'Black top to the head, whiteish body, forked tail. It must be the sooty shearwater, Bob!'

'No, it's not, but you're beginning to notice properly. Terns, those are.'

I quenched the rapid firework display of possible puns that broke out in my mind. For Dennis it might have made an amusing show, but then Dennis would have been ready with the French word for tern, as well as prepared no doubt for some schoolboy nonsense from me about *terne.* It would all mean nothing to Bob. Because he was much simpler, it was going to be much harder, I foresaw. Or perhaps I had just become weary of myself, of playing roles: of being alone. Maybe I ought to join the Junior Ornithological Club.

It would be something, and at present I had nothing. I was suspended in the void of Wixton Reservoir, meaning and hoping that Bob would rescue me. Please, please, I felt like muttering when at last we tramped off to eat our lunch on a bare patch of earth at the foot of a green-painted upright pole. On it hung suspended, like a grim, warning relic, virtually a petrified wreath, one mouldering life-belt. Pinned to it, in *in memoriam* fashion, was a card of bleached ink capitals: For emergencies only.

I wondered if many people jumped into reservoirs: disturbing for the bird-watchers, I thought, while I listened dutifully to Bob itemising the various types of tern as we lay and ate.

'Sandwich is quite funny, in the circumstances', I said. 'But the arctic roseate sounds even better – sort of pink ice-cream, I suppose.'

'Arctic and roseate are two different sorts; I'll show you in a book when we get home. Not too tired, are you?' He added suddenly, 'It's been quite a long morning.'

I scrabbled my foot in the sandy soil, hot and easily friable: earth to earth, the vicar would be booming out with relish tomorrow, strangely re-vitalised, I anticipated, by burying his own curate. The sun had emerged out of early morning mistiness, and it was warm where we sat exposed to it, with our parkas and haversacks discarded. Bob had taken off his sweater, to reveal a vest so white that it made his skin appear almost orange. Unaccustomed *pudeur*, some instinct, something, made me keep on my now clammy sweater, under which I was wearing nothing.

'I've enjoyed it,' I said.

'Me too. Made a change – coming with someone.' He paused to unwrap his Mars. 'Or were you just saying that to be nice? It's not what you're used to, is it, being with us?'

'I'm enjoying it,' I said stubbornly. 'And I'm not often nice. I might become so if I lived with you and Edna.'

He took out a pocket-knife and began to cut the Mars into neat sections while I rather sleepily watched. We were sprawled like a couple of Breughel peasants – or a pair of grave-diggers, *Hamlet*-style, pausing before we got down to the spade work.

'Being my hobby,' he was saying. 'But people don't always want to hear about your hobbies, you see. Even Edna gets a bit fed-up, I think, though course she never says so. But even when I was a kid, I liked birds – and I don't mean pinching their eggs. Want a slice of Mars?'

'I've got my own, thanks.' I groped towards my haversack but then felt too inert to go on stretching. Weakly, I took the piece he extended on the point of the knife. 'Thanks,' I repeated.

'Yes, even as a small kid,' he said. 'Perhaps because I was left rather on my own. Brought up by my grandparents, living down here. My parents were killed in the last war, a V2 raid, if you know what that was – and my brother was too.'

'Did you always want to be a policeman?'

'My father was. I wanted to be like him.'

'I expect you're good,' I said drowsily, licking the last traces of sticky toffee from my lips.

He laughed. 'As a policeman, you mean?'

'As a person.'

We lay there, lapsing into silence; and though I had closed my eyes against the dazzle of his vest, I still seemed to see it shimmering like a white breastplate: the badge of my personal life-saver, with nothing artificial, I hoped, about the respiration.

'God,' I said at last, more vehemently than I'd intended. 'I wish there was no tomorrow.'

'Monday morning.' He made a sympathetic noise. 'Back to life really, isn't it? But can't be helped.'

'More like back to death. I've got a funeral and you – you've got your crime.'

'Bit of a puzzle, that is. Well, perhaps we ought to be thinking of moving. Shall we swap bikes?'

'No. You'd look even funnier on Edna's.' Besides, I thought, I may fall off, break my ankle, have to be put to bed – or anyway be put out of action.

Briefly it seemed possible, though not by the next morning as I sat in Jim Latimer's glossy pink and purple van ('Your Upholstery Noo Through our Shampoo') and watched un-loved Spenn steadily approaching in the brilliant sunlight.

I'd half expected the driver to be a page boy in pink and purple, with matching pillbox hat, but Jim Latimer was almost middle-aged, balding, fat and smiling in creased jeans and tartan wool shirt.

'No trouble,' he said as I climbed in and started my speech of thanks. It was all he had to say.

He drove fast, and far better than Bob did. No chance of an accident.

'You've a lovely day, anyway,' Edna had said before I left the house. 'It looks really settled.'

Both she and Bob were subdued and formal at breakfast. I felt calm, calm and clean, disconcerted only by the fact that they insisted I wear a tie. It was a black one of Bob's that I fingered for a moment's assurance, as we stopped outside the picturesque lych-gate of the parish church, slightly blocked by the semi-circle of long, black snouts of the hearse-like cars, all pointing inwards as if respectfully alert to the thunderous solemnity of the organ playing. The grey walls of the church rose as squarely as if made out of slotted cardboard, tastefully splashed with streaks of lichen aglow in the sun. A huddle of professionally lugubrious, black-clad men, gamblers in mourning, shot their cuffs and directed a concentrated gaze of aggrieved disapproval at me and Jim Latimer's van as I got out and he accelerated away with a cheerful toot on the horn.

'It's the resurrection and the life – for your carpets,' I ought to have said, before walking a little more stiffly than I meant to up the steps into the already crowded church.

All I realised was that the service had begun. The congregation was rising cheerfully, prepared to sing, and there was a florist's shop of flowers in the nave where the coffin must be. Somebody official draped in white with a stave showed me severely into a pew very near the front, and I sat down automatically before I remembered I should be standing. Then I just sat there. I didn't want to hear anything, or see anything. I clutched at the cheap, slippery material of Bob's tie, comforted by its feel, loosening the knot as I bowed my head and willed the whole stupid charade to stop.

Only by the reverential shuffling and a muting of the organ did I sense it had. Beside me in the aisle a sallow man with hair as subfusc as his clothes was murmuring in faintly threatening tones about 'Mrs Danvers', which seemed apposite in a literary sort of way.

' … If you would ride with the family mourner, sir, in the first limousine.'

'Where are we going?' I asked, puzzled.

He looked at me with respectful shock, whispering firmly, 'To the interment itself.'

I struggled out of the pew and up the church. Now I could see people gathered there under the garish once-modern stained-glass window, executed in wine-gums and lead piping about 1950 and apparently depicting Christ the Aviator. Mrs Rainbow, it must be, crushed under some sort of plum-coloured plush helmet accompanied by Rainbow bow-legged in a green-checked shirt, speaking to blanched, bony Mr Cherry from the grocer's, a walking cadaver chained by what seemed a high celluloid collar. Amid the too-familiar faces I actually saw Sadie, who shyly touched my hand; she looked absurdly sexy, with mauve tights topped by a rag of black satin dress like a spoof of a Thirties waitress. 'Man, I'm real sorry for you,' she said softly.

A thin, sinister-looking woman I didn't know was shifting around impatiently in the porch. Her straight, neatly-parted dark hair and almost military-style neat dark-blue suit suggested a superior sort of chauffeuse, or housekeeper. She gave me rather a hard stare and then strode over.

'You're Nicholas, of course. You don't know me from Adam. I'm Jean Danvers – Phil's cousin, well second cousin if you want to be pedantic. Hope you don't mind giving me a bit of moral support. I'd feel a prize ass riding alone in one of those things. Let's be off, shall we.'

I followed her out into the sunshine and down to where the black flies buzzed about with wreaths, making minute adjustments, I could see only too well, to the set of the shiny, light-wood coffin in the back of the leading vehicle.

'It's a bit grim, all this,' she said, as we were mutely escorted into our own car and the door was closed on us with sympathetic bowing. 'But it must have been pretty bad for you, finding Phil like that. It's no use pretending I'm bowled over with grief. I hope that doesn't shock you. We didn't meet much. I just happen to be all the family that's left.'

As though with muffled drum-beats, the car engines began

to throb, and almost imperceptibly our sealed glass box sedately started to move with us propped there, trying to settle back on its over-pneumatic pearly-grey cushions. I was tempted to wave graciously at any peasantry lining the route, but nothing offered apart from a gratifying glimpse of Len abruptly sobered in his middle-of-the-road cycling antics as our cortège slid by, leaving him staring open-mouthed, grasping a bleeding brown-paper parcel of somebody's next meal.

'I came dashing back from holiday in Devon,' Jean Danvers was telling me. 'Felt I must. I don't know how the police down here strike you, but my feeling is they haven't a clue. I saw that man Grice last night – came to my hotel – and he just nattered on about suspicious circumstances until I wondered if he thought I'd done poor old Phil in.'

'They haven't told me what happened, though I've kept asking.'

She smoothed her unruffled hair and tugged at the collar of her tunic-style jacket.

'I gather they think there was an attempt to strangle him with some sort of scarf. Then he had a heart attack. God knows why anyone should try to kill Phil, of all people. Still, you can't make much sense of today's world, can you? Rape, murder, bombing, you name it. We've got it.'

'Mrs Danvers—'

'Oh, call me Jean. Anyway, I'm not Mrs anything – thanks. I've got a better half, Molly, and damn grateful I am for her. Talking of which, as it were, no chance I suppose of meeting your Ma here today, is there? I know who she is, of course, and I was wondering if she'd care to do a couple of television programmes I'm producing.'

'She's in Portugal at present,' I said, looking apprehensively out of the window. 'And I think this is the cemetery.'

'More later, then. I'm a bit keyed up: expect you are, too. I won't go faint on you or anything but I might be glad of an arm to grasp if this is very grisly. Personally, give me cremation every time.'

A gloved hand had the car door open, and I clambered out reluctantly into the hot, sickly sunshine. Jean Danvers had gone very pale but she gave me a brave grin.

'It's the flowers I can't stand,' she muttered as we walked as slowly as possible towards the gaping hole of the grave.

'They're so bloody pointless. I can't see Phil minding about flowers.'

'At least they aren't in the form of sculls – I mean oars,' I said. She emitted a whinnying titter, checked by a reproving, pious, clearing of the throat from the vicar, tuning up and obviously eager to begin. His beautifully washed white hair was an advertisement in itself, and he had an other-worldly, detached air which made it hard to remember that his next engagement would be lunch. I watched his big, well-shod feet plant themselves on the very verge of the grave, without any danger of slipping in, and tried to distract myself as he started mouthing away resonantly, masticating his sentences as if they were religious chewing-gum.

'Forasmuch as it hath pleased Almighty God ...'

He's easily pleased, I thought.

' ... to take unto himself the soul of our dear brother Philip.'

Earth fell on the coffin, and I clutched Jean Danvers's arm as a tremor ran through us both.

'... and to hasten thy kingdom (chops for lunch at the vicarage) ... our perfect consummation (thank you, Len) and bliss both in body and soul ... through Jesus Christ our Lord. Amen.'

Jean Danvers turned aside, and I released her arm. The vicar nodded in a vaguely benevolent way at me and shook her hand. A short litany of consolation flowed from his lips: grave loss to the parish, simple faith, highly esteemed, bereaved family ... deplorable circumstances.

'I'm not Phil's sister,' I heard her cutting in brusquely, 'but thanks very much. No, I'm going back to Devon straight away. Yes, it is lovely, though I'm only there on holiday. No, I've never been to Cornwall; I ought to one year.'

'A very grievous experience for one so young,' he said to me, 'but we must trust to time.'

'It's a great healer,' I said.

He frowned at the interruption. 'And your own good sense.'

'I ought to dash. Sorry I can't offer you a drink, Nicholas,' Jean Danvers said. 'But at least I'll give you a lift back to Spenn.'

'Might it be to Trencham Croke, please? Where I'm staying.'

'Fine by me.' As we were shown into the car, still being

116

handled like two flasks of precious glass, she added, 'I just had to get away from that. Sorry if the vicar's a chum of yours. Now, where is this Trencham what-not?'

'It's a village quite near. They'll know it. I hope it won't take too much time, but if you're in a hurry—'

She looked at her elegant dark blue enamelled watch. 'It'll be all right. I'm going to snatch a bite at Paddington and then get the train to Exeter. Thank God, thank God, that's over. Not my idea of fun. Still, we both kept a stiff upper lip, didn't we? And you looked so sweet – so lonely in the church. Your Ma would have been very proud of you.'

'What is it you want her to do?'

'Well, it sounds like cheek really, but might appeal. I'm doing some kiddiwinks' programmes on the box – nursery rhymes and things – and I wondered if she'd care to be involved.'

'She'd make a wonderful Mother Hubbard for you, only she hates dogs.'

'Oh, I shan't use a real one. In fact, I'm going to have a dear little man – Toby Morris. Bless his cotton socks. He was such a pet in *Richard III*. Anyway, what are you going to do? Be an actor?'

'No, I'm not – though I am resting at the moment. I've definitely left school. My education's complete.'

'Good for you,' she said rather absently, I thought.

'I suppose I was killing time at Spenn – with Philip. I don't want to do anything ordinary. I'd like to astonish people – seriously. I mean that,' I added, after a pause when she made no response, 'but it's not easy to explain.'

'Look,' she said, shifting her gaze from the window. 'About Phil. I gather he's left no will – didn't expect to peg out so suddenly. But is there something you'd like: some memento of him?'

'No, thank you; I wouldn't.'

'I don't imagine he went in much for possessions, but something might occur to you later on. You needn't feel shy of saying so. Quite the contrary. You know, it must be almost ten years since I saw old Phil. We never had much in common. He thought the world of your father, and I expect he thought the world of you too.'

The car halted gently. The glass panel between us and the driver slid back, and without turning round he enunciated with mournful clarity, 'Trencham Croke, madam.'

'It looks like the back of beyond,' she said crisply. 'I hope that dreary pub isn't where you're staying.'

'Oh, no,' I began.

'Well, cheerio, thanks and so on.' She kept her hands neatly folded over her blue patent-leather purse. 'Sorry we had to meet in such rotten circumstances. And look us up if ever you're in town – I'm in the phone-book.'

Obscurely disappointed, I stood at the roadside while the car pulled silently away. It was like regarding, without solving, a problem in geometry to see the dark oval of her head framed in the rectangle of the rear window and bisected by the line of dangling blind cord.

There was nothing to do but stagger back in the heat to Bob and Edna's. I took off his tie and tore open my shirt, but even if I stripped totally and started turning somersaults I wouldn't make any impact on Trencham Croke's sleeping-sickness. All that would happen would be more tightly drawn curtains and a deeper, more hopeless silence.

'Forasmuch as it hath pleased Almighty God,' I bawled. 'Almighty God is mighty pleased. Trencham Croke is super in his sight. It's a cesspool of Heshbon. Amen. It's the back of beyond, for ever and ever. Amen. Man that is born in Trencham Croke is full of misery; he will be cut down like the gladioli and end up on an eternal compost heap.'

A silver and scarlet motor-bike suddenly shot past me, carrying a pillion passenger who turned to stare back, goggle-eyed. I dropped to the ground as quickly as I could: another casualty of dangerous driving, but I didn't seem to have convinced them. No respect for mental health either, it appeared, from the impudent wave I got – as if I was the village idiot.

'It's your funeral,' I bellowed hopefully, listening for the crash as they hurtled round the bend and disappeared from sight.

I picked myself up and dusted Bob's tie which had dropped with me. I hadn't raised the roofs of the red brick box houses of Trencham Croke. If only I had thought to let Bob's tie fall into the pit of Philip's grave and be buried there – which would have been a nice touch. I hadn't even squeezed the slim blue tube of Jean Danvers: not really impinged, though I had held her arm. But I must do something. Edna, it would

118

have to be, whom I seized and whirled into a hectic, hopeless, violent dance, in and out among the tombstones, stamping down the freshly-turned earth in our crazy course.

She met me in the hall, her broad bare arms thickly covered in soap suds. 'You're earlier than I expected, but lunch is nearly ready. We're having something special – hare with chocolate. Did you ever have that before?'

I shook my head.

'You'll enjoy it. And I've done a big wash, as it's such a good drying day – took your shirts and things.'

From my room, I thought, but I said nothing.

We walked into the kitchen, and I sat down at the table. She stood there, wiping her arms with an apron and looking expectantly at me. 'Guess what. A lovely piece of news for you, after this morning. Your mother telephoned – all the way from Lisbon, in Portugal. She spoke to me so nicely too. She's flying back in a day or so and coming down here to fetch you.'

I burst into tears.

8

'Well,' she said, sitting down heavily opposite me. 'And I felt sure you'd be pleased. The line was so clear; your mother might have been next door.'

'She probably was,' I said through desperate, degrading sniffs. 'Mother's little joke – staying with Mr Latimer.'

'How do you mean?'

I blew my nose. 'I've caught a graveyard cold – that's all. Hay-fever from the filthy, fucking flowers: *blossomitis morbidis*. It affects the brain. I'm too young to die, Edna.'

'Too young to use that sort of language,' she said.

'Yes, it's not like me – whatever that may be.'

A gust of misery so intense welled up inside my head, as if a

119

hose had been turned on at full force: no wonder tears gushed from my eyes. This time, beyond humiliation, I just let them flow.

'A funeral's no place for a young lad, in my opinion,' she said, getting up. 'It's bound to be upsetting, and what's the use? Life's no joking matter at the best of times. Anyway, it's all behind you, and your mother'll soon be arriving. Now, I must be stirring my stumps if we're to have any lunch.'

'Did she say when she was leaving Lisbon?'

'Your mother? Not exactly, and it wasn't for me to ask. But she's getting the first flight or whatever she possibly can, and she'll telephone again when she reaches London.'

'I'll lay the table,' I said, tilting my head up as I rose, so as to check the water trickling idiotically down my cheeks. 'Are we having any pudding?'

'Of course there's pudding,' she said indignantly. 'Summer pudding, that's all. The raspberries have been so good this year. It's one of Bob's favourites. We must try and leave some for him.'

I meant to explain I wasn't hungry: too exhausted to eat, too queasy at the thought of the wretched hare which I kept seeing coming to the table in Easter-guise, coated in chocolate and so dreadfully life-like that I didn't dare break off or nibble even one of its ears.

'Enjoyed it, didn't you?' Edna said, not waiting for me to reply as at the end of the meal I poured myself some more cider as she indicated, though declining, into a moulded glass goblet. 'I knew it was what you needed.'

'I'm surprised you haven't got some Yorkshire saying about feed a funeral and starve a wedding.'

'I'd always like guests of mine to have sufficient, whatever the occasion. That's the way I was brought up. Not to waste food, mind you, but to be sure everyone has plenty. It's only right and proper. And maybe you do need something extra after a funeral – grief takes more out of you, and you feel empty. That makes sense enough.'

'But Edna, a wedding must be awfully sad, too. Think of the feeling of no-escape for the bridegroom – got to go through with it, in front of a lot of ghastly people, and then the shock: this is your wife. That could be really sad.'

'Go on,' she said. 'Wait till it's your own.'

'That's a long wait, I suspect.'

'Oh, yes. Boys always talk like that, I know. You'll meet someone when you're older and then you'll change your tune.'

'I'm not talking about love. That's different. I mean marriage – human bondage, for worse and poorer and for the procreation of children and that sort of stuff.'

She smiled. 'I thought your mother had such a nice voice – really friendly, she sounded. And she went out of her way to thank me. For nothing, I said. It's been someone young in the place, to spoil a bit.'

I remained silent, staring at my plate rimmed by a pattern of big brown and blue overblown flowers.

'If you'd seen more of Bob, of course … Not so easy to make friends in his position, I always think. Still, there's the age gap. A man needs his cronies, and there's no one much around here for Bob.

'Now at home, my home, our father's got lots of good friends. He's never lonely. He was a good husband too, but he always liked to slip down to the pub – just for a pint, mind you – to get away from a household of womenfolk, he said. That was only his way of talking; still, there's something in it.'

'Thank you for everything,' I said. 'Including the loan of Bob's tie. I am grateful. Mother is grateful. He, she and it are grateful.'

'Well, you're not off yet, are you?' she said conversationally.

'Aren't I? I feel I've been sealed, stamped and posted off – en route to God knows where. Who cares?'

'I'd love to travel – see places, meet people. I expect your Mother travels a lot.'

'Without ever arriving – that's Mother.'

'It's funny, but do you know where I'd like to go most? India. Ever since I was a little girl I've dreamt about going to India. I can't explain it. I just feel I want to see India before I die.'

'All right. I'll take you to India, Edna. We'll go together.'

'Oh, yes. On your magic carpet, I suppose. What we can do together is the washing up.'

Over it, she broke off to say, 'I'm going in to Spenn this

afternoon to change my library books. You'd better stay in in case your Mother telephones again. She was sorry to miss you. I'll be home for tea.'

'If you can't go to India, come to Portugal. I'll have to fly back there with Mother. You need a holiday. You could see Lisbon or come swimming at Estoril. No, I do mean it, Edna; you could be our guest – Mother's way of thanking you for having me, if you want an excuse. Have you ever been abroad?'

'No, I haven't,' she said slowly, handing me a glass. 'They come up with a real sparkle, those, if you dry them properly. Anyway, thank you very much, but I'd never go anywhere like that without Bob. He couldn't get leave with the case. And, besides, your Mother wouldn't want me – us – when you're there. We'd just be in the way. But it was nice of you to think of it, Nicholas. You send us a postcard. I'd appreciate that; we both would.'

'They're such misleading things – postcards. Nothing ever looks like what it is, and the message is seldom much better.'

'We don't get so many that yours wouldn't be welcome, whatever you wrote. Those go on the second shelf of the cabinet in the sitting-room. They were a wedding present.'

As I opened the spindly cabinet and put the glasses gingerly back, to join the matching set that occupied a shelf below the one where lay a highly-modelled porcelain carnation stem and bud, I felt the finality of it all. It was like the last hours of the holidays. Every item – even the plastic-bound cover of *Baltic Falcon* – now had its familiar charm. It seemed dreadful to be leaving any of it. Without me, Bob and Edna would draw up their big chairs in the evenings, pull the curtains and settle down to their hobbies. My postcard from Portugal – it might just as well be from Peru – would be propped for a while on the mantelpiece (Having a marvellous time here – bathing super. Often think of Trencham Croke and all your kindness. Mother sends regards ... Mother joins me in sending ... we both send our love and thanks [or a postal-order, come to that]. How's the bird-watching, Bob? Hope the knitting goes well, Edna! P.S. Did they you ever find out about Philip's death?) In the end, Edna would decide when dusting one day that it could be thrown away, and Bob would probably never notice its disappearance.

I shall dream of Philip's death tonight, I thought, still standing in the room after Edna had bicycled off to Spenn, looking entirely at ease, even dignified, as she rode past the window.

'He was strangled, I learnt that at the funeral today.'

I had waited until after supper, until we were back in the sitting-room (two more nights to go) before I said anything to Bob.

'The inquest's on Thursday,' he said (three more nights, then). 'I'll give you the details, and the Boss says I can drive you there: probably just a formal hearing, to be resumed later. You won't need to say more than two sentences. The Coroner will be very understanding – it's Dr Mason.'

'Apart from myself, who is assisting the police in their enquiries? Or can't I be told even that?'

'We're speaking to a number of people,' he said, flushing. 'We've seen Mrs Rainbow again – to check the time-factor. Some other things have come up, partly gossip. But your evidence was very helpful.'

Edna put down her book. She had returned from Spenn with something that looked drearily Tudor and domestic, *Love's Chequerboard,* and also *Throne of Glass* – apparently set in Renaissance Navarre at a period when a woman's whim could splinter a kingdom or inflame a human heart.

'Are you finding it dull?' I asked, seeing the cover again as she closed it on her knee.

'No, it's lovely. It's a new one – only just come in. The heroine is called Marguerite.'

'A daisy,' I said.

'You know, Bob, Nicholas will be leaving in a day or two, once his mother gets home. I'm sure he's sensible enough not to repeat anything you feel you can tell him. But of course you know best.'

'Leaving us, are you?' he said.

'Well,' I began awkwardly. 'I can't thank you both enough ...'

'Yes,' he said. 'I can see you'll be glad to get away from it all. Nothing to stay for, really.'

'I'm still keen to know what happened – to Philip.'

'We'd like to know too. Some funny things are turning up, I don't mind saying.'

He looked as if he did, however, and I tried not to seem exasperated. I realised it wasn't the moment for any *'étonne-moi'* patronage, nor for too much display of eagerness.

'I don't want to shock you,' he said earnestly. 'After all, he was a clergyman, as well as being your godfather. And tonight, on the very day he's been buried – talking about him doesn't seem right, somehow.'

'I'd rather know,' I said, with equal earnestness.

'Well, of course, he was fond of racing – going to horse-races, wasn't he? Now, maybe that's not so unusual. It's no crime, anyway. Nor's betting in itself. But he hadn't a large income, you see, and it looks as if he got badly into debt. He owed Bert Rainbow money, for one. Now there's talk of his owing a bookmaker up in Doncaster – that's being investigated. He may have run into trouble of some sort with a race-course gang; it's crossed the Boss's mind that he might have.'

Maigret aux courses was it going to be? I should guess Grice would be lucky if someone didn't commit another crime and nick his wallet (pigskin, with gilt-metal corners), just as mine had been on that sodden occasion when Philip introduced me to the rigours of racing.

'What proof has Rainbow that Philip actually owed him anything?'

'He showed us some IOUs in your godfather's writing.'

'Dated, were they?'

'Hey,' he said, smiling across at me for the first time. 'Are you going to be a policeman? They were dated, all right. Some of them go back to three years ago. Of course, they're not for big amounts, but it's all part of the picture, as we see it.'

'Doesn't Mrs Rainbow have any IOUs? IOU for the most indigestible meal anyone's ever prepared: tin tacks in sauce tartare. I suppose it wasn't hard for Rainbow to lead Philip into losing his head over a horse once Mrs Rainbow had sabotaged his stomach.'

'She seems genuinely upset by his death, in her way. I'm not so sure about her attitude to you.'

'I am. It's virulent hatred crossed with demented loathing.'

'Perhaps you'd been rude to her, Nicholas,' Edna said calmly, taking up her knitting.

'Not sufficiently rude. Try as I would. She was at the funeral, and I just didn't have the energy to push her under the hearse; that might have helped.'

'There's something else,' Bob said, frowning. 'Quite different, and it's more delicate. But I'm afraid it's bound to come out. Your godfather had a bit of a reputation – I expect you know – for having a weakness where young girls were concerned. I don't mean very young girls, of course, but, well, youngish. Perhaps there wasn't much in it really, but with his being unmarried ... Some of them wrote to him or came to see him. I'm sure he always meant to be helpful.'

'And?' I prompted, after he had stopped, still frowning.

'There was Lesley Coombe, for instance.'

'Your Boss, Mr Grice, went over all that with me, Bob.'

'Not quite all. It's not a nice thing, this; but the fact is she now says she's pregnant and that it's Mr Kerr's child. I may as well tell you she denies coming to see him last Wednesday, and her mother bears her out. She was moping at home the whole evening. Mr Kerr had sent her a note, kicking her out of the choir.'

He paused and brushed, rather self-consciously, at his moustache, as though uncomfortable at the silence he had created, while I tried to absorb calmly the implications, and Edna too seemed still absorbed by what he had said.

'Philip had made her pregnant?' I said at last, slowly and incredulously. 'I'd heard silly Spenn gossip naturally, but I think that's absolutely and utterly untypical of Philip. In fact, I don't believe it. So there.'

'I thought it would be a shock. I'm sorry I told you, but you were keen. It often happens like that: someone dies and it's only then that the relatives discover the sort of life they've been leading. All sorts of things start to fall out of the woodwork.'

'I'm not exactly shocked,' I said.

'Well, you sounded very upset. It's not surprising.'

'What about the baby, Bob?' Edna asked. 'Is she going to have it?'

'We're not certain yet that she is pregnant.'

'And even if she is, that doesn't prove Philip made her so. Or have Hengist and Horsa unearthed Philip's secret account in some local sperm bank? Perhaps he despatched her a test-tube of spermatozoa and she did it herself. She ought to sell her story to the Sunday papers: "Ex-chorister claims postal impregnation by deceased curate." Yes. "Schoolgirl's astounding account convinces local police-force." '

'Nobody's convinced of anything so far.'

'Oh, good,' I said. 'It's "Police still seek solution in riddle of country clergyman's killing", is it? Sorry, sorry; I'm deathly tired. I must go to bed.'

And dream even more horribly now, I thought, as I pulled myself like a cripple up the stairs. Sad to see a boy's life blighted by a Byronic defect: an angel face on a twisted satyr trunk ... Nobody was watching, so it seemed easiest to bow to exhaustion and cross the landing on my knees. *Mutilé de la guerre – de la vie* – I ought to have tried to open my door with wrists only but the effort was too much. And after all that, even daring my mind to take me back to the verge of the grave, to that rattle of earth on the flimsy coffin lid, I slept deeply and dreamlessly.

'I might go somewhere and see a porno-pic, do something,' I told Edna the next morning. The weather was dull, like me. 'Anywhere except smiling, sun-drenched Spenn, I mean, where old meets new in a typically English rural compromise of thatched barns and nuclear missiles.'

'That's right,' she said, moving towards the sitting-room with a checked duster in her hand and another tied high round her head, increasing her gypsy-queen air. 'You don't want to be frowsting around here when you could be out and about. If you'd stayed longer, I expect Bob might have suggested you both went swimming. But that's not much fun on your own. There's probably a nice film on at Amersham, only you'd have to borrow my bike. Or if you wait till tomorrow you can catch the bus.'

'A bus actually stops at Trencham Croke? What is it, the local mortuary van?'

'And brings you back,' she went on, 'by supper-time. Only on Wednesdays, of course.'

'I'll go tomorrow. Today I'll be a domestic slave, obedient to your commands. Let me dust the dado or paint the kitchen pink. If you showed me how, I expect I could manage to bake a cake.'

'Have you made your own bed?'

'I have – but I've no wish to lie on it, at present anyway.'

'If you want to be helpful,' she said, almost glowering at me in a dark way I enjoyed, and which, I guessed, she too did, 'you can start by picking me some runner beans. It looks as though it might rain, but you won't melt, will you?'

'To hear is to obey.' – Sultana, I felt like adding; but she might have misunderstood.

'After that, there's the glory-hole of the cupboard under the stairs, if you're really looking for work to do. A lot of Bob's mess in there needs a good clear-out.'

By lunchtime I had become soothingly exhausted. Empty or irreparably encrusted pots of paint, a pair of old boots without laces, two cans of paraffin and some torn and stained dungarees were only a few of the objects I had laid at Edna's feet and been ordered to throw out or destroy. 'Bob on the beat,' I said, feeling rather like a human puppy as I dragged the dusty boots before her.

'They can go,' she said.

Crouching at the sloped back of the cupboard, I wondered if Philip's possessions were being gone through as thoroughly. Or perhaps Miss Danvers had already decided to send everything to the local Oxfam shop? I moved aside a metal ladder with one missing rung and found what I thought at first was a bright blue painted clothes-horse propped folded against the wall. Something rattled as I shifted it, and I realised it was a play-pen, by the look of it not quite new.

Bob bought it from a colleague, I could hear Edna explaining to me. No. It was Bob's as a baby, and he's kept it all this time. It's all he has from his childhood; you know, his parents were bombed in the last war. He wanted to keep it for his child.

'Not suffocating, are you?' Edna called out briskly as she tramped past with a long-handled broom. 'We'll have our elevenses soon.'

Instinct told me not to confront her with the play-pen. I put it back where it had been, leaving my finger-prints on it, of course: guilty of reticence, for once, I would admit when they arrested me.

It was barely a thought. I seemed to have been without any coherent thought all day, and it was as part of the regimen of brainlessness that I tried to peruse *Love's Chequerboard* that evening before I went upstairs. I listened to Edna praising my helpfulness to Bob during supper, though I noticed he seemed rather indifferent. He too was tired, or dispirited. Grice must have chewed him up, I thought – the verb *juste* for those gleaming teeth sinking into Bob's sleeve, if not skin.

Young Harry Tudor, I read tiredly: golden, glamorous and already a little fleshy, he strode or rode somewhere, while Lady Margery Pauncefoote laid aside her lute or flute, adjusted her pomander and sent a waiting-woman for her daughter, Lettice. I could see Bob as Harry Tudor, if I trimmed his moustache a bit, and perhaps Lettice would resemble Lesley Coombe without the sunglasses. I just bet her fair hair rippled like corn down her back, but I couldn't be bothered to find out.

Eventually I went to bed, pleased with my day. But it was as if I came awake only as I fell asleep. I found myself in some sort of natural history museum with row upon row of glass cases of stuffed birds. Somebody – it must be Bob – was standing close beside me, calling out the names of the birds as I bent to look at the labels: gannet, skua, shag, cormorant, scaup, auk ... The names started scraping themselves painfully on my ear-drum, and the birds looked hard and ugly on their simulated outcrops of cliff and rock. He opened a case and showed me how one of the birds could be made to swing from a wire fixed to the low ceiling of the gallery where we stood. I didn't want him to demonstrate but he insisted, and as the dead-looking feathered bundle flew across the room it caught me on the mouth. The dehydrated chemical smell was nauseating, and hair wisps of plumage curled and clung round my lips. In panic I beat at the body that seemed gummed suffocatingly to my mouth. It softly exploded into a storm of stiff feathers falling so thickly that my senses began to be blotted out. As I struggled, I could hear Bob urging me to do something, banging and shouting until I woke up to actual noise.

It was knocking at the door; but I lay for a moment, relieved to be breathing freely, before I staggered across in the darkness and opened it. Bob stood there in green-and-white wide striped pyjamas, his hair rumpled, speaking half savagely without my at first hearing a word.

'Your mother,' he kept saying. 'On the telephone – downstairs.'

128

'God,' I groaned. 'What on earth is the time?'

'It's gone midnight,' he said, looking at me briefly and then glancing away. I realised I was standing naked in front of him under the harsh landing light. I smoothed down my own disarranged hair, trying to be at ease, feeling almost nervous of encountering a feather.

'I'm sorry,' I said obscurely. 'I'll go down. I'm sorry she's rung so late. Please apologise to Edna.'

I turned back to snatch a pair of jeans, though there seemed no time to put them on as I ran down the stairs and into the sitting-room. They lay on my knees while I picked up the telephone, panting, excited and still shuttling mentally between my dream and the abrupt impact of reality.

'Hallo,' I said tentatively into the mouthpiece as though experimenting with a new device which might administer an electric shock or take a pincer-grip on my chin.

'Darling boy, how delightful to hear you. How are you?'

The instrument was vibrant with Mother's tones. It might have been bathed in its own spotlight, while from it streamed her voice, frothy with dark resonance below, suggestive of a tap of Guinness set flowing through the decorous yet desolate room where I sat hunched rather guiltily. Tonight, Bob and Edna's wedding photograph looked like a relic from a previous era, faded, stiff and disapproving of my being planted nude by night in the centre of their home.

'You sounded quite out of breath, darling, or was it just rapture? I had to ring, to let you know where I am. But I had such a nice talk the other day with Mrs P. – your landlady or whoever. She said you'd been an absolute trump over Philip's death; and, darling, I am truly shocked about that, especially for you. It seemed so Agatha Christie – which is awful, I know, and I loved him, in his way, though it was a funny sort of life down there, wasn't it, for a man?'

'Mother, it's past midnight, and the Parrotts go to bed early. We were all asleep. Are you at Heathrow?'

'I'm at the airport in Amsterdam. It's such a bore, darling, but we were diverted – absurd word for what happened. I'm lucky not to be in the Azores. I love your remark about the Parrotts – in a dear little cage. We're flying to London first thing tomorrow, and of course we'll be down for the wretched inquest and then whirl you away. Oh, it's lovely to hear your voice, though you don't sound overjoyed to hear me.'

'Who's "we"?' I asked suspiciously.

'Well, Barney has very sweetly said she'll come down. I think Hugh might offer too, but Barney's so much more sensible. Now, when and where do we come?'

'It's at the old Infants' School in Spenn,' I said. 'Quite early on Thursday morning—'

'Old infants sound so dear. I can picture them in Kate Greenaway pinafores, can't you?'

'Mother, everything is totally un-dear and un-sweet – in fact, beastly and bloody and worse than boring. Philip's death is being investigated by the police. And I've been interrogated or cross-questioned anyway.'

'Darling, I do understand. That's exactly why I'm coming down to rescue you. After all, I have flown back for absolutely no other reason. Frankly, it's not tremendous fun being in transit at Amsterdam, but I wanted you to know your Mother's on the way. I'll deal with the police if they're being ridiculous. Don't let them bully you. You do have rights even though you are a schoolboy. Now, darling, I must dash and try and get some shut-eye. What time exactly is the inquest on Thursday?'

'At 10.30,' I said. 'But, listen, before you go. You may as well know that I'm not going back to school. I've simply had school. It's nothing to do with what happened to Philip; I'd already decided. I was going to tell you.'

'Well, it seems sensible – if you feel so strongly – but do let's all talk about it when we meet. I'm looking forward so much, my darling boy, to seeing you again. I feel something lovely's going to happen, truly, to make up for this awful thing. Anyway, we'll have a super time, I promise you, in Portugal. You'll adore it. Till Thursday, darling – at the old Infants. And I'll have my sleeves rolled up to take on the fuzz.'

'You sound very euphoric, Mother, even for you. Are you alone?'

'Am I what? If you mean, did I pick someone up on the plane, the answer is no. Terribly scruffy lot of mainly middle-aged couples. But, darling, sad though everything's been for you, you must stop glooming on like the Dane. Sleep well, and lots of love.'

'Same to you. Of course I'm longing to see you – I have been, for ages. And thanks for your card; it reached me at Philip's. It's just tonight you're near and yet miles away, and so much seems to have happened, and I'm not properly awake, sitting here with no clothes on.'

'Alone?' she asked with ironical emphasis.

'Bob and Edna are watching me from their photograph.'

'It sounds like a new party-game, but tell me more on Thursday. I'm absolutely dropping. *Dieu vous blesse*, darling boy.'

'*Dieu vous blesse*,' I echoed, feeling my features crinkling at the familiar childhood joke, and continuing to gaze fondly at the inert, now silent and lustreless telephone.

I was in no mood for turning off the lights and tip-toeing quietly back to bed. Several trumpet voluntaries at full quadrophonic blast might have matched my sensations. It was overture *Ma Mère*, with hints of the warhorse and the warlord – maybe even warlock – as she rode into Spenn with banners flying and cannon firing. I saw her hitting Heathrow in style, going through the red channel, if necessary, to declare only that it was open; marching up to Inspector Grice, with one arm round me and the other shaking a finger under his quivering, alarmed nose (Mother as Constance in *King John*, though I was merely posing as soppy, dripping wet Prince Arthur).

Tomorrow to Amersham, I thought, when at last I lay in bed, unable to sleep, conducting a brass band welcome for Mother to the beat of my over-stimulated heart.

For relaxation I rehearsed my descent on Amersham, a shy, youthful, enquiring tourist. 'Pardon, Madame, où se trouve le sex-shop? Vraiment? Quel dommage; merci, Madame. Je m'excuse, Monsieur, mais il y a dans la ville un amusement-arcade assez louche? ... Je le regrette aussi. C'est par là pour le centre paedophilique? Moi, je suis jeune travailleur.'

But as I got off the bus there early the next afternoon, I felt not even Mother could have blistered the paint on its sunlit, spotless façades, where the brickwork too had the smooth surface of well-applied paint. Amersham sniffed an alien invader and repulsed me, before I had had a chance to break any of its unwritten laws against loitering with intent to live. A pity my space-capsule wasn't calling until 4.45 p.m. to

carry me back to Trencham Croke, the capital of Zombie-
land where no human being had ever penetrated before. Too
young to enjoy a pub, too old for the ice-cream parlour, I
resigned myself to being accosted if I hung around long
enough outside Woolworths – or perhaps ran the risk rather
of being requested by some frantic woman to keep an eye on
her pram while she rushed and bought some tights.

'Who on earth would want to steal it?' I'd enquire
ungraciously, peering at the contents. 'Anyway, I'm waiting
for my Mum.'

Edna's prophecy of a nice film being on appeared depress-
ingly accurate. I could think of nothing I'd generally release
in Amersham except the wild beasts advertised in the
travelling circus poster outside the high-class poulterer's
('Breasts at attractive prices'). *Hotel Inferno* at first appeared
promising – unforgettable terror for a holiday family – but it
seemed to have a happy ending. I couldn't face *Balls-up*,
'poetic, zany, I defy you not to guffaw, (*The Guardian*), about a
disabled American lawyer whose small son introduces him to
a roller-skating competition where he meets his divorced first
wife. It wasn't clear whether *Hatchet*, 'based on the TV series',
was a man or a weapon but nobody was going in to find out. I
decided not to risk it. The person who might pick me up in an
empty cinema during that kind of film could easily be a
sadist; my hobbies might include lechery, but not butchery.

'Did you have a good time, then?' Edna asked when she
came to the door on my return.

She sounded polite rather than particularly interested. She
had on the dark green dress in which I had first seen her, and
it was perhaps that which made me feel she had reverted to
her initial shyly stately manner.

Although I now looked forward eagerly to Mother's arrival,
I found it hard to see beyond that: to grasp that I was leaving
Bob and Edna, and must find the moment to formalise the
fact, speak my thanks – and say goodbye. During my time-
wasting afternoon in Amersham, I had searched the shops for
an object to speak for me, convinced while staring into *Polly's
Curios* at the jumble of Victorian glass ornaments and
needle-cases, lockets and fob-seals that I would find an item
eloquent enough to convey what I could not. What, anyway,
was it I wanted to say? Anything I tried to see through Edna's

eyes as a candidate for the sitting-room cabinet, rapidly shrank to being ludicrous or extravagant, a cause not for delight but for deploring the expenditure on it of 'good money'. A bulging turquoise vase with tinkling pendant lustres might only have made her laugh – something her mother threw out at her mother's death – before she recovered herself and told me that it was the thought that counted. There was a big jet brooch that would have suited Edna's bosom, though I wouldn't care to say so, and a heavy signet ring with a flat dull stone, that I should have liked to slide onto Bob's finger.

Drifting away from the window, I wondered why my nerve was failing. If it had been not Amersham but Auxerre, I would be bolder: imposed my gifts, however outrageous, and left them grateful, if puzzled.

I paused outside a wine-merchant's. Virtually at my elbow was Mother indicating that a bottle of champagne would cheer the evening – if they chose to open it: give your Parrotts a drink, darling. They probably only touch it once a year, if that, and it will be such fun for them – though do get a decent brand. Never drink those disgusting substitutes, and never, ever, be tempted to buy pink champagne: it's revolting.

Yet I hadn't walked up the garden path with a bottle of anything, and I funked delivering my speech of thanks which I had assured myself would take place over supper. Edna and Bob seemed increasingly aloof, speaking more to each other than to me. An air of departure, I suppose it was, hung almost palpably in the kitchen where we ate, as depressing as if we sat under a rack of dripping laundry. There is tomorrow, I thought, and I'll pick up my suitcase after the inquest. I'll say goodbye to Edna then, properly. I must thank Bob in the car in the morning. And I can send them something from Portugal: it will be more of a surprise.

'I promised Mr Latimer I'd drop in on him before it got dark,' Bob said. 'He's set on altering his rockery, and though he wouldn't say as much I don't think he wants to move those big stones by himself.'

'Well,' Edna said, 'you take care too. Sharp and nasty some of them are, as well as heavy.'

'I don't mind helping,' I said.

'Oh, it's only a few stones.'

'You've your packing, after all,' Edna reminded me.

'That's only a few clothes.'

There was silence. The light outside was still intense enough to make the back garden a glowing, fiercely green jungle, but it was less easy to distinguish faces round the table. I felt how strong, in different ways, the presence of each of them, Bob and Edna, was: how solid, and even how similar in their slow, deep voices and large, muscular limbs, their broad bare arms – fair and dark – propped side by side, not quite touching.

'I wish it could have been for longer,' I mumbled, but they paid no attention. I had to go on, rushed on. 'You've been so kind to me. Thank you very much. I'm enormously grateful; for everything.' That means, I wanted to say, the two of you, and I ought to have had a graceful phrase ready, not be reduced to the half-sulky, stammering banality of: 'All I'm trying to do is say thank you.'

I put out my hands instinctively and for a second, in the gathering twilight, they might seem to brush, caress almost, the flesh propped there the more firmly and more reassuringly as the light wavered and started to fade.

'That's all right,' Bob said haltingly, when I had been expecting Edna's voice. 'It's not easy saying what you feel. We don't want thanks. Our pleasure.'

'I just am grateful,' but I felt it was repetitious and stale to continue. The moment, for me at least, had fled.

'Now, Bob,' Edna said after a pause, in a tone that dispelled whatever was shadowy around the trio of us. 'If you're to help Mr Latimer this evening, you'd best be on your feet and off.'

9

'She's here,' I exclaimed, startling Bob into such a jerky halt that our cheeky little striped police car nearly mounted the satin-smooth inclined boot of the Rolls drawing in ahead at the kerb.

'Do you mind,' said the driver gruffly, glaring out at Bob and then noticing me. It was Barney Burnham, a cap askew on her inky curls. 'How's tricks, Nick?'

And there was Mother stepping on to the pavement and almost willing applause from the sprinkling of assembled Spennites: a mauve and grey cloud, with suggestions of lace curtain veiling, that might have started out as Mrs Gandhi but ended up nearer the spirit of Lilac Fairy Air Freshener. Odours vanish; fragrance blossoms. It really did too, as she clasped me to her muffled bosom, murmuring something.

'God, am I glad to see you,' I said.

'Mother lives,' she proclaimed. 'My poor boy. You're looking dreadfully pale.'

'You look stunning. But this is an inquest – not the local fête.'

'Darling, I'm in half-mourning.'

'And half out,' I said, bending to retrieve a pale grey scarf that had drifted to the ground.

'Got some decent lunch plans, once this is over,' Barney muttered to me as we moved towards the Gothic stone school porch which seemed built on such a doll's house scale that none of us – least of all Barney, thin and tall as a loft-ladder – would be able to fit inside.

'Alone, I hope,' I muttered back.

'How do you mean?'

'No bastard Stephen.'

She laughed. 'He's not a bad lad. Anyway, Norah left him sunning himself in Portugal.'

'I can imagine.'

But, try as I might, it wasn't easy this morning to stir my imagination to do anything. Some sort of lurking fright, like incipient stomach-ache, had kept it from functioning ever since I woke up. Although my packed suitcase was left in the bedroom at Trencham Croke, after Edna handed over solemnly two shirts overlooked in the airing-cupboard, I felt that the day might unwind without my actually returning for it – and it hardly seemed to matter. I followed Mother's billowing draperies into the dark, cramped school, as I supposed I should go on following her, now she had arrived and taken charge. Somehow I had lost sight of Bob, though I saw Grice talking in the doorway to a fat, cheerful man in a boldly-checked ginger jacket (a bookmaker come to give evidence?). Then we were taking our seats in a bare room where a few people were already sitting, gazing respectfully at an expanse of built-in, faintly greenish blackboard that stretched along the brick wall behind the Coroner's desk. Our arrival provided a distraction.

'It's just like *Oliver Twist,*' Mother said resonantly, smiling round comfortably as she adjusted her counterpane-style sari. 'I knew it would be.'

'You mean *Nicholas Nickleby,*' Barney said.

I half-expected a ghostly bell to ring out for Assembly – or at least someone shouting 'silence in court', but the proceedings were underway before I quite realised it, so quietly and informally did they begin. White-haired Dr Mason was nature's Coroner, country-flavour, Edwardian-period, a mountain of wheezing benevolence, dressed in a vast dark suit draped with an almost mayoral-size watch-chain and with jowls that called for the support of a wing collar.

Instead of being a star witness – still less dramatically accused or arraigned, trapped through the trumped-up evidence of Mrs Rainbow – I had only the briefest part, restricted to nodding and saying 'Yes' to discovering the body, to having recognised it straightaway as Philip's and to having summoned the police. Dr Mason rewarded me by a return nod that combined a hint of headmasterly dismissal with silent sympathy. Then I had stepped down and was going back to my place to receive one of Mother's hugging glances as if I had just won first prize for something, elocution perhaps.

I looked at my grey flannel knees, flanked on one side by Barney's more pointed, navy blue denim ones, and on the other by the soft mound of Mother, whose hand on her lap suddenly stopped undulating that scarf I had retrieved, while we all listened to the fruity voice of Dr Metcalfe, and I heard again the tones I had heard speaking to Grice on that first morning as I sat at Philip's empty breakfast table. We had reached the approximate time of death, shortly before 7 p.m., and the post-mortem established that a meal laid out on a tray close to the television set had not been consumed. Some sort of struggle must have occurred. Bruising of the neck was evident. There had apparently been an attempt at strangulation. 'With a scarf or something of a similar nature, although it was not in itself the direct cause of death. That was undoubtedly a heart-attack. The deceased had no history, I am led to understand, of heart trouble. Nevertheless ...'

It was surprising to find Dr Metcalfe so physically small, drab and unimpressive, when his voice suggested a towering presence and massive, highly-polished, brown – fruity brown – brogue shoes. No duel but a duet arose between him and the Coroner, softer-voiced yet equally versed in a vocabulary that seemed to bury Philip more effectively than had the Vicar and leave themselves untouched in every organ.

'Precisely,' Dr Metcalfe responded, gratified by one of the Coroner's questions. 'They are not totally surprising symptoms, possibly increased by the deceased's build. Some strain on the heart may have been sustained at a quite early age. As a young man he showed, I believe, distinct prowess in rowing.'

I bent my head. Nobody but I could see the dusty, slightly crooked photographs on the stairs, and even for me the words blunted and blotted out – almost as if they were meant to – Philip on the college barge, or wrapped in layers of sweater, brandishing an oar and grimacing a little self-consciously. At that moment it was odd rather than at all distressing to think that Philip had once existed and had now ceased to do so. Yet when I thought of him it was of him in the distant past – as I had never known him. He had always seemed dead to me; I suppose that was part of the trouble.

'You okay?' Barney was whispering, gripping my knee hard. I sensed the rallying note. I must not fall out of line, faint on parade, let the side down.

'Fine,' I said. I turned my head and looked into her healthy brown eyes. At least she would see no sign of tears in mine. She grinned, relieved. We were mates again on the good ship 'Chin up', where every emotion was trimly stowed away well below decks.

Then it was Grice's turn. Suit and manner were matched and modelled as perfect inquest wear. It looked as if today's tie was dark blue, not black, knitted silk, and the slightly serrated line of white handkerchief was like a set of separate teeth matching the gleam from his mouth as he spoke and smiled respectfully. Everything was being pursued and investigated. Machinery set in motion hummed with efficiency (it was probably equipped with something for leaving no stone unturned) and his team had adopted a rigorous line of enquiry likely to yield results. Hiscock and Horder on all fours was about the sum of it – leaving aside Bob – but it sounded good and clearly impressed Dr Mason.

'In the light of continuing police enquiries,' he said, deepening his voice gravely and glowering out at us like an aged white-maned lion pretending to be at bay, 'I have decided to adjourn the inquest.'

'Don't clap,' I said to Mother, whose hands really did seem raised for the purpose.

'What a sweet old buffer,' she said. 'He deserves a kiss. And such a relief for you, darling, that it's all over.'

'Let's go.' Barney put her cap on decisively and thrust her hands into the pockets of her safari jacket. 'You must be dying of hunger, Nick. I am. Aren't you, Norah?'

'Ought we to thank anyone?' Mother asked, as we moved towards the doorway and people fell back before her, smiling rather nervously at finding themselves blocking her route. 'Thank you,' she said vaguely but benevolently, scattering invisible largesse which seemed to be welcome. 'Thank you so much,' she added with more force, negotiating an obstacle that became visible as Grice, in the porch once again. He was standing gazing at the rain just starting to fall over the asphalt playground. I mentally challenged him to speak – and so he did, not to me but to Mother.

'May I offer you an umbrella, madam?'

'I've got one in the car,' Barney said.

'How terribly kind,' Mother answered, and so I had to introduce him, as curtly as I could. Instead of the umbrella he produced the ginger-jacketed fat man: 'Chief Inspector Catesby, from Aylesbury.'

'Very sad and distressing business.' Catesby tried not to look cheerful, but it was clearly an effort. 'Sorry for your youngster finding himself involved.'

'But he spoke up so splendidly,' Mother said. 'And he's

coped so well. I'm getting him away to toast on some glorious beach and forget. I feel he deserves it.'

'Jolly good idea,' Catesby said. 'Wish we could all get away from this beastly weather. It's hard enough to fit in a round of golf, even if there wasn't this sad case – sad and puzzling, you know. Still, we mustn't detain you.'

Finally Grice had his umbrella ready, holding it up over Mother at a high, tilted angle that seemed more ornamental than useful, increasing Indian associations, as they stepped across the wet surface of the playground while Barney and I followed slowly, as if lugging ceremonial garlands. Mother laughed playfully at something Grice said – I couldn't conceive what – and I thought she might take his arm if the walk went on any longer. I made a face at Barney.

'He's the one who's been grilling me. I want Mother to give him a rocket – not go dancing with him.'

'Don't ask me how, Nick my boy, but your mother is someone who can do both. You bet if she just kicked him in the goolies, he'll be ever so grateful. Hopes to see more of her foot.'

'Listen,' I said, stopping. 'This Stephen—'

'Keep it till lunch,' she said hastily. 'They're waiting for us.'

'And I do so wish you luck, Inspector,' I heard Mother saying as we came up and Barney unlocked the car. 'But you ought to try Portugal one year – just for a change.'

'I shall certainly bear it in mind.' Grice was bent uncomfortably under the umbrella at the car window, bowing without quite backing away, condemned to crouch there while the rain steadily caned him, and Mother settled back increasingly dismissively. Perhaps I only imagined the car splashing him, since Barney drove off so smoothly. But it was definitely goodbye to Spenn.

'That's that,' Mother said, as though guessing my feelings. She put her arm round me and I felt glad of the firm, featherbed physical contact.

'I do hope he takes my tip,' she went on. 'It seems too silly to go to Benidorm each year. It's his wife's idea, of course. And now I've discovered Portugal, I want to convert everyone.'

'I'm surprised he's not coming with us,' I said. 'You were

doing so well.'

'Nice teeth,' she said reflectively, 'though he's rather too conscious of them. I'm sure he meant well, darling, and never intended to frighten you. He knows how upset you must be.'

'He did not frighten me.'

'Well, bully you, then. I think he's terribly conscientious, and he very sweetly said he'd discouraged the media from being there this morning.'

'How thoughtful,' Barney called, without turning round.

Mother laughed. 'At least it shows he's not cynical – unlike some people. Besides, it could have been awfully awkward. Of course, I'm sorry for Philip. It's horrible, sad, grotesque really. But it's you, darling, I feel most for. Now, we're going to cheer you up. Don't you wonder where we're going?'

'To lunch, I trust. And to talk about things.'

'There'll be lots of time for that later. Yes, we're on our way to an absolutely fascinating place. Well, it sounds it. Clever Barney realised how near it was. It's "Flavours" – a fabulous sort of country house restaurant, run by two absolutely dear old things.'

I groaned.

'No, I oughtn't to say that. They wouldn't thank me for it, though Estelle must be seventy, mustn't she, Barney? And dear Freddie was over seventy when they left the stage. I actually saw them once – in Leeds, in *Floradora*. Or perhaps it was at Harrogate in *White Horse Inn*. I know it sounds absurd, but the fact is that Freddie was marvellous. Even then. He really could sing, which I rather doubt if Estelle ever could.'

'Prettier too, judging from the photographs,' Barney grunted. 'Not that one should.'

'I suppose you couldn't call them very famous, but they kept going. That's what I admire.' Mother paused, shifting her arm. 'And they've stuck together. It's touching really. Think of starting a restaurant in some mouldering old place, down here, at their age. I'm surprised they didn't call it "Darby and Joan". And now it's all lavender bushes and topiary work, somebody told us.'

'Not in the food, I hope.'

'Oh, I don't know, darling. Lavender soup might be fun, to look at, anyway. But we'll have a tremendous celebration lunch, only poor Barney can't drink too much, and drive back to town. We're staying at a hotel. I somehow didn't think you'd want to stay at Margot's. And I long to hear all about how you became friendly with your Parrotts – and so on.'

Amid the untidy bundle of wrapping rather than mere wraps, she beamed out, confident and shimmering, even shiny, without any contrivance of smiling, pink-cheeked and jewel-eyed, round-eyed to the point of seeming to have only those blue-glass pupils. Norah, you're a doll, people probably still said, without any apologies to Ibsen. And I had never before seen how true it was, if a doll could be as well-sprung and upholstered as the car we sat in. Mother disarmed even while she appeared to do nothing. I narrowed my eyes to give her a harder, sapphire stare in return.

'I told you I'd decided to leave school, didn't I?'

'You said something on the phone, but, darling, little conventional though I am, I can't help wondering.'

'What?'

She gave me an amused yet not unexasperated glance: it stung, and at the same time it punctured the buoyant feeling I had had as we slid together, snugly, dryly, through the damp countryside.

'Well, whether it's a madly sensible thing to do. That's all. But do let's wait till we've reached "Flavours". That can't be its real name, can it?'

'I expect it was originally called "Favours"', I said. 'Charles II gave it to Nell Gwynne or some other tart. And now everything on the menu has names like "milady's petticoat" and turns out to be rice pudding.'

'Built about 1907.' Barney had slowed down, and through the rain we could see a not very large pseudo-Elizabethan house, creeper-clad and ruthlessly asymmetrical with twisted chimneys, a sodden-looking and deserted dove-cote standing in the centre of its formal garden. 'But it's got its own ghost, Nick. A stockbroker once shot himself here.'

'I ought to have guessed. Havanas fell; so did he. He probably haunts ye gilt-edged Bears room.'

As we drove or wove, in a stately pavan, past a row of lead statues in bedraggled topiary niches, a gaunt figure in a pirate-style shirt appeared at the main doorway, waving cheerfully with his left hand. He had his right arm in a sling and a patch over one eye.

'It's the Vagabond King,' I said, waiting for a burst of song as he extended his free arm to embrace Mother. 'Seriously, Barney, we can't talk here.'

'Well, we can eat. I think they've just won a British Heritage award for their cuisine.'

'You cooked this up,' I said. 'And I don't apologise for the metaphor.'

'Enjoy the meal, then,' she said brusquely, striding forward and sticking out a hand to shake Freddie's, while deftly avoiding his attempt to kiss her. 'I'm Barney Burnham, Norah's agent. You don't know me.'

'But I know all about you, darling,' he boomed gallantly. 'I know Norah's a lucky lady. When I think of what Estelle and I started out with as an agent.'

Down memory lane, I thought ruefully, as he led the way inside, still talking. The hall had rafters, of course, and gave additional volume to his voice. From the panelled walls protruded big-game trophies, with thrusting snouts and glass-eyes, and horns curled like vast Edwardian moustachios, so that without incongruity they could have included a mounted stockbroker's head, self-bagged circa 1910.

But it was Mother I myself was stalking. I was well enough used to her natural trouper behaviour, which proximity to other, especially old, troupers always enhanced. Now she had an almost physical sheen to her, which seemed greater than usual. I had seen it immediately she had stepped out of the car. Freddie could sense it, I suspected; perhaps even Grice had. 'Yes,' I could have whispered. 'And you've won something too.'

We had had to pause reverently and admire the parchment-style Heritage culinary certificate, with its English oak framing and giant unconvincing sealing-wax seal, awarded by the all-party Parliamentary Gastronomic Group. It was while we stood there that Estelle, seeming hardly taller than a Christmas-tree fairy, had run up to greet us in vivacious silvery tones that matched her high-heeled silver sandals. Rafter-ringing time had begun, and I felt quite ancient and stoic as the quartet played and prattled around me. Anyone lunching quietly that day at 'Flavours' would be getting a free performance accompanying the meal.

With deadly blankness I stared at Freddie's sudden observation to me, man to man, that England were all out for something. Perhaps a mocking laugh would have been the best reply. Still, I thought I ought to linger gallantly over the minute, skeletal hand Estelle extended: let's make an operetta.

'Charming,' she said, tipping up her tiny, shrivelled face and giving a shivery shrug that admirers must once have called delicious. 'So nice to see good manners again. But look at my poor Freddie,' she cried, whirling round in a way that set her pleated skirt swinging. 'Hasn't he been in the wars? We had the most terrible thing a few nights ago. A real break-in. Isn't life appalling nowadays? Even down here. Freddie was so brave, and the dreadful punk, or whatever, fled of course. He would. But Freddie got fearfully bruised, and I was absolutely panic-stricken. And now we've heard that over at Spenn the Vicar's actually been murdered by a burglar. Can you believe it?'

'It was the curate, dear heart,' Freddie said.

'Well, it's still awful, I think.'

'But what a success you've obviously made of this.' Mother gesticulated to include rafters, big-game trophies and the certificate. 'It looks so peaceful and lovely.'

'Nick and I are just here for your lovely food,' Barney said. 'Aren't we, Nick?'

They all laughed, turning to me. I felt faintly betrayed by Barney. Adult nervousness, I had long ago decided, must lie behind the constant assumption that anyone under twenty-one is permanently starving. All I was experiencing at the moment was an increasing ache in the stomach.

'Gosh, I'm hungry,' I said. It got another laugh and made the signal for us to go through to the dining-room.

'Listen,' I managed to hiss at Mother as we stopped to duck on the low-beamed threshold of what promised to be a décor of tapestry and tapers. But it was Freddie's attention I had caught.

'Want the Gents?' he asked.

'Not particularly.' I looked round, though, just to check if its logo was a codpiece stencilled at the heart of a Tudor rose.

Before I could say another word to Mother, Estelle had skipped back to us. 'Congratulations,' she trilled, holding out both claw-like hands. 'Barney's just told me, darling. Oh, that's so exciting for you. We must celebrate.'

I knew it: knew it, I repeated to myself in a sort of raging despair of certainty, as if a long suspected avalanche had broken, engulfing me as it swept on. I trembled, and I seemed still to be trembling within well after Mother had averted the avalanche with one airy wave of scarf.

'Nothing's settled,' she said. 'It never is nowadays with films. But of course I'd love to do it. It's such a challenge. Play Mrs Siddons, darling,' she said to me. 'Though I know I haven't the nose. Well, who has?'

Of course they had to produce champagne, and my dread of being expected to quaff mead subsided. I was going to ask for old English water, if it had come to that. And eventually we were alone in our niche by the mullioned window, at least by the time we came to the syllabub (garnished on the menu with an Elizabethan quotation, unattributed, about 'Love's sweete sugar'd sop'). Across the room a Japanese family carried out the British lunch ceremony in smiling silence and three youngish business men drank cups of coffee in a resentfully subdued way, trying not to stare at us and keeping their flagging conversation alive by snorts and bursts of synthetic cheerfulness, mingled with frenzied over-use of first names, suggesting they scarcely knew each other. I guessed they had expected saucy wenches bursting out of period bodices, not the slow, pseudo-grandmothers who clucked around like aged hens.

'Stopped raining,' Barney said. 'It'll make driving back easier. We must remember to pick up your suitcase, Nick.' She got up abruptly from the table. 'Just want to check something with Freddie.'

Mother put her hand on mine, glancing fondly at me as she did so.

'Can we talk?' I said, smiling and putting my other hand on top of hers, warm and plump. 'About my not going back to school. I may not know what I want to do, except that I don't want to go back there. And I don't mean a different school. You've brought me up not to need school any more.'

'We'll have days to talk about it on the beach, darling – simply days. I want to talk to you about something else.'

'Mother, do please understand that talking about it on the

beach, or anywhere else, won't change my mind. I am too old for school. Voilà, c'est tout.'

'Well, your future,' she began. 'It's not wrong to talk about that. In fact, I want to talk about the future for all of us, before you meet Steve.'

'Why?' I asked, genuinely puzzled.

'Let's slip into the garden for a few minutes, shall we? It looks rather quaint, and now it's stopped raining.'

'It looks to me like a bad set for *Twelfth Night.*'

'Do you know, darling, I've never understood why nobody ever asked me to play Maria. I'm sure I could have done, and still could. You can be any age really for the part. It's such a good one. Now, let's have a quick glance at the garden.'

'Why the sudden passion for the open air?' I asked. 'It's not like you, Mother.'

'Oh, I don't know.' She laughed, very effectively, but I thought I detected a sub-nervousness.

'What is like me, anyway? Or like you, come to that. Or like Barney. Everybody's an individual, darling, and that means being very peculiar sometimes.'

'Perhaps I'm peculiar all the time,' I said.

'Oh, darling. If so it must be my fault.'

'It's not a fault at all.' I gazed across the table at her, meaning to see her as she really was, but familiarity blinded me. I thought I could have seen her more clearly if she hadn't sat so palpably before me: it was like trying to see behind a large neon sign saying "Mother" – a neon sign in an ethnic quilt, I told myself affectionately.

'Mother,' I said aloud, though I felt too proud, too old to go on with the appeal: I need you, and otherwise I am most awfully alone. Yes, let me get it out; I'll be my own dentist, and once I've told her everything, it will stop hurting and seem nothing.

I suppose it must have been when I was about thirteen that after an endless, weary week-end of agonising toothache at school, I eventually found I was staring still numb at the object like a rice grain held up cheerfully by the local dentist. 'That's the little fellow that was causing all the trouble. Want to keep it?'

'You're looking much better already,' Mother said. 'Do you know that, darling? Much less white than when we met.'

'I feel a bit white inside still, to be frank. I wonder if there has to be an inquest when a Coroner dies? It's rather like wondering about the burial of one of those people called funeral directors.'

'Well, don't. I want you to forget everything that's happened recently, and I'm sure you will once we're in Portugal.'

'In Portugal,' I began, 'with—'

We were no longer alone. At first I thought it was Barney returned, but the hovering presence was moth-like in rustic brown-and-white linen, with a muslin cap and an usherette's tray of what seemed to be clumsy basket-work.

'I am the English Cheesemaid,' she giggled as she rushed on with her recitation. 'May I suggest you sample one of our native cheeses? We like visitors to England to experience and enjoy our finest produce, and a portion of English cheese rounds off even the tastiest meal.'

'Mon dieu,' I moaned as exasperatedly as I felt. Any minute now a bevy of Milk Marketing Board moppets would be lowered from the Edwardian beams and shower the table with dainty vouchers for double cream. 'We're trying to have a private conversation, for Christ's sake.'

'It was a lovely lunch, dear,' Mother said. 'But I couldn't touch another thing, thank you. And have you been doing this long? I do hope you're enjoying it.'

'S'better than being in an office.' The Cheesemaid giggled again. She might have been Sadie's Anglo-Saxon sister, as skinny and pretty, dipped not in cocoa but flour.

'Don't be shy with people, dear, and never, never mumble. You want to sweep up and surprise them.'

'She did that well enough,' I said.

' "I am the Cheese Lady",' Mother declaimed. 'Make it sound nice and clear, and unhurried, especially if you really are speaking to foreigners. Don't forget it's your title, isn't it? "The Cheese Lady". You want to feel proud of it. We're going out for a few moments' stroll, but I think you should approach that sweet Japanese family in the corner, and remember what I've told you, dear. You look very charming and you want to sound charming as well. It's all a matter of confidence. Now, darling, where are we?'

'In the garden, I suppose.'

146

She took my arm as the Cheesemaid retreated with the hint of a curtsey, her eyes not on me but on Mother. At another time I would have asserted my presence, not have hidden, as it were, behind Mother's skirts, but I was still sore and apprehensive, very much like a page-in-waiting, literally, at her side. I decided to say nothing as we stepped from the dining-room on to the sodden gravel bordered by a high yew hedge in which raindrops hung.

'I've been thinking,' Mother said slowly, and we seemed to move at the same rhythm as her words, advancing very gradually down a dark vista of hedgerow. 'Thinking hard, darling, ever since I left Steve.' She squeezed my arm. 'And not by any means only about him. About you, and about us. I want you to like him, you see, from the first.'

'Is it so vital?'

'You haven't always liked my men, have you? Do you remember nearly poisoning that dreadful stick, Desmond, the barrister, with your chemistry set? Oh, I suppose that wasn't so much jealousy as a boyish urge to experiment.'

'I don't have a chemistry set any longer.'

'Just as well perhaps. No, seriously, darling, I want you to like Steve and I want to talk about him – about us – before you meet. Your old mother feels distinctly old sometimes. And lonely. You're growing up, grown up, virtually, I suppose. You talk of leaving school, and so on. Your future is before you. I've often felt I didn't have a future.'

'Mother.' I flamed angrily, hurt on her behalf, at her misrepresentation of herself. 'That's rubbish. Why, only before lunch we were all toasting your next film. I bet it comes off. You'd be wonderful as Mrs Siddons. You are Mrs Siddons as far as I'm concerned.'

'Thank you, darling. I don't think she had a very happy private life.'

'Who cares?'

She stopped and looked round. 'I wonder if this is a maze? We don't want to get lost. The fact is that not only am I rather shamefully in love with Steve but the poor dear boy is – I almost blush to say it – totally in love with me. That's why, this time, it's not quite the same old story. Darling, I never thought I'd come to it again, but we are actually thinking about marriage. I feel quite silly uttering the word, even to you. Of course, nobody else knows as yet.'

For a moment I thought I was unwounded. I felt nothing; and then gradually the pain and misery of it rose and spread, excluding every other sensation. Even as I stood there, I could detect an inner crumpling. I couldn't even quite call the news a surprise.

'Did you have to tell me?' I asked miserably, staring at the tall, stupid stretch of tailored hedge around us.

'But, darling, I wanted you to know exactly how things were before you met Steve. No secrets. Anyway, you'd have guessed, and then felt I ought to have told you before. Haven't we always been honest with each other? I'm happy, and I'm telling you why. Isn't that sensible?'

I moved away, tempted momentarily to plunge into the furry green barrier before me and flee. The very word had a wonderful sense of release: away from the manoeuvring Mother had contrived.

'Well?' she said, not pulling on the line, just a calm, assured fisherwoman who knew she had hooked her son.

'Why marriage?' I queried as sullenly as I dared. 'I thought you didn't believe in marriage.'

'I only said it was on the cards.' Add some earrings and Mother turned gypsy, shuffled the pack and told your fortune. 'Steve's rather romantic and conventional in some ways. He'd feel more sure of me married. I know it sounds ridiculous. I ought to be the one demanding marriage lines from him.'

'It's very sudden.'

'Darling, that's heavenly. You sound like some delicious father in a very old-fashioned play. I don't actually need permission to get married.'

'But it's all taken for granted, isn't it? You and he shacking up together. What about me? We haven't discussed that, have we? Suppose I hate his guts?'

'I don't think you will, somehow.' She had not budged, though I seemed to have revolved around her only to return so close I could smell her scent in the damp air. 'Steve would be hard to hate, I think, though obviously I'm biased. You'll see for yourself.'

'And what if he hates me?'

'Oh,' she said, calmly smiling. 'I'm sure you'd be able to

148

deal with that. Not that it's terribly likely. Perhaps we ought to be thinking of going. Barney wants to be back in London not too late.'

It was my turn to stand still. 'I don't want to go.' In time I'd change into one of those grotty lead statues, weeping in the rain, patched by lichen and prematurely aged by snow. I was the boy with a leaden heart, out of some sad, unsuitable, children's folktale. It was Mother who had done it. That was the hardest thing to understand or bear.

'You don't want me in Portugal,' I said. 'That's fine. I'm glad I know. If I didn't hate your Steve person I'd certainly hate the *ménage à trois.* '

'Well, darling, would you like to bring someone?'

'God, no. Anyway who is there?'

'We needn't be *à trois* all the time. In fact there are some very sweet people we've met already, and I'm sure lots of people of your age are about. It'll be fun for you, and we can have plenty of talk together on our own.'

'But you'll marry him, won't you? That's really what it comes to. He's going to be in our lives from now onwards, regardless of what I feel. That's it, isn't it? I haven't any choice - except I choose to stay here.'

'You can't be serious, my darling child. And we must go in.' She put her arm consolingly yet compellingly round me, and I stumbled reluctantly along at her side, carving great troughs in the gravel with my feet. 'You're at a perfect age.' I groaned. 'No, please listen. I don't have to treat you like some awful adolescent in love with his Mum, do I? That would be so hackneyed and utterly unlike you. We're not going to live together - in any sense of the word, darling - and you've got your life before you. How could you help me? What's left of my life could be horribly lonely, desolate without Steve. Think of it. No need to envy Estelle with her Freddie. The answer to a middle-aged actress's prayer. Normal, handsome and loving - and not even a bad actor. I'm so sick of being an old bag in life, never mind in art. And don't forget I'm growing older. Maybe it sounds absurd to you, but one day I'll be blind and batty, senile or something. Oh, I shan't expect him to nurse me. But at least I'll know he loved me. That'll do. Don't begrudge me it. God knows it's rare enough in my experience - actual love. So there's a good chance I'll die happy. What more can anyone ask?'

We had reached the glass doors of the dining-room. She took me in her arms. 'Now do you understand?' she said. 'Let's have a kiss.'

I clung to her silently, confused and begging mutely for her to understand me, tell me where I was, though all the time I knew. I recalled the instant I'd seen her stepping from the Rolls, when I'd have liked to set off the police siren in salute. How warmly her voice had poured through the sitting-room at Bob and Edna's as I sat naked, crouched there, many nights ago, it seemed. Words like senility and death had no more meaning than her talk of Stephen – Steve. She would go on; I wanted her to go on, and that's what I thought of as real love. Only, somehow, she would go on for Steve, not me: stolid, solid, sexy Steve. I believed it without seeing him. And my belief made me feel very old and sad, far older certainly than Mother would ever be.

'I give you my blessing.' I tried to say it cheerfully as we drew apart. 'On one condition.'

'Agreed,' she cried happily.

'That I don't come to Portugal. And don't say you want me to, because that can't really be true. I'll meet him over here, in London, in the autumn.'

'But, darling, what will you do meanwhile? I know you're splendid at coping, though I can't leave you on your own, and after all that's happened ... You must be longing for a change.'

'Not that one.' I held open the door with a gesture of finality. She paused to gather her floating robes, glancing at me anxiously and yet underneath – I could, if not positively see, detect – relieved, pleased even and then ashamed of being so. Steve rushed to greet her at Lisbon airport. He probably referred to me as the kid (young Hamlet, when he was feeling facetious, and privately to himself, young Nero). 'Not to worry,' he'd tell her when she broke the good news. 'The kids nowadays ... it's all so different ... independent little buggers, sweetheart, from the word go. Believe you me.'

'I'll get by,' I said as she still paused. 'I usually do.'

'Oh, I can't go off without you, darling, really and truly. I do long for you to meet Steve, and the beaches there are heaven. And I've talked so much about our having this holiday together. It wouldn't be the same without you, would it?'

'Nope.' It seemed more ironic than a genteel mere 'no'.

'Barney's got your ticket too. We'll talk to her on the way back. You'll listen to her, if not to me, darling, won't you? She's got her head screwed on so sensibly. You know that.'

'You make her sound like a bottle of lemonade. Yes, I like her. But all the same, I'm not going back with you, Mother. J'y suis, j'y reste.'

'But, darling, what would you do down here? It's the last place for you. We can't ask Freddie and Estelle to put you up.'

'I have my plans,' I said proudly. She should never guess how desperate I felt. I looked at my watch, and for some reason I remembered the day at school when I discovered its glass had slipped out, and, though ticking on, its hands had become horribly mangled, squashed on the bare face like a couple of entwined insects. My first impulse was despairingly to throw it away.

'Oh, I don't know,' I said, talking to give myself courage. 'There are lots of things I might do. After all, there's Philip's death. I could always hinder the police with their enquiries.'

10

The front door I approached boldly enough, I hoped, to show Mother and Barney I knew what I was doing. I did not intend to turn round, whether or not the car waited. The ride back had become almost perturbing in the high spirits the three of us displayed; and Mother remained buoyant even after Barney had failed to second her. 'It's your life, chum,' Barney said, giving me a parting wink of encouragement and perhaps challenge.

I needed a good dose of that, as well as time to control my

absurdly racing pulse. The path seemed too short to provide a breathing space, and without any luggage my hands were strangely unoccupied. It was even hard to walk quite straight. Mr Latimer ought to be looking out, confirmed in his belief that drink or drugs intoxicated the youth of today, their minds blown, out of wilful idleness, whereas in his day ...

'No, I shan't ring,' I'd told Mother twice. 'You wouldn't understand – they're not telephone people. It'll be much less alarming if I just turn up.'

Still, I had promised to telephone her that evening. It would set her heart at rest, she said; and I found the phrase oddly troubling, more poignant than her earlier talk of old age. I didn't like to think of her heart being rested.

The front door was ajar, which I had not foreseen. I half stepped in, knocking as I did so. The red hall-tiles looked as if they had been polished again since Bob and I had crossed them that morning. The house was quite silent, faintly fragrant with elusive domestic smells that seemed familiar. And yet I felt an intruder.

'Oh, it's you, is it?' Edna had come out of the kitchen, straight from the garden I guessed, holding a colander full of unshelled peas. 'I thought you'd be back sooner. You'll find your suitcase on the landing.'

'Edna,' I said. It was far more difficult than I had realised. I was positively shivering. 'I want to ask a favour. It's all a bit complicated, but could you put me up for a few more days? I mean, obviously I'd pay. It's just that I don't think I am off to Portugal, and I'd love to stay on here – if you'll let me.'

I suppose I hadn't thought she would quite rush to embrace me but I had anticipated some sign of pleasure. She remained where she was, impassive, even threatening, with the colander held like a weapon at the ready.

'I'm not running a boarding-house, you know,' she said. 'I took the sheets off your bed first thing after you left. Have you quarrelled with your mother or something?'

'No, of course not. It's just that – oh, I'd rather stay here. With you and Bob. But not if I'm a nuisance. Anyway, may I stay for tonight? I can always sleep on the floor.'

'Oh yes. Then what'll you do? Join the Army or something? It all seems a funny carry-on to me. I thought you wanted to be with your mother.'

'It's become very complicated, as I told you. I haven't anywhere to go – well, where I want to go. I might possibly go abroad with a friend, Dennis; but I'd have to get in touch with him first.

'We had the inquest this morning,' I reminded her after a pause, hoping to stir some interest or at least movement. 'It's adjourned. I met the Chief Inspector over from Aylesbury,' I added.

'Mr Catesby, is it? Bob says he's good at his job. They were bound to adjourn the inquest; Bob knew that. Not sufficient evidence so far, that's the problem.'

'Oh, really?'

'Well,' she said. 'I've plenty to see about, especially if you're staying – as I suppose you are.'

'Not if you don't want me,' I said. 'I could easily go to London, or somewhere, tomorrow. And I'll ring my mother tonight. I'm sorry to be putting you to such inconvenience.' My voice trailed away. I couldn't think what else to say, unless I fell on the tiles at her feet – near enough – and bared my bleeding heart. Something like that must have happened to Wanda in Renaissance Riga with Ladislas or Stanislas. Edna's reaction would be to get out the Band-aid and tell me to take that shirt off, soak it straightaway in cold water so it wouldn't stain.

I meant to be the prodigal son returned, but I seemed to have chosen the wrong day, or even the wrong household. My hasty improvisation about Dennis might come to be the humiliating only alternative. Or, wildly for a moment as I still hovered on the threshold, I thought of Jean Danvers; after all, I could remind her mordantly, we met over Philip.

'Well,' Edna said again, dismissively. 'You know your way around. I'll bring you up some clean sheets once I've done these peas. And we'll see what Bob says when he's home.'

Guiltily I moved towards the staircase, turning myself near invisible as I trod delicately to mask and disarrange the minimum by my presence. One thing school did teach was how to become physically unobtrusive during an abrupt wave of unpopularity, when you had yet got to go on doing things communally. The day had dwindled to being like that, and with not feigned but real weariness I climbed the stairs and contemplated my grey suitcase propped on the landing. It

153

needed no 'to be called for' label to betray it was out of place; and even its sleek, silver-buckled elegance was a reproach of ostentation – almost as bad as if I had left a five-pound note on the bedside table.

Grabbing it furtively, I pushed open the door of what had been my room. At first glance it was unchanged. But neat and orderly as it had been, it had never possessed the desolate impersonal orderliness it now showed. The flat naked mattress and folded counterpane, and the wide-opened windows from which the curtains were drawn back to their fullest extent, suggested the sequel to a death. It had been visited either by undertakers or a wood-worm firm. The rug no longer lay on the floor. The chest of drawers stood half-open, and even the blue pottery donkey had vanished from the windowsill. Only the view of Whitby Bay survived.

'Super,' I muttered, slinging my suitcase on to the bed where it sat like a dumb animal beside me. If I'd had bubonic plague, Edna could not have worked harder to expunge my occupancy. I suppose if I'd left a worn-out sock in one corner of the chest-of-drawers she'd have carried it downstairs on a broom-handle and ritually burnt it in Bob's incinerator outside the kitchen door.

It was a pleasure, however pointless, savagely to unpack and spread everything in a confused pile over the mattress. I meant to go further and strip myself, so that I just sprawled there amid the confusion until Bob came home. He begged me to stay for ever, but I shoved him aside and ran down to telephone Margot. Sooner or later Mopsa had to return from Greece. So much had happened since we'd parted in Knights-bridge; I flushed to think how childish and stupid I'd then been: childish, stupid and odious. But during the summer I had grown older and wiser. Mopsa more than half-loved me already, and instead of fighting Simon Sinclair I would now be subtle, tolerant, even friendly, if we had to meet again. It was the policy of Néron with Britannicus: 'J'embrasse mon rival, mais c'est pour l'étouffer.'

I wasn't prepared for Edna's sudden appearance in the doorway, carrying an offering of folded sheets and towels. It made me jump; but it was easier to dispose of my reverie than of the litter scattered across the bed.

'It's quite parky in here now,' she said. 'You'd better shut the windows. And unless you want to sleep on the floor, you can make up the bed.'

'Thanks.' Still embarrassed, I took the sheets from her. 'I'm glad to be back, Edna. Thank you. And glad to have this room again. I like the blue walls.'

'Settling in, I see. If the room's not very inviting, it's because I didn't expect to use it again after you left.'

'It's the guest-room, I suppose,' I said, conscious of the stilted remark.

'You and your posh ideas. I don't have guests that way – not to stay. It'd be a long journey for our father now, and anyway he wouldn't want to come south. And my sisters are all tied up with their families. No, Bob and I always thought of this room for if we had—' She broke off and went and straightened the Whitby view which could scarcely have been hanging crooked. 'If we had a family of our own.' She turned from the wall. 'Nice clothes yours, aren't they? I like a man to have nice things. I always buy Bob good shirts and what they call leisure wear. That's a nice scarf there; I never saw you wear that.'

'What scarf?'

'The yellow sporty one.'

'It's not a scarf.' I spoke quickly yet casually. 'It's a shirt – one I'm not keen on and hardly ever wear. Anyway, I'm sorry about this mess. I'll tidy it up; I don't quite know why I unpacked everything. I wasn't thinking.'

'Perhaps that's your trouble,' she said, standing in the doorway and watching as I knelt up on the bed, cramming my clothes back into the suitcase. I stopped, gaping at her in surprise.

'What on earth do you mean? I'm not exactly stupid.'

'I didn't say you were. You're not daft. More thoughtless, if you ask me. Well, talking won't change you. It's none of my affair, and I've supper to get ready.'

'No, Edna, seriously.' I clambered off the bed, feeling somehow that I must literally stand up to her, or at least stand up for whatever medicine she meant me to take. Her bulk filled the doorway, not diminished by the short-sleeved, boldly-floral, autumnal-coloured overall she wore, and she went on regarding me so gravely that I flinched – or felt I did – even while I tried to meet her eye. It's like a firing-squad must be, I thought: certainly it was unlike anything I could envisage, and I wouldn't have minded the offer to be blindfolded.

'What's my crime?' I said, before realising she couldn't know the train of association. 'I mean, in what way am I so thoughtless? I've apologised for coming back like this, haven't I? I am truly sorry and I quite see it was a mistake. I'll be off tomorrow. And I won't ever forget all the kindness you and Bob showed me. I am grateful. I always will be. Please believe that.'

'Oh.' She sounded disdainful now. 'Bob and I don't want thanks. It wasn't much we did. And talking about ever and always at your age – that's just stuff. Anyway, I ought to have kept my big mouth shut. Bob wouldn't be pleased if he knew what I've said, so don't you tell him.'

'Of course I won't. But, Edna, at least please tell me—'

'Tell you what?' she asked sharply. 'Why should you need telling if you're such a clever one? I'm not going to make long speeches about my feelings, but if you must know – and then that's an end of it – I never liked your way with Bob. I always thought you were making fun of him – underneath.'

'Making fun of him? That's ludicrous. Nothing could be further from the truth.'

'So you say now. Young lads of your age don't care much for the police, do they? And Bob's just a sergeant down here in the country, living quietly. You can't know what he's like or how good he is – I mean, really good. I know. And he was fond of you. Still is, I expect, more's the pity. But you didn't want to go bird-watching with him, did you? Just made jokes about you and me going off together to India or whatever. One day you're away to Portugal with your mother. Next minute you're back here with a fresh tale. Very different from us you are, and don't expect me to keep track of it all.'

'I thought I fitted in,' I said sadly. 'I like being with you both – both,' I repeated. 'Yes, Edna.' Suddenly I felt there was nothing to be lost. I might as well throw down the equivalent of a lighted match in the emotion-soaked room. It was as if I had never before been so earnest for anything in my life. I looked, no longer flinching, at her brawny arms, sizing up the struggle that might physically take place before we finished. 'That's the truth. I can't help whether you realise it or not, but I'm going to say it before I go. It's nothing to do with my being different from you and Bob. All right. I am. My background's different. And I'm not simple or good or fond of the countryside. And you're so right, I don't want to watch birds – or be a bloody bricklayer, come to that. But does it matter?

'I wasn't mad at first about staying here, I admit, but I hadn't anywhere else to go after Philip's death. Actually, I dreaded it, and then when I arrived it wasn't what I'd expected. You were kind to me, and I liked you. You and Bob. That's not so common with me. Now, my mother's getting married – re-married, I learnt today. I thought I'd rather come back here. You'd made me welcome before. Must I go on?' But it was myself I was asking. She never shifted her stance in the doorway, and her face hung large, brooding, perplexed, with no sign that I had made an impression on its graven features.

'Perhaps it began as a game,' I said. 'Okay, it was convenient. I wanted to be around to see the police fail to solve it – solve Philip's death. But I never despised Bob. If I'm uneasy with him, it's because of too much feeling – not too little. I thought both of you wanted me, wanted me really as sort of your child. I suppose I wanted it too. How's that for fucking frankness?'

She gave me a long, dark look, almost tragic in its intensity. I was so exhausted that I hardly quivered when she put her heavy hands on my shoulders; it simply seemed one of several possibilities that they would close round my neck, and after all without a struggle I should end up strangled on the bare floor. There was little to disarrange in the suitably bare room. She probably was sufficiently strong to carry my body downstairs and dispose of it before Bob returned. The back of the cupboard under the stairs, close to the playpen perhaps, would do well enough to stow it overnight.

'You're an odd lad,' she said slowly, as if passing judgement. 'Let me talk to Bob when he gets in. You have a wash.' She took her hands away as if conscious my neck and shirt collar had become dirty. 'And I'd better see to supper if we're not all to go hungry to bed.'

'Stoke a quarrel,' I might have shouted after her, but I was beyond shouting anything. I rather wished she had left me as a janitress, locked safely in my cell, so that I did not have to encounter her or Bob until the morning. When I thought of how much had been revealed, even if she had not fully understood it while I was speaking, the next morning seemed no solution; it would be better to creep away tonight. I had no appetite for food, or for further exchanges.

In the end, of course, there was no alternative but to go downstairs. I had washed, as told, and changed into cream-coloured jeans and a bleached tee shirt – my whited-sepulcre uniform – so as to achieve cleanliness without purity. Candid was the suggestion I meant to convey – meant to be, purged after all I had disclosed before Edna. I am corrupt, sophisti-cated and a little confused, as well as quite clever – do you still want me, had been my challenge. By declining to answer, Edna won the contest. That was why I made my plimsolls – sneakers wasn't actually such a bad word for them – squeak on the stairs for mercy, or in warning.

Bob had come in. I could hear his voice rumbling in the kitchen and at the sound I held back, desperately, untypically shy. I, who ought to be able to manage anything by now, longed to lose all sensation: just propel myself into the room like a package, gift-wrapped, and leave them to savour the contents. Mother could do this, I thought; people called it giving, though what Mother gave, confident it would always be welcome, was her unblemished self.

But for that you had to know exactly who you were. When Bob looked up at me from the table, as I entered with false élan, I hadn't got myself sufficiently in focus to feel more than a blur. Perhaps he felt it too. He was in shirt-sleeves and slightly rumpled, as if barely off-duty, solemn, respectful almost, physically more ordinary than I had ever seen him. He started to get up and subsided, greeting me with 'Hullo' in a very neutral tone.

Now that I came to think of it, I had never heard him use my name. Suddenly that seemed significant.

Edna presided over the meal with all the politeness I associate with the aftermath of a bitter row. The Japanese at lunch had been riotous by comparison. Bob hardly said anything, except that he was tired and looking foward to a holiday in September. Bird-watching? I would have asked, even one evening ago. Now I was silent. It seemed incredible that we had all sat there such a short time before, when I had clumsily tried to thank them.

I was expecting Bob to say something as soon as possible about going off to help Mr Latimer. Edna, I foresaw, would probably reject any offer of mine about the washing up. I could go and telephone Mother. I should ask her to ask Barney to put me up for a couple of nights in her house at Putney (it was always full of stray visitors, arriving from America or leaving for Australia, but nobody was permitted to stay long). Then I would ring Margot, and I might even contact Dennis – anything, I intended, rather than have to take that flight to Lisbon.

'Care to walk down to the pub?'

'Now?' I said stupidly, when I at last realised Bob had been addressing me.

'No time like the present.'

Edna said nothing, and I couldn't tell whether she had been prepared or not. Once away from her, I determined, I would become more at ease with Bob. I would slip into being what he wanted – if, of course, he knew.

As we strolled out of the house, it was still light but the air was humid, sprinkled with rain, or so I imagined from the slight prickings on my forehead. Trencham Croke lay in its usual death-swoon. Edward VI, not VII, I amended as the monarch whose initials ought to be on the solitary pillar-box from which no letter surely was ever sent. And when was the last instance of breaking and entering around here, I might have once asked Bob, the *Belle au bois dormant* case?

'Look, about this morning, I'm sorry. No, please.' For he had begun at virtually the same moment to speak.

'Nothing much,' he said apologetically. 'Just going to say Edna and I have got a wedding anniversary coming up next month. Yes; we'll have been married ten years.'

'Have you always lived here?' I asked with the simulated eagerness of an interviewer. Perhaps that was my future: roaming the streets with a clip-board and asking passers-by if they'd travelled to work that morning by car.

'No, at first we just had rooms in Spenn – a flat over the grocer's, Mr Cherry's. We were lucky when this place came up. More space and everything, with the garden. Suits us very nicely, though some people might find it dull.'

'I suppose that depends.' It was about the verbal equivalent of munching the neck of my tee-shirt. The next thing would be to touch my hair and wonder if it was raining. I could hear Dennis at his most clipped, clipping me not so metaphorically over the head for any remark as banal. 'Observations on the weather are not conversation. There's no weather, is there, in Racine or Molière? Even Baudelaire ...' Perhaps during the summer I had grown too old for Dennis ('eternal master seeks eternal pupil' ran the advertisement, but sadly there aren't any eternal pupils). Still, he loved me, had loved me anyway. And I was fond and grateful. What more, as Mother would say, can you ask?

The Old Wheatsheaf looked as raw and newly-built as usual; I had not previously noticed the free-standing cement wheatsheaf, crudely hatched with what seemed more like ears of barley, positioned at the Public Bar entrance, the result probably of a brewery firm's sponsorship of living sculpture.

'Don't you want a drink?' Bob asked, seeing me pause.

'Of course. But am I coming in?'

'Why not? You're over sixteen, aren't you?'

Inside, the pub was mercifully empty – of atmosphere and customers. The juke box stood silent, and only a single strip of horse-brasses dangled over the table where two aged men sat sipping pints. Bob greeted them and they grunted back, paying no attention to me. Very slowly, one of them started to light his pipe, patiently applying match after match from the box in front of him and carefully putting back the spent ones. We leant on the deserted bar, and I played with a beer-mat. Life in an old people's home must be like this, I thought, as time congealed.

'Edna was saying,' Bob began, as if asserting himself against the silence, but a smiling girl appeared and he stopped.

'Sorry to have kept you waiting.'

Her freckled froggy face and blue eyes were so cheerful that I had to smile back. She was plump and quite assured in a shapeless, smocked peppermint-green shift that dipped to reveal her very white breasts. I felt ashamed in front of Bob of the sudden attraction I felt as she propped herself there and re-arranged, with a direct smile at me, the beer-mat and a stretch of silly fringed velour cloth I had rucked up.

Bob was looking enquiringly at me. 'I'll have some cider,' I said, and waited. He seemed unflustered.

'A pint of draft cider and a pint of bitter, please,' he said.

The girl moved away; I watched her pulling cheerfully though not very expertly at the levers, pushing back her long, reddish-brown hair from nearly bare shoulders. She could not be much older than I was. Why hadn't I seen her before? Between us we could have created the Trencham Croke Youth Club.

'You know, Bob,' I said, still staring beyond him. 'You're committing an offence. Oughtn't mine to have been a ginger-beer or something?'

'Did you want one?'

'I hate it, and always have.'

'Well, you'll pass as not under age, and the landlord's safe enough with me, just for this once. That girl's new,' he added. 'New, aren't you?' he said when she brought the tankards to us.

'Let me pay,' I said, but he intervened. I might have asked her if she'd like a drink.

'Only helping out,' she said. Her pale, plump arm briefly lay alongside mine, and I was tempted to put my hand on it, so soft and inviting did it look. She didn't mind the proximity, I could tell, and when she went on talking it seemed more to me than to Bob. 'Only for a few days, while Geoff who works here is on holiday. Not my part of the world at all, I'm afraid, and I'm not much good as a barmaid, even if I do look the part.' She gave me a grin. 'Haven't seen you in before.'

'Well,' Bob said heavily, causing a conscious break by carrying the drinks to a table opposite the two drowsing old men.

'Where are you from?' I lingered at the bar.

'London. Can't wait to get back, though this has been an experience. Are you local?'

'God, no.'

Somebody called her from the other bar, and there was nothing to do but go over and join Bob. He had sat down, looking mournful or thoughtful.

'Cheers,' he said.

'Oh, cheers.'

'Edna was saying before supper about how you'd come back.'

'I thought she would. I'm sorry about it, but don't worry. I'll be off your hands – finally – tomorrow.'

'Well, we never went swimming, did we? Just one of those things. It was bound to be quiet for you but it was company for Edna. She gets lonely down here, I mean, she hasn't got her roots in the south. She misses her family; they're very close, and she's not one for making many friends.'

'Edna said you thought the inquest would be adjourned.'

'That's what the Boss wanted, and now Mr Catesby's taking an interest. We'll get to the bottom of it, never fear. Seems quite a while ago, doesn't it, since – since that morning when we met?' He smoothed his moustache with a touchingly uncertain gesture; perhaps it was a little ragged. Did he trim it himself, or was it Edna who did that for him? As though asserting his palpable, fleshly existence he put his shirt-sleeved elbows on the table. I looked at his biggish hand, with the broad band of wedding ring gleaming amid the slight, glinting gold hairs, as he grasped his pint: he is good, Edna's voice seemed to go on echoing.

'But I think she's got fond of you.' He startled me by the coincidence of thought. 'Maybe it's not like her to show it. She doesn't talk much about her feelings. Sometimes people don't understand her down here, because she's not one for a lot of chat. It's a good thing in a policeman's wife.'

'She's been very kind,' I mumbled. 'You both have.'

He sipped the beer, making it last. 'And you're off tomorrow?'

'Oh, Bob, I was going to be off, as you put it, today. You know that. Everything's suddenly much more complicated; I can't explain. I'm sorry. It's not so unusual, with me, or my mother.'

'But you're not in trouble, are you?'

'Well, I'm not a waif or stray – not yet quite.'

'You don't seem to have a proper home, that's all. I know it's not my business, but that's what strikes me.'

'Should I have an improper one? No, seriously, I'm surviving pretty well. Home anyway is only something you leave. Besides, Mother lives a life of short leases, if you must

162

know, and borrowing other people's houses and never settling down for long. At least, that's been her tendency so far. It quite suits me.'

'So you came down to Spenn to stay with your godfather?'

'I often did. God, haven't we been through all this before, Bob, as part of my evidence or statement or whatever? I came, saw and was bored to death – all much as usual.'

'And now what?'

'The world is before me. At least, so people have always told me. It's my oyster, but I happen not to eat oysters. Youth is opportunity, I've heard a hundred times. The opportunity to do what? The only nice thing about a career is the word: it sounds so wonderfully speedy. My career is probably to be brilliant and burnt-out by the age of twenty. And that's not the cider speaking. I see myself glittering and falling, but I want a period of glitter before you start mourning over my premature death.'

'I only meant, what'll you do in the next few weeks. Because we're happy enough if you want to stay on a bit. Only if it suits you, though. I know Edna would like it, and I'd like to think she had someone around. You can call it selfish.'

'Yes,' I said meditatively. 'There's that in its favour.'

I drained the rest of my cider and peered into the distorting prism of the empty tankard. Actually, I did feel rather light-headed, pleasantly so, obscurely as relaxed as if I'd scored with both the barmaid and Bob, and was shifting comfortably between them in bed, having regretfully closed the door on Edna. ('Sorry, we're busy. Be down for meal later. Could you bear to wash these clothes?')

'Another drink?' I said to Bob, victorious yet magnanimous: young Icarus giving a helping hand to Daedalus (he only flew near the sun to get away from his father's droning platitudes).

'Halves, I think, if we have anything. But I'll get them.'

'No. Let me.'

We were still amiably, aimlessly wrangling when the door banged open and a figure in motor-cycle gear swaggered in. The entrance must have been TV-inspired; it called for a shot of a noisy pub falling quiet. As he marched to the bar and started rapping with a coin, I saw it was bloody, bleeding Len from the butcher's. He had dyed his fair hair puce, and it certainly matched his acne.

'What about a bit of service?' he shouted. 'Wake up. Oh, hullo, darling. A packet of fags, a packet of crisps and an orange-juice. Have one yourself.'

'Hey,' I said, hurrying to the bar. 'I'd just asked her to have a drink with me. When I ordered those halves of bitter and cider,' I said to her, nodding.

'That so?' He lounged against the bar, glancing threateningly round the room though not at me, his leather-clad bulk expanding to exclude my presence without quite touching me. Now we were so near, I realised he was quite short, with a thin head like a cockatoo's, pecking and glaring on the broad perch of his shoulders. I could call a policeman, I thought, if this becomes a real brawl.

'An orange juice, a cider, a half of bitter,' the girl said demurely behind us, 'a packet of crisps and twenty cigarettes. That'll be – but you're not together, are you?'

We both swung round. Bob, I was annoyed to see, had got up and come and joined us: reinforcements before I called for them. But it was the girl Len and I were mutely interrogating. She looked calmly at Len and then at me. My sword was out in a flash. Clasping her in one arm – wonderfully soft and clinging she was, yet no impediment – I sliced his gear open from neck to navel, without doing more than leave on him a stinging whiplash line of reddened skin.

'Thanks,' she said. 'But I'm not drinking anything.'

'I'll be in tomorrow night', Len said, knocking back the orange juice noisily and stowing the crisps and cigarettes in some zippered pocket. 'That's a promise, darling.' He threw down a pound note.

'And 38p,' she said.

He dug reluctantly for it, nearly jostling me as he did so. One sticky contact with that leather, I decided, and this glassful will be all over you.

'Won't you really have a drink?' I asked her as he clattered out (on his way perhaps to Sadie?) and the two old men still slumbered on. Bob was hovering anxiously, but now I hunched myself to keep him excluded or at least waiting. Her smile was friendly as she shook her head, making the hair swing slightly on either side of her face. Only a shake or two more, and the shift would slip off, and underneath she would be naked. Well, meet me later, I ought to have suggested. She must have a room somewhere in the building.

'Thanks all the same,' she said. 'Even though it is my last night.'

'Student type,' Bob said, when finally we came out of the pub, and began walking slowly through the dusk. The girl had disappeared after I paid for our drinks, and we sat on silently long after they were finished. The two old men got up, for some reason shook hands with each other and went out together, though clearly parting.

'That's my bet about her,' he added, as though consoling me for a disappointment. 'Earning a bit of money in her holidays, I reckon.'

We walked on. Once or twice I stumbled as I followed him along the uneven, dusty grass verge, trying to avoid the tall stinging-nettles that leant from the rank hedgerow and seemed likely to slap my face.

We were in sight of the two cottages. Mr Latimer's was in total darkness, but a pinkish light glowed and showed where Edna must be sitting by a lamp; or she had gone to bed and left that beacon shining out, to guide us back and sober us up. Or might she be waiting at the top of the stairs, in a flannel dressing-gown, armed with the traditional rolling-pin? I suppressed a giggle at the thought, and next time I dodged the nettles and stumbled, I let myself clutch at Bob, almost surprised at his warmth and solidity under the thin shirt.

'Okay?' he asked amusedly, steadying me as I hung there.

'If you are,' I said. I felt too excited to hiccup, just hanging there, weighing him down until he uneasily shifted. 'Too much for you, am I?'

'Well, it's only a few steps now.'

'Could you care less whether I go or stay? You personally? Oh, don't bother to answer.'

'Course I'd like you to stay, Nick.' He said it half-angrily, roughly hauling me upright as he spoke. Still, he had said it, perhaps unaware it had slipped out. 'But why ask me? Make up your own mind. Come on.'

'You might be sorry – Robert.'

He laughed. 'I'll be sorry if we're found drunk and disorderly. Now, come on.'

'Let's go swimming,' I babbled, in mock confusion, stumbling after him as he reached the gate and raised the latch. The front door looked inexorably closed, but Bob could open it and I would walk in.

It must have been nearly midnight when I got through to Mother. It was never too late for her, but she seemed unusually distraite, literally distant, repeating, 'Oh, good, good, darling,' while I told her how the Parrotts seemed only too pleased ... 'Barney can always get you a ticket, don't forget,' she interrupted at last. 'If you do change your mind or your Parrotts start moulting. Darling, I don't mean that unkindly. I'm virtually coming apart at the seams. We did have an odd day, didn't we, but don't let's start discussing it. Just tell me you are all right.'

'I'm fine.' I felt it as I spoke: perhaps I seemed too fine, finer anyway than I ought to sound, and my sparky assertion caused no answering spark. I was lying prone on the carpet, whispering close into the clammy mouthpiece of the telephone as if conducting a nefarious love-affair in the room over which Bob and Edna were sleeping.

'Dieu vous blesse,' I said more desperately, as though to catch Mother before she drifted far out of earshot and was lost to me. 'You – and Steve.'

I rolled over and lay for a while, staring up at the ceiling.

11

Although Edna replaced the rug in my room, she did not put the donkey back on the window-sill.

I never had to make any declaration about staying on; it was obvious that she and Bob had talked – were perhaps still talking while I telephoned Mother that night. Meanwhile, the house filled up with bunches of larkspur handed over the fence by Mr Latimer, who received in exchange gifts of new potatoes and rhubarb.

I unpacked most of my things, and wondered how the girl from the pub would get back to London. I saw her standing for ever at the solitary bus stop of Trencham Croke, in the green shift and with a bulging suitcase, until eventually a passing motorist picked her up. When I walked that way I still stupidly thought of her being there, and the banks of nettles basking in the sun looked the more forlorn and meaningless.

At first I felt Edna did not want me around the house; or it was I who felt uneasy, glad to make some excuse after breakfast, take a book and explore the fields that lay beyond the back garden. Sometimes I thought, or imagined, she glanced at me with a residue of suspicion. I wondered what exactly – and how much – she had told Bob. It was not merely that I couldn't forget her reception of me on my return; our conversation upstairs seemed to haunt me, unresolved as it was and went on being. Nor was it the weather to stage any grand remonstrance. The days had become oppressively hot, damply so, sapping energy and making even eating an effort.

'You could sit outside the kitchen,' Edna had said one morning as I dutifully finished the drying-up and replaced on its hook the 'Windsor Castle' tea-towel, itself faded a little so that its scrolled border now read only 'centuries old ... of our ... archy.'

'On the verandah,' I murmured, ruefully conscious that I had never volunteered to help Bob continue its building.

But though Edna had made a concession, and I went and sat for a while within the low brick enclosure and close to the hot-smelling currant bushes, I remained not totally at ease. The buzz of the radio she liked to listen to was almost a summer noise and yet irritating. I picked up and put down *The Tale of Genji*. I had forgotten where I was in the book, and it never seemed to matter. Adjusting his sleeves and calling for another shade of tinted paper before despatching a one-line note to another lady appeared to sum up the activities of Genji. Everyone admired him; I suppose I did myself. He was the first of the fin-de-siècle dandies, whenever the book was actually written.

'Have a gooseberry,' Edna said, passing by later. 'They're dessert ones – nice and sweet.'

167

Not like me, I thought, putting one to my lips. She dropped two more on to my lap as she went inside. I picked up *Genji* again, though the pages had got creased and I couldn't pretend to concentrate. To think – if that was what I wanted to do – I had to be further away.

The next morning I went to the end of the garden. A gate in the low fence led into the field beyond, through which the Croke trickled, looking no more than a now dried-up muddy stream. It was hard to believe that further down it became a river. Go for a swim this coming week-end if nothing crops up, Bob had said the evening before. He had seemed pre-occupied or harassed when he came home, saying something to Edna which I didn't hear except for the word 'demo'. Just before we went to bed he turned to me as if seeing me properly for the first time that evening. Edna had left the room, taking a tray of glasses with her. I tended to be less constrained when the three of us were not together.

'Well, you weren't so wrong about one thing where your godfather was concerned. I forgot to tell you yesterday. That Lesley Coombe made it all up about being pregnant. The Boss thinks she's nothing to do with the case.'

'Oh, really? Didn't Mrs Rainbow let someone in to see Philip before she went home?'

'Someone, yes. But we know it wasn't the Coombe girl. Who it was still isn't clear. Nobody's come forward. That could be a clue of sorts.'

Throughout the evening I had felt dazed from too much exposure to the sun, but now I became suddenly alert.

'I don't see that, Bob. In what way a clue?'

Edna had entered the room again, crossing over to snap out the standard lamp and somehow simultaneously causing the conversation to be extinguished.

As I wandered along the Croke, thinking hard, I felt I must enshrine the boyhood of several British historical figures. I had encountered nothing but two donkeys who stood gazing at me, large-eyed though not much interested, from under the speckled shade of a scrubby, indeterminate tree. From just such a background of amorphous, undistinguished country-side destiny would call anyone – and anyone would gladly answer the call, if only to get away.

Yet, with the stream widened and a line possibly of poplars to run beside it, it might become the scene of Maigret's retirement. From some half-glimpsed bicoque, he would be in the habit of coming here to fish, less to catch anything than to savour the tranquillity and the opportunities to meditate, or doze, he had long promised himself. Was it, if he was truthful, somewhat boring? One last case should by chance come his way. The death of a curé de campagne continues to baffle local police, and half-unwillingly Maigret is drawn into the affair, meets the few people involved, starts once again to exercise his imagination: *La dernière enquête de Maigret*.

Inevitably, I would, in one language or the other, assist. And if to me he sometimes seemed to drop, without warning, into a trough of old age, grow sleepy at the very moment one expected the keenest response, there would be little to disconcert him about me. Nearly fifty years earlier, with a very dissimilar upbringing, less quick-witted and certainly never good-looking, had he been at heart so very different?

I stayed out all day, obscurely on guard against Edna, perhaps punishing her a little, though I knew she liked someone to talk to when she had her 'sit down' at teatime. If some sand had mysteriously crept into the works of our once smooth relationship, accumulating overnight and making each day's breakfast a task of beginning again, it usually disappeared, dissolved, over the teacups and newly-baked bread. I began to think it was my invention, though by supper and Bob's imminent return, fine grains of it were falling again, hardly perceived as I sat on, turning the pages of Edna's photograph album, identifying her tall elder sisters, Marion and Angela as dark as she, and Elspeth the fair one. Their father, she told me, disliked being photographed. By now Edna's knitting had changed its colour, I noticed, from pink to blue, though the garment seemed to be much the same jacket affair, destined presumably for another of the blurred babies who surrounded the sisters in snapshots, and it disappeared before Bob came home.

I found him already seated at the kitchen table when I got back at last, and Edna (distrusting the refrigerator for most things except butter and milk) was bringing a cold pie out of the larder. I interrupted no conversation – only a silence which I couldn't interpret, or which was merely accidental.

'You look hot, Nick,' Bob said. His face never disguised anything. He looked washed, if not bathed, even to his slightly fuzzy hair, and content, whereas I felt gloomy and was hot.

I panted floppily, to mime agreement. Then I hastily splashed my hands and face with water at the sink, which I thought a homely, rustic, no-nonsense action.

'That towel's none too clean,' Edna said warningly, as I dried myself on the roller towel behind the door.

'Cleaner than I am,' I said.

'Where have you been?' Bob asked, helping me to a giant piece of pie. 'Oh, that reminds me.' He got up and left the room, and the silence seemed to start seeping back.

'Got a letter for you.' He came in, handing it across as he spoke. 'Sent to you care of Mr Kerr. Nobody's opened it,' he added, seeing that I was scrutinising it in the poor light. Outside the sky had turned a dull, thundery colour, I could tell, though my back was to the window.

'I'll read it later.' It was from Dennis.

Upstairs in my bedroom, just before I went to sleep, I unhurriedly opened it. With admittedly less choice of papers than Genji, Dennis nevertheless had a natural pedagogic penchant for half sheets of ruled foolscap that effortlessly spoke of the classroom and the team-list. I was surprised he didn't include a drawing-pin with the missive, as ever neatly written, opening without a greeting and curt in its conceal-ment of emotion: 'Since you have not cared to be in touch, I assume you have no interest in going to France this summer. Perhaps you might consider visiting me later in the year, if your plans permit, as I have taken at short notice a teaching post in Geneva. I shall be there for at least a year, starting in October. A friend of mine, Bernard d'Albert, already teaches there; I think you might like him. As ever I wish you well.'

No love and kisses: just curlicued initials to sign off with, housemaster style. It could – if not exactly go up on the games-board – at least be read out in court without sending the judge into an orgasm of indignation over monsters like Dennis, abusing (and he emphasised that verb with all the gravity at his command) a young boy's natural, affectionate respect for a gifted teacher. Something told me that Bernard d'Albert might be rather less discreet: perhaps along the lines

170

of the classics master who amused himself and teased Dennis at some previous school by sending him in class a boy with a note marked 'urgent': 'I think this one is rather pretty, don't you?'

I bet the boy opened that note on the way. I grinned as I switched the room into darkness, but there was some bravery behind the grin. Dennis, indicating it as neatly as he wrote, detached himself just at the moment I was debating whether to re-attach him. He was moving on. I would be welcome to go and stay in Geneva perhaps at Easter, but I shouldn't be too disconcerted to meet also an attractive collégien, with long eyelashes and a passion for English literature. 'I do hope you two will become friends.' We might, Dennis, we might ...

'Thought up to the last minute I might have to be on duty,' Bob said as we set out walking along the Croke. Today the donkeys had disappeared, and the morning was overcast, almost sullen, far from ideal in fact for swimming. I wrapped my towel shawl-like round my shoulders and wondered how much further we had to go. 'Yes,' he went on. 'They keep threatening to stage a demo on Spenn Common. The CND lot. Against having nuclear weapons here, you see.'

'Or anywhere.'

'What? Oh, I suppose so, but they feel it more strongly round here. The Common's a beauty spot, after all. I can understand their feelings.'

'Oughtn't we to join the demo then? Us versus Grice – I bet he's pro every sort of nuclear weapon. Ban the demo and keep the bomb.'

'Well,' he said cheerily, 'there hasn't been a demo yet, has there? Anyway, there's something to be said on both sides. We all agree about keeping the world peaceful, but how d'you do that best? That's the problem.'

'I can think of lots of other problems – beginning with, where's this super bathing spot? Never mind the beauty spot, a hideous term anyway.'

'Not much further. You'll be surprised.'

As we followed a bend, the Croke widened quite dramatically amid dull fields where a few cattle were grazing. Even the weather seemed brightening in a slow, reluctant way. Bob

171

led me over a rickety iron fence and past some bramble bushes; I stopped briefly to inspect them, but the blackberries, though fat and glossy, were still red.

'This is it,' he said.

'God. We're not alone, exactly.'

I looked round the expanse of grass and river. A group of boys of about eleven or twelve were shouting and chasing each other into the water and up the slope of the opposite bank.

'They won't bother us.'

I stood there uncertainly. Bob had already unrolled his towel and started to undress. He was revealed oddly patched, with his brown forearms and white chest and white legs, rather slimmer than I had anticipated. As he stepped out of his trousers I saw he wore swimming shorts of a glinting metallic blue, almost gunmetal colour in the sunlight, with three narrow, closely-set chalk-stripes diagonally across them (special police issue, bullet-proof, sergeants for the use of?).

Grudgingly I sat down and slowly took off my tee shirt, then my canvas shoes and socks. The sun was thinly brilliant, though not very warming, and I could understand why those boys rushed up and down, flapped their towels at each other and shrieked as they fled splashing in and out of the river. It was true they appeared to ignore our presence, but as fervently as possible I wished them away, invoking a scoutmaster, bandmaster, choirmaster, or anyone to lead them off to some Sunday duty. 'What's the matter?' Bob asked. 'Aren't you coming in?'

I stood up again. 'I think the zip's jammed on these jeans.'

'Let me try.'

He set one hand partly on the waistband and partly on the bare flesh of my thigh above, and it slightly goose-pimpled at the contact.

'Sorry,' he said. 'I'll be careful.'

He bent to put his other hand to the zip, while I stood there, my arms by my side, not consciously seeing anything, seeming barely to breathe. For a second I thought I was losing my balance, and my fingers reached out instinctively to steady myself by resting lightly on his faintly freckled, broad shoulder.

Cries and whoops echoed around us, and at each smacking

172

impact the surface of the river seemed to shiver and break into painfully bright aural as well as visual flashes. We went on standing there, and I thought how vulnerable Bob's bent, reddened nape of neck looked. He straightened up, his face red too, taking away the hand that had released the zip.

'That's it. It was nothing – just seemed awkward.'

'Thanks very much.'

I had stopped touching his shoulder, but I did not shift, and only after a pause did he remove his other hand. I didn't want to look directly at him, shook the jeans off and plunged down the tufted uneven bank into the shockingly icy water. 'Like the wolf on the fold,' I chattered as he splashed in behind me and we began swimming, though I could still feel the weeds and muddy bottom shelving away under my feet.

'Don't go too far upstream,' Bob panted after me. 'There's a nasty current. Those kids are local and play safe.'

Most of them appeared by now to have scrambled out and be sitting, knees clasped or absently pulling on clothing, as if spectators silently absorbed at some impromptu swimming gala.

'Go on,' one shouted piercingly. 'Push him under when you catch him.'

Shrill laughter and more cries, encouraging Bob presumably, rose as I swam away fast, and upstream, glad to find my feet free of entangling weed. The water felt chill but less icy now, and it was a wonderful sensation to be cleaving through it, as if through cold steel, with intermittent flushes of warmth as the sun fell on a portion of exposed skin. I slid on to my back, letting the water churn and swell into a liquid cushion, to see Bob swimming an earnest breast-stroke, falling behind, though we seemed mercifully to have swum out of sight of the Boys' Brigade.

Trees began to overhang the water, the occasional branch dangling, broken off, and I let myself be carried by the tug of current into the centre of the river, but I had every intention shortly of turning back. Bob's face, with hair wetly plastered down, rose and hailed me anxiously, calling 'Nick' hoarsely and I kicked my legs up in a foam of response.

It would be the Victorian school story of all time if only as he staggered on shore, clasping the burden of my drowned body, his tears mingled with the water streaming over him, did he realise in that proximity the depth of his love. And it would be too late. Even years afterwards, strangers at evening might encounter a grizzled figure, dignified, manly in bearing, grieving by a tombstone in a lonely Buckinghamshire churchyard, and be tempted to pause, to learn more of the tragedy lying behind a few simple lines incised on the mossy stone.

I dipped and shook my head, spitting out the sour yet unchlorinated water, and then turned swiftly back towards Bob, while the current fought to drag me the other way. I didn't feel like fooling with it – or with him. Swimming was something I had always done effortlessly, enjoyably, but I always detested ducking, fake panics and schoolboy antics in the baths.

But it was tiring, fighting back, and perhaps I was out of practice. My shoulder muscles ached as I swam firmly in Bob's direction, and his face looked pale, strained, when I overhauled him at last. I staggered the final few yards, almost relieved to be out of the water and collapsed, face upwards, gasping on the hot grass.

Wearily, it seemed, he plodded up the bank and fell, heaving heavily, beside me, his head propped on his arms.

'Well, it was fun,' I said, shielding my face from the sunlight and squinting down at my foreshortened already drying body and yellow and black hooped trunks. Mother gave them to me (did she get them in New York?) and she had a similar costume of her own. The heat brought a faint odour of cowpats with it. It wasn't exactly Estoril, but after all I had chosen to be here: J'y suis, j'y reste.

I shut my eyes as Bob remained silent, and the sun went on pinning me hotly to the hard, uncomfortable ground.

Then I felt through my trunks the additional heat of his hand, exploring, imploring rather. I eased myself lazily, but as I moved so did the hand and a suppressed noise came from his still buried head.

'It won't sting, you know,' I said airily.

He made another inarticulate sound. Very gently I leant over and took hold of his ear-lobe protruding from the mass of damp, now darkened hair and he reluctantly turned his creased, flushed face to look briefly into mine before looking away.

'It's disgusting,' he stammered up at me.

'What a charming thing to say. I've had every sort of proposition but none couched – the mot juste for the occasion – in such tempting terms. No, Bob. It, whatever it may be, is not disgusting. Nor, I hope, am I.'

'I am. I am. It's me. Forgive me. I got a fright in the river – '

'You make it sound like something from Dr Freud's casebook. Was it when you were a small boy? Apropos which, I trust we have lost the Sunday School outing, or whatever it was.'

'They've gone. Just now in the river, I mean. I thought you'd get into difficulties and I'm not much of a swimmer, really, and I realised then ...' His voice died away.

I sat watching his shoulders working, almost as though he was some stranded sea-creature trying to swim on dry land, and as though the wave of affection which flowed from me was exactly that, setting him afloat again. It would be easy to fling myself against those solid-seeming shoulders, cling to him as to a merman and beg to be borne off for ever to some safe, secure, underwater grotto of love. Easy and fatal. Such baroque urging could only disturb him more profoundly. And as if my musing glance had stung him, he rolled round abruptly, fixing me with a wild glare. 'Look, you must believe me.'

'Oh, I do, Bob.'

'I've never felt like this before. I'm horrified. I can't understand it. And I swear to you I've never even wanted to touch a man or a boy – never mind actually doing something like that. If I thought I was like that, I'd resign tomorrow – I'd go away; I don't know what I'd do. It's criminal. You wouldn't, would you, ever tell Edna? I couldn't stand it. Please promise me that. It would be the end of everything.' He sat up and laid his head on his knees in an attitude of despair. 'We both liked you so much, wanted you to like us. And now this. I just feel sick at myself but don't despise me, Nick. Try to forget it and forgive me, won't you?'

'For what?'

'Don't ask me to put it into words. I can't.'

'Now, listen to me, Bob. To begin with, you are not disgusting.' I put my hand on his knee, wondering as soon as I did so whether this Barney-like gesture of reassurance was itself too intimate. But he clasped my fingers convulsively and held on to them, his head still bent. 'And secondly, there is nothing disgusting about our being fond of each other. Well, is there? If we like each other, love each other, let's say, it is not only not criminal to want to touch each other but it's utterly natural.'

He shook his head, murmuring something inarticulate.

'Does it help,' I went on, 'if I tell you you didn't shock or disgust me? Quite the contrary. I'm glad about what happened. I am fond of you, Bob.'

'I never meant it to be like this,' he burst out. 'It's got so muddled, I don't know why. You see.' He raised his head and glanced fearfully, almost furtively, at me. Though I smiled back into his deeply creased features, with moustache bedraggled and rather bloodshot eyes, I felt the force of what I had awoken. No longer a toy animal or some mythical sea-creature, he breathed and heaved so desperately beside me that it seemed as if my rôle really was rescue of a drowning man.

'You see, we haven't got children, Edna and me. Perhaps it's my fault. We don't talk about it much nowadays. It's one of those things, but we keep hoping in the way people do. I think Edna would love a daughter, and I've always wanted a son. Seems funny to you now, I expect, but one day you'll feel the same yourself, or something like it. Somebody young about the place – oh, we aren't old, I know, but sometimes I think about the future, and ... It was wrong, selfish really, suggesting you stayed with us. You're a cut above us, me anyway. But somehow I liked you, though of course never for a moment ... It was caring, you see, for someone, as well as for Edna naturally. Maybe I didn't always understand you. You made me feel stupid sometimes. I expect even parents do. Edna often said you'd got an old head on young shoulders.'

'Oh, Bob.' My smile had long vanished. I began to feel Edna's adjectives were the wrong way round.

'It was when you swam upstream after I'd mentioned the current. I knew somehow you would. I suppose I thought you were lost then. You'd drown. I wouldn't be able to save you. Then when we came out of the water, I suddenly got such a strong feeling, relief, love you could call it ... You were still

176

here. That's no excuse, though.'

'You don't need an excuse – or apologies. At least grasp that. And shouldn't you be pleased I care for you? Perhaps I'm looking for someone too. Perhaps I've got problems too. One of them is that my hand's either crushed or gone to sleep.'

He released it without speaking.

'Oh, cheer up,' I said. 'I'm the one who's moody, difficult and dangerous – quite apart from anything else. But from the first, almost, you appealed to me. I meant you to care for me. But I'm glad to know you do.'

'I never would,' he said slowly, hardly listening. 'It would never have crossed my mind, I reckon, whatever I felt, if your zip hadn't stuck. That's what did it.'

'Yes.' I jumped up and put my hands on his shoulders: we might have been about to demonstrate our acrobatic skills. 'And if Cleopatra's nose had been a bit shorter. No, I can't explain it. But lunch definitely calls, and Edna was making rhubarb crumble.'

I started to dress. He still sat on, hunched, looking out, unseeing, across the stretch of river. I knelt down beside him, partly to tie a shoe-lace and partly to convey comfort by my physical proximity.

'What shall I tell her,' he said at last. 'I can't think what to say. I can't face lunch. I feel so sick – dirty, really.'

'This is your shirt,' I said, picking up what had obviously been a choice of Edna's – rambler roses, virtually, all over a pale ochre ground. 'Put it on. And let's get moving. Fond as I am, I can't be expected to dress you. Even love has limits.'

'You don't understand.' But he began somnambulistically thrusting his arms into the sleeves of the shirt. 'It's easy for you, I suppose.'

'And I'll see that it's easy for you.'

'But how can I tell Edna? What would she think of me?'

'It won't arise. You were begging me a few minutes ago not to tell her, so obviously you don't want her to know. Anyway, there isn't a great deal to tell. You're not being charged with rape or child molestation. In fact, you're not being charged at all.'

'I don't like hearing you speak like that,' he said, as slowly he fumbled with the rest of his clothes. 'And I've never kept things from Edna – never.' He picked up his towel and began mournfully and unenergetically pushing it backwards and forwards over his hair.

'Do you think,' I asked, looking down impatiently as he rolled up the towel and then adjusted the red leather belt of his fawn trousers, pulling at the crotch to ease their fit, 'she's always told you everything? Have you talked a lot about me, for example? Do you know what we had for tea on Friday? Or if I've seen the photographs of her family?'

'That's different. Anyway, we haven't talked all that much about you, if you're so interested. We both know how we feel – without a lot of chat,' he added proudly.

'Fine. Nobody's hurt, and nobody needs to be. We all love each other and can shut up, then, can't we? And enjoy our lunch if of course we get back in time for any. Bob, you must be the slowest dresser in the world – constantly being late for everything at school, I expect. Take a hundred lines, Parrott.'

He glowered abruptly up at me, and I felt as pleased as if a dying fire had revived. Getting him into shape for lunch was my first task, so that he didn't sit there glooming and appetiteless until Edna started to think we had violently quarrelled – or that somehow I had behaved badly. A flick or two of mental towel would do no harm, perk him up a bit, perhaps ease that typical adult guilt that so often follows their turning fantasy into reality.

Bob would never understand it in those terms. Indeed, acting as his physician, I should not advise him to try and understand *it* at all. Let's get you on your feet first must be the brisk tone, accompanied by some ritual rubbing or washing of hands. After that, medically cautious, we'll see.

And so I led him back, not exactly leading him a dance but tacitly inviting him to join the dance. My mock-turtle, I thought, with an inward smile. Any tears shed, however, must be mopped up before we entered the garden, not precisely hand-in-hand – more's the pity – but shoulder to shoulder, agreeably exhausted and suitably hungry after our Sunday morning swim, just as might, I suppose, a real father and son.

As we drew nearer I quietened down, growing docile, domestic almost. It seemed wiser now Bob, though silent, was recovering. Nobody knew better than I how tricky these shifts of mood were to gauge. Even with Dennis I used occasionally to get it wrong, or became restless myself. And Bob's was a case of much greater complexity, outside, I was forced to admit, my usual range. A flip tone, any touch of too experienced boy tart (not to speak of the camp) could be dangerous at this stage; like too free a gesture, it ran the risk of making me disgusting. Yet too great a normal, boisterous, boyish emphasis on a smashing swim mixed with anticipations of tons of grub, might set oscillating again sensations of disgust with himself as the most perverted of all paternal figures.

Encountering Edna could of course bring on an attack anyway, and I was still debating quite how to steer through lunch and its somnolent aftermath when she appeared at the kitchen door, beckoning us urgently. (Grice taken hostage by a CND guerilla group was my first hope; or maybe divine service at Spenn church had been celebrated by someone with aesthetic sensibility chucking a brick through that Christ the Aviator window).

'Sorry we're late,' Bob began, flushing – or perhaps already we were both flushed.

'I didn't expect you any earlier,' Edna said. 'You weren't to know.' She was clearly excited, though not alarmed. Only when she had got us into the kitchen, and closed the door, did she announce with a sort of hushed intensity: 'It's Mr Latimer. We mustn't be too long over lunch. He told me first thing after you left, came round to tell us himself. Give me those wet towels. He's getting married again. She's a lady from Colchester, I think he said, and she's coming this afternoon, and we're bid to tea with her. What do you think of that, Bob?'

'I've a previous engagement,' I said. 'My bad luck.'

'Mr Latimer specially mentioned you,' she said triumphantly.

'Oh, I'm sure he did.'

'Who'd have thought it? Getting married again. And he's kept it so quiet; nobody ever guessed. Help Bob with those plates, Nicholas, and let's start or we'll never finish. He met her on holiday last year.'

'He never said anything to me, not a hint, when I was doing the rockery for him,' Bob said, absently handing me a bowl of potato salad sprinkled with chives.

'Well,' she said, still pitching her voice low. 'He's always been one for keeping himself to himself, hasn't he? I wonder what Jim thinks, though. You can't ask, but getting a new mother at his age. I wouldn't like it, whoever she was.'

I started laughing hysterically, and nothing seemed to stop it – not even Edna's quelling frowns at the disturbance possibly reaching Mr Latimer's ears – though I tried to change gear into whooping cough (too ill surely to meet his fiancée) and subsided into hiccuping at intervals for the rest of the meal. But I had ceased to impinge, hiccuping or not. Instead of gulping water, I ought to be gratefully toasting the happy topic that pre-occupied Edna and to a lesser extent Bob.

Actually to be raising a cut-glass glass of medium sherry in Mr Latimer's front parlour was not, however, what I had intended. Yet there I was a few hours later, reflected in a mahogany-framed mirror, amid wine-coloured moquette chairs and vases of flowers arranged in order of size, as if for judging at the village show, joining the muttered congratula-tions, along with Mr Latimer's Jim, his pale, nervous wife and a baby whose jelly-like obstinate fingers had grabbed at the lapels of my grey suit, while it dribblingly lisped 'Dada', to Bob's amusement. Edna had not noticed. The occasion excited her too much, and at the toast her glass quivered as she stood like an overgrown bridesmaid, her voice far higher than usual, exclaiming 'Mr Latimer and Gwen.'

The pair looked not merely married but twinned: as like as two pearls. She, whose name Edna had speedily discovered, was as pinkly white as he, and hardly younger, in a heliotrope and silver tunic, with a rope of white beads and wide white trousers. Edna seemed unconscious of her patronage ('such good-hearted people, I hear,' the Gwen person had said to me, nodding her well-coiffed head towards Bob and Edna as though vetting them for domestic service: 'Are you with them as a P.G.?') and impressed by her clothes.

'She comes from Chichester, not Colchester,' Edna told me, when eventually we managed to leave. 'And been married twice before. There's a daughter from the first marriage.'

'Jim's kid thought Nick was his father,' Bob said giving me a playful nudge-cum-punch in a way he had never done before. Ah, mon beau monstre: you like to think me potent.

'Too ugly to be mine,' I said. 'As well as obviously myopic.'

'Looks aren't everything,' Edna said, comfortably. 'Oh, I do hope they'll be happy.' We had reached the front door, and Bob and I stood back for her to go through. 'Now what's funny?' she demanded, as a snort of rising laughter seized me. 'Is it the drink? I should have thought it took more than a glass of sherry to get you tight.'

'It does – normally. But I'm celebrating, celebrating.'

'Well, come inside for goodness' sake.' She tugged me not too earnestly over the threshold. 'What will the Latimers think of us?'

We all went upstairs to change, but a mood of festivity lingered, perhaps in part relief that the official occasion was over. Once or twice Edna wondered aloud if they would stay on next door; or might they move to Chichester? But she put her knitting aside after supper and agreed with Bob that there would be no harm in a glass of parsnip wine (giving me a heavily ironic look as she did so).

'My sisters can't understand being without the telly,' she said, pondering over the plate of biscuits Bob had brought in with the wine. 'But it's not something I'd ever want, not even in the winter. And we never had it at home when we were all young. Had to amuse ourselves as best we could, and we always had lots of games and plenty of fun.'

'Care to play Scrabble?' Bob asked me. 'We often do.'

'I shouldn't think Nicholas would be one for Scrabble,' Edna said. 'But we can play.'

'I'll play,' I said. 'And beat you both.'

'Don't you be so sure,' Bob said. 'Edna's a devil at it, aren't you?'

We had some more parsnip wine and started to play. Of course, Edna won. Bob was still pleased about it at breakfast the next day: a negative sort of day it looked. He went off quite jauntily, giving Edna his usual, somewhat formal embrace and me a slightly shy glance which I returned shyly but with sufficient intensity to recall the previous morning.

What happened next, nobody could say. Maybe there was no next, except that sooner rather than later I should leave. Behind me would be only whatever gift I finally found for them: for your wedding anniversary, I should explain, to justify its extravagance. Or were they each to have a gift, it would prompt private memories for each. I saw again that brooch and ring, though I knew I could not really give them those; but I thought of winter coming, another summer, Bob and Edna remaining whether or not the Latimers moved, and of some solid tokens they could finger that recalled for each personally that summer when *he* was here.

Still musing in *Genji*-style, I obeyed quite happily Edna's request to go into the garden and pick the remaining red currants for the jelly she planned to make (perhaps a pot of it would travel with me when I left: a pot of preserve). I was crouched under the netting when I heard her calling me, sounding untypically flustered. The telephone no doubt: Margot, Barney, even conceivably Mother? She came almost running into the garden.

'It's Chief Inspector Catesby. For you.'

I walked into the house and opened the sitting-room door. It was a shock to find Catesby himself standing there, blocking the light.

'Hope I haven't disturbed you,' he said cheerfully. 'I thought I might drop in for a little chat. Following up the inquest, you know, and just trying to tie up a few loose ends. I'd be very glad if you could spare me a few minutes. I'm sure Mrs Parrott will understand.'

'Yes, of course.' I was still bewildered, but on guard against his wash-leather glove manner and bluff, buff-jerkin tone. My hands felt sticky and I longed to wipe them against something, even my jeans.

'Not much of a morning, I'm afraid, but I wondered if you'd care for a spin? My car's outside and we could probably talk more easily in it. I'm a great admirer of Mrs Parrott – and her husband too, of course. I'd heard you'd got a billet with them.

'Come in,' he called unhesitatingly as Edna tapped at the door with the offer of coffee. 'That's very kind. Nothing I'd like more,' he said, 'but I don't think we've time for it. Our young friend and myself are just off for a short joy-ride. I wouldn't deprive him if I didn't know he'd plenty of chances of enjoying your hospitality – and he'll be back for a good lunch, I can assure you. Lucky dog.'

He laughed boisterously but it was laughter to accompany our leaving as distinctly as if he had handcuffed me to him.

We walked down the path to the oddly humped-back, old-fashioned black car (without, I noticed, a driver), though there was hardly room for us to walk side by side. Catesby was big as well as fat, and made more so by his gingery tweed jacket with its knobbly leather buttons. His red face looked almost vacuous in its cheerfulness, and yellowish whiskers running like traces of curry powder from ear to cheek increased the jovial appearance.

'Unusual name yours, if you don't mind my saying. Gonville,' he said as we drove off. 'There was a chap R. Q. Gonville once. Gifted golfer. I saw him play a round of 64 at Muirfield that made you want to go home and put your clubs away for ever. In a thousand years I'd never come near it. Sad business, though. He died quite young.'

I stared out through the windscreen at the greyish, dusty road. 'R. Q. Gonville was my father. He hated his first names, Roland Quentin.'

'Well, well. What a coincidence.' I couldn't detect whether or not he had known. 'It must have been a real tragedy for you – and for your mother. But he was a great player, take it from me. Someone to be proud of, all right. I expect you've got his trophies at home. Do you play yourself? Or perhaps it's not your game.'

'I don't. There was a bag of clubs at Philip's – Mr Kerr's – in my room. I've often wondered if they belonged to my father.'

'I suppose your mother would know, wouldn't she?'

'Not necessarily. They were divorced some time before he died. He re-married and most of his cups and things are with her – his second wife.'

Catesby settled deeper into the flabby driving seat which seemed to have been shaped by his bulk, humming absently and relaxed. Just as I expected, he drove with a show of casualness but very competently.

'Do you know,' he said suddenly, smacking his lips as though recalling a delicious meal, 'he'd take an iron some-times where most other golfers, even good ones, mark you, would use a wood. I shouldn't have minded seeing that bag of clubs. As a matter of fact, I was thinking we might tool along to what was your godfather's place, if that's all right with you – not too distressing for you?'

'Fine by me,' I said curtly. 'I expect the clubs will have gone, though. Philip's cousin—'

'Ah, yes. Still, it might help us in other ways, going over the ground. It's not very clear in my mind, I'm afraid.' He laughed, paused and then said, 'You and your godfather must have been quite close, with your own father out of it, as it were. He always seemed a nice chap, though I barely knew him. The vicar certainly thought highly of him. On good terms, were you? That's probably a silly question.'

'With the vicar?'

'With your godfather.'

'Easy terms,' I said. 'Not particularly close ones. He was usually kind to me, even if he didn't understand me. But he wasn't my idea of a father, or a father-substitute.'

'I think we turn off here, don't we? Rather bumpy, but it can't damage this jallopy of mine. My difficulty is, if I may be frank, that I don't know what happened and I can't quite follow what I've been told.'

I kept my hands stickily together in my lap and watched impassively as the yellow slice of Philip's house came bouncing into view. It looked bleak, tenantless and alien after what seemed so long, yet I could effortlessly visualise its interior, and it was almost surprising not to find Mrs Rainbow's snout poking suspiciously round the front door. Inside, now stripped, dark, it was smaller and shabbier than I had realised. It had become a specimen; a few discarded flash bulbs lay on the floor, and I noticed here and there mysterious stick-on-arrows, pointing at smudges, as if part of a trail.

Catesby unfolded a plan, presumably, and started to frown over it. Then, pushing down the maroon and blue silk handkerchief in his breast-pocket, he drew out a pair of enormous horn-rimmed spectacles, giving them a dust with a corner of it before putting them on.

'Let's go in the study first, shall we? I'll just unlock it. Needn't worry about leaving our fingerprints. That's all straightforward – up to a point. Now,' leading the way. 'You found your godfather lying there, like that. Sorry if this is the nasty part. We needn't be in here long and what I'm after, if you could try and recollect, is your impression of the room – in general.'

'Well.' I glanced at the floorboards and the outline in tape not chalk, the bare mantelpiece and the tightly closed windows. 'It looked as though there'd been a struggle of some sort. There were ornaments all over the floor – and the sherry decanter was smashed. And I think a window was open. That's about all I can remember.'

'Splendid.' He beamed at me through the property-like spectacles. 'A great help. Now, the odd thing is that, according to the housekeeper, Mrs Rainbow, nothing was missing. Do you follow me?'

'I'm not sure.'

'Nothing was stolen, to begin with. So we can forget any motive of theft, can't we?'

'Well, I suppose there could have been something we don't know about, like a letter, for example. It might have been incriminating. Or thought to be. Possibly something to do with Philip's racing debts.'

'You know all about them, I see. It's a possibility, though perhaps only a very quixotic thief would come here to steal the evidence of your godfather's debts from him.'

'Mightn't somebody do it for blackmail?'

'That's ingenious. They might. Still, from all I hear, your godfather wasn't much blessed with this world's goods. And, assuming you or I were looking for a letter or some papers, we wouldn't need to sweep the ornaments off the mantelpiece, nor surely break a decanter. Perhaps I've got this wrong, but I think Mrs Rainbow said it was the mantelpiece ornaments that were all over the floor – the ones you saw as you looked in. By the way, I'm a bit puzzled about the study door. It was ajar, wasn't it, when you came down in the morning?'

'Yes.'

'But closed – or apparently closed – when you came down the previous evening? I'm sorry if I've got this muddled. I'll check what you told Mr Grice; don't trouble. It's only a detail, one of several I ought to check.'

'It appeared closed, but I obviously wasn't thinking much about it at the time.'

'Of course not. Why should you?' He took off the spectacles and smiled vaguely around the empty room. 'I'm not as methodical as I should be, I don't mind admitting. A lot of police work lies in hunches, to let you into a secret. There's plenty of hard slog as well, of course, but nowadays I let others do that.' He laughed.

I paused before asking coolly, 'And you have a hunch about the struggle?'

He had gone towards the window, unfolding the piece of paper again and then trimming up his whiskers pensively with one hand, humming while he did so. When he turned it was difficult to see his expression but his voice retained all its bluff overtones.

'I beg your pardon. You were asking about hunches? I mustn't claim too much for them, and the trouble is that often enough you can't prove what you guess. But I'll give you one, if you like. What you saw when you put your head into the room wasn't the evidence of any struggle. Why should there have been a struggle?'

'Well, if Philip was suddenly attacked …'

'Oh, it wasn't that sort of attack. Nobody who gets near enough to slip a handkerchief or something similar round his neck is going to have a fight with him first, is he? And afterwards it isn't necessary. Anyway, your godfather would more likely shout for help. But you heard nothing, did you? Yet it's a very small house.'

'You mean, there was no struggle? I can't see how you're so sure. Anyway, it is a fact that I saw what I've described.'

'You saw it and so did other people, but it was an amateur attempt to suggest a struggle. I'd go as far as saying it was thoroughly short-sighted, though another sense is involved. Suppose you'd come downstairs feeling a bit hungry or worried by something, about ten o'clock that night. You'd have smelt the sherry through the open door, gone to investigate – and telephoned for us.'

'I follow that. Would it have helped, significantly?'

'You're going to chuckle, I'm afraid, because this is just another hunch, but yes, I think so. Still, that really is surmise. I wonder if we might just go up to your bedroom, as was, more to give me a clue to the geography.' He began moving towards the door, taking care to avoid treading on the outline on the floor. I watched his big suede shoes stepping deftly, as though in some Highland dance or children's game, and it was impossible not to fill the outline with Philip's flung-out body; I thought if we stayed much longer I should detect the aroma of sherry in the airless room. For the first time, since that morning, I felt panic. I couldn't move, or only as far as the bottom of the stairs. Now it seemed no momentary sensation but one that nothing would ever banish.

'Something's upset you,' Catesby said sympathetically, hastily crossing the room and taking my arm in a friendly grip which actually made me shudder. 'It's my fault, I've been thoughtless. Mrs Parrott will scold me, quite rightly. We'll forget about upstairs this morning. I'm rushing you, and that's the last thing I intended. But I want to get to the bottom of this, you'll be the first to appreciate.'

As though I was physically stricken, he tried to help me out of the house and into the car, murmuring a mixture of reproaches to himself and encouragement to me. 'It's quite all right,' I said. 'I'm not going to be sick or anything. I never am.'

He drove fast, much faster than on the way there, occasionally glancing at me as if he feared I wouldn't last out until Trencham Croke.

'Perhaps I'll be able to show you that bag of clubs next time,' I said.

'Who knows? But if they really are your father's, you ought to have them even if you don't play. Something to remember him by. Now, can you manage? Make my apologies to Mrs Parrott, if she asks, and let's see how you feel in a day or two. Cheerybye.'

It was a relief to be out of the car and away from him. I stood at the gate, making sure the black hump of it had disappeared before walking up the familiar, flagged path, revived sufficiently to smile in retrospect about yesterday's return from chez Latimer. Slam the front door on Catesby was my impulse, and refuse to see him again.

The sight of Edna seated at the kitchen table, propped over a huge copper saucepan, was instantly comforting: Edna, preserve me.

'Redcurrant jelly time,' I carolled, but she did not turn. Only very gradually, as I skirted the table, with its mound of unstripped currants, did she lift her face. It looked dreadfully heavy, almost ugly in its drained, sallow colour, against which her eyes were blank, darker than ever under the thick, dishevelled hair. She put up a juice-stained palm to push back a strand of it or rest her forehead. 'Edna,' I said, half embarrassed at the nakedness I saw, afraid she must be ill.

Her lips quivered, and for a moment I thought she could not speak. She gestured at the table, where beside the still-life of saucepan, earthenware bowl piled high with sugar and a silver fork, its prongs holding a cluster of currants, lay a half-folded telegram.

'It's our father,' she whispered, as I hesitated to read. 'They've sent for me. He's had a stroke.'

She seemed too big, too daunting in her misery, for me to put my arms round. But I knew I ought to. It was no use just standing there, silently saying her name, willing the pain of it all to disappear. I sat down and reached across the table. She bowed her head, as if a child in disgrace, and I felt rather than saw a tear fall on the smooth slope of the sugar.

It roused her in some way. She straightened up, moved the bowl and took the fork, shaking her head stiffly as she did so. She even gave me a tight grimace meant to reassure, though the effect was ghastly. She gazed at the heap of currants in despair and then laid down the fork again.

'Edna,' I said. 'Please.'

'It's no good.' She stared at me wildly, pleading with me to contradict her. 'He's going to die.'

12

It was a strange sensation, sad and yet secretly exhilarating to stand at the foot of the staircase and inhale the fact that I was alone. The front door had closed behind Edna (driven away to Spenn station by Mr Latimer's Jim) and it would not open again until the return of Bob.

Edna had come down the stairs grimly composed, practical and somehow remote, already on her journey, in a brown straw hat, thick-looking brown coat over her arm, holding a suitcase and a large red handbag. Tonelessly she gave me instructions and showed me there were provisions enough –

for Noah's ark, I might have remarked at another time. Yes, I had said unsmiling, almost as tonelessly, I know Bob likes his tea strong; I can put a casserole in the oven; I think I do know how to make a salad. I feel sure we shan't starve. About the milk, I would certainly be able to explain to the milkman where she had gone, and why.

When, however, she handed over the knitted purse with the house-keeping money, I felt my eyes abruptly pricking – tactlessly so, since there was now a stately resoluteness about her, forbidding emotion. Solemnly I was charged with the keeping of her fortress; and at that moment I saw myself kneeling in fealty, scrubbing the floors as I knelt, and baking, ironing, polishing, until it was time to surrender the purse of office.

'I'll come to the station,' I said, when Jim Latimer rang the bell. 'Carry your bag, at least.'

'No. Bob's meeting me there.'

'Actually, I could easily travel up and see you across London. And what about food? Will you eat at King's Cross or on the train? Won't you be very late getting into Darlington?'

'I hope at my age I can manage alone across London. And find myself a bite to eat,' she said, with a touch of her usual vigour. 'It's good of you, Nicholas, but you stay here. You take care – of everything.'

When she had gone, I just went on standing there. With Edna, it had seemed absolutely right not to proffer a farewell kiss – I was sure she did not wish it, might even dislike it – but how to receive Bob was less obvious and instinctive. Not, anyway, with anything as overt as a kiss.

Thinking about Bob led unwillingly to Catesby. There was nothing amusing or exhilarating about the memory of him, though I felt my anger should be directed less at Catesby than at my own weakness. He ought not to frighten me with his bluff, bluffing manner and the hints I had sensed quickly enough under the over-acted jovial, casual air of real menace. Even the spectacles were probably to mislead: poor old purblind Catesby, pottering along with an apologetic hunch or two, suddenly turns from hedgehog into hawk, to drop with sickening accuracy on his prey. Next time he would not find me so helplessly quivering.

I hadn't, it was true, encountered anyone before quite like

Catesby. He didn't fit in with my experience of school teachers, though he might have run a private school somewhere on principles more sado – than masochistic. He looked and dressed like the archetypical bursar but that was only another aspect of his disingenuousness. A policeman was what he was; it couldn't ultimately be disguised.

And Bob was another, wedded not to Edna but to law and order. He would never really join a demo on Spenn Common. Even if there was a threat to pollute Wixton Reservoir, he would probably see good-humouredly two points of view and then not hesitate to line up with authority on whichever side it was. He wanted to be good, without having to think.

Twenty years hence he would be a sort of countryfied Catesby, lower ranking no doubt, less acute but with a much nicer nature. I didn't expect to be around, but supposing someone like me came his way again, would he be any better at understanding that boy – or himself? Catesby played at being ordinary, with an ordinary hobby of the most disarming kind (I shouldn't be totally surprised if he'd never visited Muirfield, though my father's 64 happened to be true). Bob, as he said, was ordinary. Perhaps it was part of the surface of his appeal for me, but paradoxically or not I wanted to dent it, if not change it, leave him less innocent and more knowing. Not a silly, sentimental piece of jewellery worn round his finger but the unforgettable pressure of my arms, my lips, my body upon his would be the lasting though invisible memorial I bequeathed at my departure. That he ought never to lose.

'I knew a young bloke rather like you once,' he would say, cross-questioning some presumed delinquent in a gentle, friendly manner (the Biblical overtones of 'knew' remaining private), and that boy's apprehensive figure would blur as he spoke, to be replaced by mine, once again standing there in the very jeans I wore at the river-side.

'Well, how was your day?' Bob asked incuriously, in the English form not expecting an answer, taking his place at the kitchen table. Almost as if aware – absurd as it would be – of how he had glowed before me in prospect, he seemed not merely doused by strain but grimy despite a quick wash, his turned-back shirt-cuffs rimmed with grey (need a good scrub, they would).

'There's a casserole,' I said, assuming the Prince of Wales oven-glove with the air of a royal falconer, before bending with a hint of reproach (twinge of my old arthritis) to extract it. 'Ich dien'.

At least I had not made the mistake of creating a sophisticated environment for an intimate little dinner à deux, with wine-glasses a-gleam in the candle-light and a single flower floating in a shallow porcelain bowl, while Vivaldi sprinkled the atmosphere. Even my getting two cans of beer out of the refrigerator, though I plonked them down resolutely enough, seemed neither to stir nor cheer Bob.

Edna, he explained, had set off all right and would telephone as soon as she could. One of her brothers-in-law would meet her at Darlington station. She would be with her father before midnight. It was a neighbour who discovered what had happened; in a panic she wired Edna, having telephoned her sisters. It was a terrible shock for Edna: she was the daughter closest to him, though the furthest away.

'It was a shock even for me,' I said. 'Especially coming after a foul morning with your Chief Superintendent Catesby. He really upset me. What a pig – if that isn't insulting pigs.'

'Catesby? He's a good bloke. Everyone likes him. You won't find a more decent Super in Southern England.'

'I'm not conducting a hunt for one, Bob. Oh, of course, he seemed friendly enough. The police always do, somehow. But underneath all the jollity he was trying to needle me about Philip's death. How's the casserole, by the way?'

'All right,' he said, pushing pieces around on his plate. 'A bit hot for me.'

'It's meant to be hot, for God's sake.'

'All right. It's very good. Did you make it?'

'I cooked it. Edna made it – this morning, I suppose. While I was being kidnapped by crafty Catesby and forced at pistol-point to confess all – standing in Philip's study, explaining how to carry out murder by numbers. And it's not over. He wants me to go back there, dig up the floorboards in my old bedroom and get out the blood-stained putter that did the deed. Pity, really, you didn't take me into custody when you first arrived.'

He paused with a skewered stub of carrot at his mouth, like an exotic chopped-off cigar. 'I don't get it. I'm sorry, Nick. I feel a bit clobbered by everything this evening. I'm just not with you. Whatever he did, Wilf Catesby's only trying to sort out how your godfather came to die. It's his job. You want to know, too, don't you?'

'And somehow I've become a prime suspect, have I? You might have told me earlier – preferably before putting your hand on my prick and swearing undying lust or whatever it was. It's my turn not to get it, as you put it.'

I heard my voice rising, as if only by shouting could I let the words escape, but escape they did, each one landing on the target opposite with almost physical effect. An intrusive ray of evening sunlight, sent like a blessing at the close of a clogging, cloudy day, illumined his face as blanched as his shirt: a round white target still reverberating from the impact of the darts hurled at it. And I couldn't stop hurling them.

'You are the absolute end, Parrott, you really are. First you tell me you hope I'll stay – have a drink, break the law, be our guest – we're so fond of you. Fancy you as my own son. Or a bit more, only that's too disgusting, isn't it? Anyway, hang around until Mr Catesby's tied this one on you. Shouldn't be too long from the way he's going. I reckon the youngster will crack in a couple of days, sergeant. You and your good lady put on a fine act – took him in, in every sense, ha, ha. Bloody funny stuff. Ha, ha, ha.'

There was complete silence. Every word is true, isn't it, I wanted to start crying out, filling the void, piling on the pressure – or ridding myself of the pressure I'd been under since Catesby confronted me in the sitting-room a few steps away. We've heard all about your shock, I could have yelled. An old man in Yorkshire may be going to die: very sad, too, I'm sure, for his family. But what the hell about me? Nobody's listened to my shock at being tricked, led on, by shows of affection and of genial old bufferish ways which will stop and drop the second the trap is sprung. And caught in it most horribly would be me. Me. So far from being seventy-seven, I am not yet seventeen.

'Nick.' I felt him hovering, near at hand: deflated, not expired. He had come round the table, as if waiting on me – or was it rather for me? Perhaps it was time for the next course. Feed the beast.

'I don't know what's for pudding. I expect there's cheese and biscuits. What d'you want?'

'I want you to listen to me. I swear—'

'Oh, save it for the witness-box. I, Sergeant Robert Parrott, do solemnly ... With luck, you and Edna should be in the *Bucks Bugler*. "How couple's hospitality snared teen-age terrorist." '

'You're no terrorist.' He was on his knees – must be to have got his head so close to mine.

'Don't say it in that soppy tone of voice. And don't be too sure.'

'Nick, listen to me. You must.'

My turn for silence, as petrifying and unyielding as I could make it.

'It's rubbish about your being a suspect. It's just not true, any more than about our pretending to care for you. Christ almighty, haven't I made it only too plain what I feel? Go ahead, throw it in my face, I don't mind. I'm sorry you've got the wrong idea about Catesby, but that's nothing to what I feel over your being so wrong about us and specially about me.

'Want to know the real truth? I'm frightened about how much I'm stirred up. Didn't I tell you I'd never had this sort of feeling before? For a bloke, I mean. I can't talk about it. Ever since yesterday, I've been—'

'Disgusted. I know.'

'Dazed, I was going to say. Can't you understand? Something about it – about how I feel? I want to help you, if you need help. Take care of you. Perhaps I could be there when Catesby sees you next. Oh, Nick, I'll do anything to convince you.'

'Of what?'

He threw his arms around my neck so fiercely that I nearly over-balanced. Who was drowning now? His face pressed against mine was hot, and an elusive tang of sweat seemed to plead his weakness. To go under together would be easy, sweet and premature. Catesby was still elusively present in the kitchen.

'Don't ask me,' he mumbled. 'Isn't it enough, as it is. You don't need telling. Good grief, what am I doing in this situation?'

'And you a police officer.' I took his arms from their stranglehold. 'Let me put the kettle on. Some strong tea will

193

help clear your head. You'll feel better after a good night's sleep.'

'You always end up making fun of me, don't you? You're the one who takes people in. First you're looking for affection or a home – or something. Then when it happens you just humiliate the person. You couldn't care less about me, and I don't suppose you give a damn for Edna. It's all just one big joke to someone like you, trading on – on everyone fancying you.'

'Not Catesby, I fear. And somehow fear's the word there.'

I took the kettle to the tap, watched sullenly by him.

'That's no joke. Nor, when you calm down and give it a thought, is my remark about a night's sleep. Alone. If I was quite so clumsy and cheap as you suppose, I'd have you in my bed tonight, followed by your agonies of remorse at breakfast tomorrow. Inaction can speak louder than words too, if you follow me.'

I wheeled round on him still crouched there, still sullen and struggling. He sprang.

'I'll make my own bloody tea, thanks.'

I yielded the kettle. 'And you can do breakfast,' I said.

No, I did not sleep well, I could have replied to an enquiry the next morning, though none was forthcoming. I couldn't have described my dreams, but they lingered as jumbled, hateful, and better stuck away in the very bottom drawer of the mind.

Bob looked as spruce as ever, too clean to touch, not much more real than the genie of the latest washing-machine ('it's easy enough *even* for Dads') and a lot less animated. Like a genie, he just vanished.

I took a duster and flicked it ritually round the sacred objects in the sitting-room, the lustre jugs, the firescreen and the wedding-photograph. When the telephone rang I rushed to it almost wishing it incorporated television: Edna would have been able to see how bravely I carried on, despite my sense of heavy emotional hangover.

'Hallo there,' came Catesby's voice, as though hailing me on a windy day from the first tee. 'I hope you're on top of things again. Could we meet up this morning, do you think? (Fit in a few holes before lunch, perhaps.) It looks a splendid day – not a cloud in the sky. How about my picking you up and our grabbing a quick coffee in Spenn before anything else?'

'I don't think I can,' I said. 'Mrs Parrott's away – she's been called away to her father – and I'm expecting her to telephone ...'

'Sorry to hear it,' he said with jovial ambiguity. I couldn't even be sure it was news to him. 'Still, I'd assume she'll get through to the police-station, so you've no cause to worry.'

Before Catesby arrived – hoarse hooting from his old-fashioned horn – I changed into an indigo tee shirt bearing the words, 'Peace and Love'. I'd meant it for Bob's return last night and was beginning to realise why I had forgotten to put it on.

'A stroke's nothing nowadays,' Catesby assured me, stirring his coffee and looking contentedly across the room filled with stout, middle-aged shoppers, to my eye cardiac cases every one, amid the warming-pans and hunting-horns of *Betty's,* second cousin once removed round the corner from *AMANDA for Chocolates.* 'He could live to a hundred, taking good care of himself. Weight's the thing to watch, and don't I know it. Not exactly your problem is it, so far? Now, with your godfather, it seems as if he'd got a bit over-weight, and then he had that dicky heart. Never mentioned any symptoms to you, did he? You know, a bit breathless, funny pains in his chest – nothing like that?'

'Nothing like that at all. He always seemed in literally the pink of health.'

He laughed appreciatively. 'Jolly good. I like your motto,' nodding towards it. 'Young people today, you seem much more idealistic than my generation, but perhaps life's easier, in a material sense. My wife and I came up the hard way – one pair of shoes, that sort of thing. Nowadays, a boy like you – if you don't mind me calling you that – could open a bank account, I shouldn't wonder. I had to save up my shillings – know what they were? – in an old Everton toffee tin.'

'I have a bank account, thanks to my mother. But only two pairs of shoes.'

'Well, well. One of my hunches goes bang. That's what comes of basing them on insufficient evidence. No kiddies of our own, you see. I'll get the bill.'

I waited until the house once more appeared, more desolate-looking than ever in the sunshine: yellow but not even a curate's egg of a house. The coffee, it must be, had keyed me up. I felt it might prove a morning for pricking the buff jerkin persona with the unprotected tip of my foil.

'Have you checked for footprints?'

'Footprints?'

'Prints of feet. I can produce my other pair of shoes if you wish. I expect you've already had a word with the local bank manager about my account.'

He stopped the car and we got out. This seemed to be becoming a routine, and I was pleased to find how confidently I entered the hall.

'Oh,' he said. 'I'm afraid we've probably been less thorough than you think. Or, at any rate, I have. Your bank account's your own affair as far as I'm concerned, and I don't know whether we'd get much in the way of footprints on this ground. An awful lot of people came and went, visiting your godfather. Or have I missed your point?'

'Mightn't footprints help over that girl who came to see Philip? Inspector Grice told me she must have been the last person to see him alive, and I think Sergeant Parrott said she hadn't been traced.'

'Get a girl's footprint, you mean, and then conduct some sort of Cinderella search? It's a nice thought, though I wonder what we'd learn at the end of the day. Well, now, what about visiting your ex-bedroom? How'd you feel about that?'

Under Catesby's tread the staircase seemed dangerously flimsy. He paused at the top, either to get his breath or in a typical show of politeness. I led the way to what had been my bedroom, surprised by how shrunken the dimensions of everything had become without furnishings. There was no golf-bag, nothing, except a few remaining flecks of the custard paint adhering to the window-panes. Catesby walked over to look out, and then went through the performance of putting on his spectacles to scrutinise the empty room.

'What's that on the door?' he asked. I turned quite sharply, as if there hung on it something grotesque or alarming.

'I chalked it up. "The future", in French; as a challenge, really, to myself.'

'A-venir,' he said slowly. 'To come, isn't it? Yes, I think I've got that. Something was coming, was it, you hoped, for you?'

I shrugged. 'Well, that was the challenge. Was it? It didn't have any particular significance,' I added, then regretted my semi-exculpatory tone.

'Not a big room,' he said.

'No – and no golf clubs, I'm afraid. They used to be in that corner. It was really Philip's lumber-room, combined with bedroom for me.'

'Just two bedrooms, aren't there? The other at the end of the corridor and the bathroom in between. Nothing else up here, I suppose. There wouldn't be any other space, would there?'

'Have you a hunch about somebody hiding up here? Perhaps I oughtn't to ask.'

'Would you think that likely – someone trying to hide up here?'

'Not very.'

'Nor would I.' He approached the door closely, raising and lowering his spectacles as if testing his eyesight. He tapped the wood and then opened the door. 'You could help me enormously,' he said, with an extenuating laugh, 'but it seems a pretty odd request. Would you mind? Could you go along to the bathroom, shutting this door behind you, then shut the bathroom door and flush the cistern for me? Oh, and before you go. The bed in here was always where these marks are, was it?'

Several questions rose in my mind, but I reserved them for my return. How many times had Catesby, I wondered, sent Hengist and Horsa along to carry out this exercise? Or even Bob. And anyway shouldn't the water be turned off? I tried a switch in the the corridor as I passed. Exactly. The electricity had been cut off.

When I went back Catesby was still studying the door and feigned to be disconcerted as I opened it on him.

'So sorry,' I said. 'I didn't intend to give you a shock.'

'Let's go downstairs,' he said. 'Just as you did that evening when you wanted something to eat from the fridge. Forget I'm with you. Just act naturally, as you did then.'

'I'm afraid I'm not a good enough actor,' I said, at the top of the stairs. 'I can't seem to manage to forget you're behind me.'

'Don't let that bother you. It's not so much how you went

as where, if you follow me.'

'Isn't it the other way round?'

He appeared to ruminate on it for a moment, giving the curry-coloured whiskers a rapid grooming, before a slyly appreciative smile spread over his face.

'I expect you ran down the stairs,' he said. 'Hungry. Just woken up, I think. Very understandable. You reach the bottom. Can we do that?'

I ran down, leaving him to plod heavily after, slightly puffing. 'Please go on. I'm watching.'

I walked over to the kitchen, went in, paused precisely where the refrigerator had stood (miming opening and closing it for verisimilitude) and walked out, clasping an imaginary carton (peach flavour, I'd reply, if interrogated).

I found Catesby squatting on the lowest step, brushing at his whiskers again, trousers hoisted to reveal bright yellow socks. My producer. He looked up as though considering whether to ask me to do it again, this time with feeling.

'You walked past the study door – had to, really. But you didn't stop, either time?'

'No, I didn't.'

'And it was – as far as you recall – closed both times?'

'Yes.'

'And you heard nothing from inside? No voices? Nothing?'

'Well, I didn't stop to listen, but I heard nothing.'

'Are you sure?'

'I heard absolutely nothing.'

'Are you sure you didn't stop?'

'Quite sure.'

He got to his feet. 'I put it to you that you did stop. Now, that's not a crime. Of course, I don't know whether it was on the way down that you stopped – I rather suspect it was. The door wasn't shut. It was ajar. You entered that room.'

'This is total nonsense. I did not enter the room. I've told you that already.'

'Have you? I don't remember when, if you did. At least, you stopped to put your hand on the door-knob, and I wondered why if the door was closed. Your fingerprints are on that knob, I must tell you. But then perhaps on reflection you think the door was ajar?'

'You talk about my fingerprints very glibly. When did I

give them to the police? That's something I don't remember. Or maybe it doesn't matter. Call them mine. Who cares? It's your hunch they're mine. Super evidence. Don't let's bother with a trial – just conviction and the sentence. I bet you really regret the abolition of capital punishment, especially for young offenders. Good way, too, to solve the problem of school-leavers.'

'You misunderstand me,' he said mildly. 'Both in general and in this particular case. And I didn't bring you here to accuse you of a capital crime.'

'Oh no? Just for a breath of fresh air, was it? Making the criminal go over his tracks, day after day. How stupid am I meant to be? I break down and confess it all.'

'Will it help,' he said, 'if I tell you something?'

'What?'

'I'm not looking for a criminal exactly. Not in the normal sense. I think I partly know what happened. Two people, two young people, I grant – one of them I can't yet put my hand on – behaved very irresponsibly and dangerously, as it turned out. Probably it'll never be proved, or never come to court. I don't think it was a conspiracy between the two, but my hunch is that you were one of them.'

'What did I do?'

'Shall I first answer your earlier question, about your fingerprints? It's an assumption, not an unreasonable one, I think you'll agree, that the prints we lifted all over the room upstairs are your own. Nobody else entered your bedroom, did they? Those prints match the main ones on the knob of the door down here.'

'And?'

'And I think it was quite late – maybe ten or eleven o'clock at night – when you came downstairs. I think the silence in the house had already struck you. No sound of doors closing or anyone using the bathroom. You'd sense you were alone. I'm really guessing now, but I believe you were frightened, perhaps came down to investigate.

'The study door was ajar. You may have called out to your godfather. There was no reply. You gripped the knob, and went in. He of course was already dead. It was a terrific shock. If you didn't exactly love him, you certainly didn't hate him. But I think you may hate the police, and you're quite proud of your own ingenuity. You smashed the ornaments and the decanter, made it look like some sort of crime, left the body and to confuse things a little more pretended to discover it the next morning. You wanted to see if we'd solve the puzzle you'd devised.'

'Marvellous. I'd never have credited you with such a splendid imagination, Chief Superintendent. Ought I to have been calling you that? It's really rich. Can you prove a word of it, incidentally?'

'Probably not. I don't think I shall even try. But I'm convinced in my own mind of two things. One, the more obvious, there was no struggle, as I told you the other day. Two, more hypothetical, you knew of the death hours before you reported it. I'd agree that there's an alternative explanation of those, to me, facts. The decanter and so on could have been broken at the time of your godfather's death. When you came down you smelled the sherry, and it was panic that made you delay reporting it. Yes, panic and shock. You probably slept badly, dashed downstairs early the next morning, carefully forgot to put on your watch – didn't want to know the time, no doubt, in case we asked you – and went through the motions of discovering your godfather was dead.'

I threw my hands apart in a feeling of sheer frustration combined with fury. I'd flung away anything as subtle as a foil. My gesture was one of violence to serve instead of actually rushing over and pummelling his pouter-pigeon tweed chest, padded as it seemed to be with hunches as flimsy but as unending as a quire of tissue-paper. And under sufficient quantities of that anyone could stifle. If there had ever been little Catesbys, parricide – justifiable parricide – would have been their sole hope of survival.

'Shall we go?' he said. 'Unless, that is, you have anything to tell me. After all, I've only been guessing. You can easily show me where I'm wrong. I'd be glad to learn. It will probably end up an open verdict, anyway.'

'Before we go, I've something to ask. The second person, what did she or he do? Or don't you want me to know?'

'Not much. I'd rather hear your story.'

'Rather arrest me, you mean.'

He laughed, but now even the wrappings of joviality were falling off. At the centre of all that paper tissue lay something lethal. If he failed to put truth drops in my coffee, he had manacles concealed in the shabby, cosy-seeming upholstery of the car outside: settle back, relax, and enjoy the steel on skin touch of collars closing round your wrists and throat.

'Incriminate yourself, would you? At your age, there'd be great leniency, I can assure you. An advantage that, being so young.'

'An advantage for you – not me.'

But he went to the front door, and the blue rectangle of sky and sunlight as he opened it was as welcome as a sudden glimpse of swimming pool.

'I'm going to tell you,' he said as we climbed into the car. 'I want you to think about it. It's about being young. I think you know your godfather had a penchant for young ladies – none too serious. Perhaps better if it had been, in a way. Mrs Rainbow knew, of course. I'm afraid she nosed out the hanky-panky when girls came to see him. And one or two wrote him silly notes, we found. All rather avuncular, but horse-play must have gone on, of a sexual tendency. A bit of teasing on both sides, I've no doubt. Pity he never managed to get married.'

'Whatever went on, I bet Philip didn't harm them,' I said.

'The girl Mrs Rainbow let in on that last evening was a stranger to her. Her eyesight's not all it might be, but at least she could describe the voice. The girl sounded foreign – had some sort of accent anyway. She might be someone's au pair. Or just putting on the accent. Hard to say. What the girl got up to with your godfather isn't clear. Mrs Rainbow took herself off. They were just fooling around, I'd say, with her sitting on his knee, it could be, and playfully putting something – a scarf or a handkerchief round his neck. No harm meant. It got pulled too tight. He began to choke. Of course, she loosened it straightaway, but his coughing brought on a heart-attack. Frightened, a bit like you, panicky, she nipped out as quickly as possible – through the open window. That's how I see it. The action of someone young and foolish. I hope we'll find her, but to some extent she concerns me less than you do.'

'Oh, of course,' I said. 'That's been clear all along. I was on the spot – in more ways than one. Maybe I should have disappeared, not reported Philip's death, or claimed I wasn't in the house that night.'

Catesby had slowed down behind a cyclist, an old man wobbling on, bent beneath what looked to be an old-fashioned scythe. The narrow road with its high hedges, today not wetly green but dry and dusty like discarded matting, was the one Bob had driven me along that stormy morning when confused emotions and proximity had made me so ill-at-ease. 'Drive on,' I ought to have cried when we reached Trencham Croke in the pelting rain. Exceed the speed limit; there's no restriction on libido. Thanks for the rescue-rape. Just what I needed.

'We'd have caught up with you, and sooner rather than later,' Catesby said calmly.

'Would you mind,' I said, no less calmly, 'letting me out here? If, that is, I'm a free agent.'

'I was taking you back to Sergeant Parrott's. Have you got some other destination in mind? I can probably still give you a lift.'

'I'm better without it, thanks. I'd rather walk – much rather.'

'Well.' He appeared dubious (on the point of asking how I felt), even disconcerted. 'This isn't a very safe road for pedestrians. I'm not sure I ought to leave you here.'

'Might I be knocked down before my next grilling session? Don't worry; I'll take care.'

He stopped the car. I hesitated, watching for a convenient moment to get out.

'Oh,' he said, smiling at me in the driving mirror. 'I wouldn't call it that. But I don't think there'll be a next anything on my side. I've given you my explanation. I'm a patient sort of chappie. I'll be waiting for yours.'

13

'Ah, Watson,' I said, walking so silently into the kitchen that

Bob, blundering with plates at the dresser, nearly dropped one. 'You don't know my methods. But you will, my dear Watson. You will.'

'A budding Sherlock, are you?' he said when he turned round, a shirt-sleeved teddy-bear (my menagerie, with blue plush rabbit and green duck, had somehow always lacked one: there might be the root of the matter). It wasn't quite a smile he offered, but the look at least not hostile. 'Going to solve something?'

'I rather think I have. And what about criminal statistics today in Spenn? Anything juicy off the record? Hiscock and Horder arrest Mr Cherry for flogging tins of exploding mushrooms?'

'As a matter of fact there was a bit of a flap. A fire in the kitchen at *Betty's* – you know, that café—'

'Know it? I was in there this morning and pretty rough it was. I can point the finger at your main suspect, fattish, red-faced man in ginger sports coat, a dangerous arsonist known as Wilf – obvious code-name. On this one I really am anxious to help the police, Bob.'

'Oh, balls. It was only an accident. Anyway, listen. I've talked to Edna on the phone. She's in much better form, and the great thing is so's her father. They think he's going to pull through. If all goes well she might be back early next week. How about that?'

'It's good news. Splendid.'

'She hoped we were getting on all right – getting enough to eat, I mean, and so on.'

'Super.'

The kitchen sink drama of the night before seemed still to hover around us, almost as palpable as the kettle. Echoes of 'my own bloody tea' might have been in the ears of us both, and I risked dispelling them by a brisk embrace, too quickly executed to be either resisted or prolonged. Not much yielding there; some teddy-bears are less soft than they seem.

'All is forgiven,' I said. 'Let's celebrate – Edna's news. And not by a trip to that local of yours, the Mortician's Rest, or is it the Old Shroud?'

'Plenty of beer in the fridge.'

'I think this calls for uncorking the home-made wine. I opt we start with elderberry, as our apéritif.'

He was hesitant, sufficiently nervous or unsure to spill some of it down his shirt front when he poured out the first glasses while together we washed lettuce and chopped tomatoes. 'Eat in the sitting-room,' I said, not waiting for a reply.

I felt agreeably in a cloud of my own creation: the last wisp of steam from my very hot bath had lingered even as I drifted downstairs, delaying long after Bob's return, dressed without anything he would notice as care.

'We've made rather a mess,' he said, sounding not un-pleased, gazing round the sitting-room where the still bright evening sky showed the litter of our supper laid out as if in a trail for training sniffer dogs. Despite my indicating the cold pie in the larder, he had opened a tin of sardines; it stood untouched but smelling profane on the arm of the big, mushroom-coloured chair in which he was sitting. I sat on the other arm, scrupulous not to let a drop fall as I filled our glasses with the last of what for the meal had become parsnip wine.

'If you mean emotionally, I might take it as an insult. And as for the room, it can wait.'

'There's something I want to ask you,' he said. 'Will you answer truthfully?'

I got off the chair, carrying my glass with me.

'Will you,' he pleaded, his voice following me as I moved away, manoeuvring among the shadowy, scattered furniture, and coming to rest, arms behind my back, upright before him.

'I might. Fire away. But don't blame me if this hurts you more than it hurts me.'

'You're making it difficult.'

'Of course.'

'Get me a beer, would you. I've a rotten thirst. I think it must be all that wine. Good.' He put a paw-like hand on mine when I gave it to him, a little tentatively but holding me so that I had to remain stooped over his slumped form. 'Last night,' he said. 'I wasn't talking just in temper. I meant a lot of it. About you. I've got to make that plain. You're mucking me about. It's a big mess all right, but it's one you'll walk out of because you aren't involved, are you? Well, are you?'

'I decline to answer on the grounds it might incriminate me.'

'A bit late for that. You're incriminated up to your neck. Playing dirty little schoolboy games with me – the sort of games that could wreck a man and his marriage.'

'I'm sure it's bad to stoop after a meal.'

'You'll stoop, if I want you to. And I do. So far it's all been me stooping to you, getting mixed up about you, afraid of my own feelings, asking you to forgive me. Christ, you forgiving me! It's you who ought to be on your knees begging me not to sling you out of this house.

'Yes, really down on your knees. I'd like that quite a lot,' he said ruminatively, twisting my arm as though experimenting with a try-your-strength machine, until I had to bend lower to alleviate the pain. 'This one is definitely going to hurt you more,' he added, half-rising to force my arm into an agonising lock behind my back. 'Typical police brutality, eh? Like to complain to Mr Catesby, perhaps?'

'Both sadists in your different ways,' I mumbled angrily, trying to avoid the thick pile of carpet brushing my mouth. With a sudden shove, my shoulder almost had him off balance. He staggered and tightened his grip, though the chair slid back, and the sardine-tin fell softly on to the floor beside me. It was too dark to see the oily stain it made but the reek of it was strong where I crouched, straddled now by his legs, the two of us posed in a David and Goliath group of unfortunately reversed rôles. Bob's head on a charger, I thought confusedly; and somehow it did seem amusing down there on the carpet to envisage his moustached face mournfully staring from a vast meat-dish, decorated possibly with sprigs of parsley, reposing on a shelf in the larder.

'Enjoying it, are you? Probably how you get your kicks, being beaten up by yobboes in some filthy alley at night. Good luck to them. I wouldn't interfere with your fun – or theirs.'

'Bob, seriously.' His hold had relaxed, and he stepped back, perhaps ashamed. I could no longer distinguish his features in the darkness accumulating which I seemed to be breathing in like smoke; gasping as I knelt there, aching, massaging my wrenched muscles. 'Calm down and listen to me. I do not enjoy being bashed up by anyone.'

'I haven't lost my temper properly with you yet.'

'Well, don't. I thought you wanted to ask a question – not

give me the third degree.'

I tried to haul myself into some sort of sitting position, my fingers scrabbling at his belt for support. He stood there, watching me, feeling my hands, I suppose, as I could feel the rapid throb of his diaphragm through the shirt material, asserting his physical existence. It was enough that he lived, was flesh and bone, solid all right, as my own bruised flesh told me. And it seemed good for me to go on kneeling there silently, in total healing contact with him. Each crease of shirt, slightly distended by his stomach above the belted-in trousers, was remarkable as being part of warm living Bob, to whom I clung in the soothing, dusk-filled room.

'Can I trust you to answer honestly?' he said, unmoving, without emotion. 'And no clever back-chat?'

'Yes,' I whispered. 'You can.'

He paused before speaking again. Only dimly could I trace the outline of his head and shoulders against the black glass of the windows. The world outside had ceased to exist. He cleared his throat, and that itself seemed affecting, intimate, almost sad. 'It's not the first time, is it, that you've made someone – a man – fancy you?' There was nothing dispassionate, now, about his voice. 'Is it? You weren't shocked when I touched you that day, were you? Any normal boy would have been. You weren't. It was just what you'd been waiting to happen. Do you deny it?'

'Why should I? I told you, I cared for you, Bob. Unlike you, I'm not ashamed of my own feelings. I'm proud of them.'

'Proud of not having them, I'd say. In what way did you care about me as me? You just want to feel fancied by men, like a cheap tart who doesn't even deliver the goods. You're much worse altogether. Men could land in jail led on by you. Perhaps that wouldn't matter if you'd an ounce of real feeling. And I'm by no means the first man you've led on, am I? Come on. Let's hear it. Am I?'

'Bob, please understand. Please.' I clutched at his waist. 'I do care about you, and that is the absolute truth. I feel everything you feel. I swear it.'

'You didn't want any swearing before. Nor do I. Just tell me – and then maybe I'll start to believe you – that this is the first time you ever had a bloke this way about you.'

'Well, be reasonable, Bob. Am I responsible for anyone—'

'You know what I mean all right. Go ahead. I want to hear.'

'It's not the first time, obviously. But – oh, for God's sake,' as I felt a tremor in his body and my fingers seized in a savage grip. 'Let me explain. It was utterly different, with people very different from you, not so innocent themselves ... with different standards—'

'Get your hands off me,' he suddenly shouted, hurling me back so violently that I crashed sideways against the sharp edge of the low table piled with dishes. Something broke. I felt a gash across my forehead, and a long gouging graze tore down my outflung arm.

'I knew it,' he said, more calmly, as I lay there, too jarred and shaken to want to move. 'You're nothing but a lousy little cock-teaser.'

No urge to protest stirred in me. I heard him going quietly out of the room, and it seemed a relief just to be left lying there prone, wrapped in a bandage of blackness. Sounds of him locking up came to me. Yes, I thought, he ought to do that. It's as well to be safe. Then he must have a look at me, which will mean turning on the light. Bob won't be afraid of blood; he'll be proficient too at first aid. If a fragment of plate cut me, it could be nasty; if it was actually in the wound ...

When gradually I realised he was not returning, I almost thought of sleeping there. Morning would banish the whole affair, affray, it might seem, though only a bit of a scuffle. A mistake, we would conclude, to mix homemade wines, and then add beer. I had slipped when reaching to spear a piece of tomato, jolted Bob, who jolted the sardine-tin ... Shouldn't take too long to clear up. Lucky, really, that more damage hadn't been done. Tentatively I moved my less painful arm and probed very gingerly at the scuffed skin of the graze stretching from wrist to elbow. At the moment of impact it had seemed to gouge into the bone but now appeared merely a graze, sore but not serious.

Even the cut, when I brought myself to explore it, felt not deep or long, though horribly wet, it or my head throbbing at my own nervous touch. I sat up and removed a curled, chill finger of lettuce pressed into my abdomen where my tee shirt rucked up as I fell. Each move was a tingling experience in the darkness, as though the atmosphere answered with electric shocks any disturbance of it. But I knew what I had to do. I must let none of my wounds grow cold.

In the bathroom, which I took so long to reach, there was no avoiding the extent of them. The mirror reported with detached, police-surgeon precision: laceration, minor contusion, superficial grazing, slight flesh wound – and the promise of a black eye. I patched the cut with sticking plaster, dabbed antiseptic over the rest of the damage and then went to knock on Bob's door.

It opened too speedily for him to have been asleep. He barred the way, his hair tousled, wearing only pyjama trousers in the wide green and white stripe I had seen before. His eye passed over my head, noted (I felt sure) every scratch and bruise, with more suspicion even than satisfaction.

'I must speak to you, Bob,' I said. 'And no, it won't keep till tomorrow morning.'

'Not in here.' He shut the door behind him.

'My room, then. I'm sorry, but I quite want to sit down.'

He leant on the chest of drawers while I tried to sit upright on the bed, longing to collapse on it and knowing how foolish that would be. It would have been far easier to have the light out, and no less foolish.

To any Trencham Croke voyeur, our two figures confronting each other in the austere blue bedroom, at whatever hour of the night it was, must have been extraordinary. Guess as he might, he could hardly have hit on the purpose of our conversation or the dryness of tone, belied by the sight of us in comparative proximity. I felt almost as if I were the voyeur, audience as well as actor, and it gave me the determination to proceed.

'I want you to listen carefully, Bob. And then think about what I've said. We are both being very stupid – in different ways. The question is, do we want to go on behaving like that?'

'You speak for yourself.'

'I am; I shall. But you're concerned too, because it's about us. I am telling the truth, Bob. I did so downstairs. Nothing would have been easier for me than to flare up at your insinuations, swear that I'd never been touched by a man, let alone encouraged one. You wouldn't hear me out, but at least you heard me answering you honestly, as I said I would. Why didn't I lie to you?'

'Oh, I was there already. You only told me what I'd guessed. Maybe I'm not what you call sophisticated, but your behaviour at the river gave the game away.'

'What I gave away was the simple truth: I love you. And I trust you. Because I love you, I wouldn't lie to you. Of course, it's surprised me. Of course, as I was trying to explain, it's new for me, just as it is for you. It's important you understand that actually because I've played around, been loved before and certainly been fond myself, I know how different I feel this time.

'I told you, frankly enough, that I needed someone to love. And that the someone was you – which doesn't exclude Edna or hurt her. We happen to have a few days to enjoy our love – you and I – before I go away. Enjoy it and cease provoking each other. Or we can stop now totally. I can ring a friend of my mother's and leave tomorrow. You won't need to chuck me out. Tell Edna anything you like – the truth, if you want to. Unlike you, Bob, I'm not ashamed, you see. Or you could blackguard me to your heart's content. You seem fairly adept at it. Why not the story of Joseph and Mrs Parrott's husband? I always got good marks for scripture, but tonight I've been super.'

'Everything about you has to be super, doesn't it? You can talk about it all right, but you still don't understand my feelings. I love Edna, for one thing.'

'I should hope so. Nobody's suggesting you divorce her and marry me.'

He crossed the few feet to the bedside, his fist raised. 'I'm a peaceable bloke normally but sometimes I could smash your bloody face in. And not be sorry.'

'I'm a walking – just – testimony to that,' I said, looking first up at him and then down at his bare feet planted on the patch of blue and buff rug. His toenails were pale and oddly stubby. Perhaps that would be the memory I took away the next morning.

'Sooner or later,' he said, still glaring over me, speaking grimly. 'It'd stop, wouldn't it? Not planning to stay here for ever, are you? One day, whatever I say, however I feel, you'll be away, won't you? Thanks so much for having me. That's it.'

'Leaving aside the form of thanks, yes. It's all a matter of time – even with the greatest love, my poor Bob. Sooner or later, if nothing else comes along, death does. Hadn't you noticed?'

'You sit there, coolly asking me to—'

'The only thing I asked you to do was to think about what I said. Now, it doesn't matter. Sorry, I must go to bed, especially if I'm leaving tomorrow.'

'You don't need to leave for me.'

'Oh, yes, I do. You're the very reason. A night or so ago you talked vehemently enough about your love for me. I took it quite seriously – thought my feelings were reciprocated. Now you make it clear they aren't, I shall indeed be off. I shan't abuse you in the way you did me, but I expect there is a word for men like you – cock-less teasers perhaps.'

He bent fiercely over me, his fists driven deep into the pillow on either side of my face. Even I could smell my own antiseptic aroma and I couldn't help flinching as he came close; not so old wounds might easily re-open, and anyway the skin round my left eye felt so fragile and swollen that it was surprising he could get his face as near mine as he had.

'I've told you,' he said threateningly, 'a thousand times how I feel. What more do you want – shouting of it from the housetops?'

'On the contrary. And bashed up though I feel – am – I think it's time for actions to speak louder than words.'

He reached out and switched off the bedside lamp.

'Oh, and Sergeant.' My arms ached too much to raise them. I could manage only to get my hands as far as the knotted cord of his pyjama trousers. 'My turn to take down your particulars.'

'I'm only telling you what he said, Nick,' Bob said.

'All right. He's got a long wait. What else happened today?' I asked lazily. I felt tired, too. The bed was not ideal for two to sleep in, and after the first night I sent him back to his own eventually, sad though it was not to wake together. He was right, of course, about their bedroom. I felt I owed it to Edna, even while carrying out the household tasks, not to go in. Besides, she would be back on Monday – or might it be Wednesday now, since she was taking the opportunity of staying a few days with her sister Marion and seeing little Edna, her godchild?

The sitting-room was orderly again, though a portion of carpet looked sinisterly dark and over-scrubbed. I moved a chair to hide it, and then pushed it back once more. Honesty, on occasion, had its charms. Bob, I suppose, had taught me that. 'I upset a tin of sardines on the carpet,' I intended to tell Edna. 'I know. It was my idea – eating supper in there. I'm very sorry.'

I shouldn't refer, however, to my effort to make a damson tart. They looked ripe to me was all I could say to Bob when he put his spoon and fork down in dismay.

'Trying to poison me, are you?' he said with a grin. 'As a first effort, I think the pastry anyway is rather good.' But I had taken the rest of the tart and tipped it into the pedal-bin under the sink.

'Edna rang,' he said, shifting to find space in the bed. 'Her father's never fully going to get back the use of his right arm, the doctor says, but luckily he's left-handed. They don't think his brain's affected at all. He's a tough old boy, I can tell you.

'Everything much as usual – routine stuff at the nick. The Boss was in a good mood, though. And I'm off on Sunday this week. What about us going swimming again?'

'We'll see,' I said absently. 'Perhaps you ought to be working in the garden. Doesn't mulching or digging-over start soon?'

He laughed. 'I don't suppose you know one from the other, do you?'

'I shall if I stay long enough.'

He was silent, his head turned away. The late light on the walls of my blue room made it an extension of the blueness outside. From the bed nothing was visible but the bloom of unbroken sky, and we might have been reclining in a private celestial ward.

Under the sheet our bodies lay juxtaposed but relaxed, twined loosely in pleasing confusion so that it was not obvious which arm and leg belonged to whom, and it seemed utterly unimportant. He stirred consciously, as though physical action was dictated by some mental one, and I stirred too, for no reason except to echo him and then again subside. Perhaps it was a raft we were on, far out at sea, drifting under a broad crystal flask of sky from which the liquid blue was gradually draining away.

'Nick,' he said. 'Oh, Nick, I wish—'

'Don't.' I put my finger to his lips, more for the sensation of ownership than anything else. 'It's a dreadful adult vice, disease really.'

'You of course don't have any wishes, do you? Least of all about us. Sometimes, even now, I wonder if you care. It's much harder for me, feeling as I do, and guilty and frightened – and I've got to go on, afterwards, as I was.'

'Better than going on without this interlude, don't you think? Or not?'

'I'll never understand you,' he said, barely turning at first, and then swivelling round to strain his gaze in slow scrutiny over me.

'I don't usually feel I have to apologise for my appearance,' I said, 'but unless sticking plaster and black eyes send you, I am a sorry sight. What shall we say? I hit my head on the table while doing the dusting?'

'Don't let's talk about it,' he muttered. 'You'll heal soon enough. You're young. It won't take long.'

'Well, gaze on. I'm better from the neck down.'

'No.' He laid his hand on mine, arresting the movement I was about to make (quick thinking, and quite right).

'So Catesby dropped in, did he?' I said dozily. 'Shows how little he thinks of your boss.'

'I didn't tell you something.' He still gazed at me with those mournful brown eyes that seemed to grow bigger when as now the fringe of his fair hair hung tousled over them, as if he had run his fingers through it while puzzling over some homework.

'What is it?' Immediately I felt alert, even while I debated whether to brush his hair aside or leave it tangled.

'About the Boss – well, his wife really. She's going to have a baby. They're very chuffed about it.'

'Oh, Bob,' I spluttered, lying back the better to digest my own laughter. 'My dear Bob.'

'Is it so very funny? Most things are to you, I know, but I see it differently. I don't think it's funny at all. Sorry, but I don't.'

I put out my hand and took his. 'You nit. I don't think it's

212

funny. It was just the way you announced it. Somehow I wasn't expecting that.'

He lay, deceptively quiescent, but I could almost hear the chugging and grinding beside me of thoughts like the wheels of a paddle-boat. Not even I, gently squeezing, physically wheedling, his fingers, twisting as I did so the cold band of wedding ring, could stop the steady, disturbing plash of them. Yet he managed some sort of return pressure, and I knew there was value in my silence.

The blue walls were losing their colour, as though the damp of night had slowly faded them. The print of Whitby Bay was reduced to a chalky glow, like an expiring lamp, and even the sheet was a ghostly stream of ectoplasm, weightless on our slightly sweating, wedged bodies.

'I want,' he began, speaking up into the shadowy ceiling.

'Wanting,' I interrupted, 'is quite different. It's more positive. I'm with you about wanting.'

'I want to be convinced you really have cared for me – if you like, needed me. Somehow, before you go, I want to feel that. It would make all the difference, later on. I'd believe it had all been worth it, I can't explain how.'

'I see,' I said softly. It seemed best to whisper. I turned on the pillow, to be sure he heard. His snub-nosed profile was there, almost too close to be visible, held rigid in the hollow formed by our heads. 'I'll try.' He went on as though I had not spoken. 'Then, I'd feel it wasn't wrong. And it would make sense, really, about your going off, moving on. I could bear it. It would happen with any bloke ordinarily. You know … if he had a son growing up, had to find his own feet …'

'Bob,' I breathed. I understood not to make any gesture, just leave my hand clasped in his, and let the metal of his ring impinge on my own flesh, like a last contact with reality.

'Oh, Nick. I've got to say it, but don't laugh this time. Don't you say anything. You're my boy.'

The final flicker on the wall of Whitby Bay had been extinguished. Only the sound of Bob, otherwise immobile, breathing heavily, suggested life in the room.

'Put your arms around me,' I murmured a long time afterwards, my hand grown slack and fallen away from his. I was drowsy, dreaming, not even quite sure until I stretched out that he was still there. I felt him slowly turning, no less drowsily; and, as his arms blindly, instinctively, sought to catch and hold me, there came the overwhelming sensation of release and protection.

'Tighter,' I begged. 'I'm tired of being alone.'

'You're not alone.' His voice was a comforting buzz in my ear.

'I know. Thank you, Bob. Have you gone to sleep?'

'Of course not. I'm here. I always will be.'

'I'll tell you something. I want to. The day Philip – my godfather, Philip – died, I was there. In the room, I mean, when it happened. It was all an accident. And a most horrible shock. He suddenly started coughing and coughing. The only thing I could think of was the stupid sherry and in my panic I knocked it over. He had collapsed on the floor almost as it spilt. He just lay there, and I knew he was dead. I was frankly more terrified than sad. I'd planned to shake Philip up, but that's how it ended.'

His arms seemed to tighten further around me, accompanied by the resonant buzzing of something indistinct, somehow demurring.

'Oh, it was my fault, though it wasn't intentional. I just wanted him to get a shock when I was shown in by Mrs Rainbow. That part was absurdly easy. One day I'd bought a horsey headscarf in Aylesbury. With a pair of dark glasses, it was easy to pass myself off as one more girl visiting Mr Kerr the curate. I wore ordinary jeans and a scruffy jacket. I took my watch off – in case old Ratbag spotted that. Five minutes after creeping out of the house, just about the time I knew she would be leaving, I rang the front door bell and in quite a decent French accent asked to see Philip. With a characteristic sniff or two, she showed me in, obviously not spotting anything wrong. Of course, I couldn't keep it up with Philip. He wasn't very amused. He felt I was getting at him. And I was.'

'Why did you do it?' Bob asked gently.

'Philip never had any real awareness of me, perhaps of anyone. I thought I'd show him. Oh, he was always giving spiritual guidance – or not so spiritual, as it turned out – to local girls. I thought I'd appear like that, wake him up, make him sit up. And it was a cry for help, if you like. He couldn't cope at all.

'God, he was at his most obtuse, flustered too, I realise. Anyway, to cut off the gabble about how at my age and so on, and how he was so amazed, I just threw the silly headscarf round his neck and gave it a playful tug – he was sitting there, and as soon as the coughing started, I let it go. But the coughing didn't stop. Or, rather, it did. But by then it was too late.'

'And the ornaments – did you break them?'

'Of course. It was an impulse. Only later, when I'd got out of the room and thought properly, I realised there was the makings of quite a puzzle. First I had to get out of the room. I was too scared to pick up the telephone, and Philip was dead. I nerved myself the next morning. I had to. I knew that. And so, in a way, something happened. Thanks to you, I came here. I never foresaw that, Bob. Now I've told you everything. I'm glad.' I gripped his arms, still holding me fast. 'Glad it was you, Bob. Something to share: our secret. And I hope you're glad. You see, I trust you.'

'I'm trying to take it all in,' he said, speaking slowly. 'I want to do the best I can for you, Nick. It doesn't affect what I feel personally. Nothing can do that, now. But why you didn't tell us at the time ... after all, in a way, you'd done nothing criminal. It was an accident, wasn't it?'

He moved an arm restively, and I let it go. Abruptly the bedside light came on, making both of us jerk up blinking.

'What's that in aid of?' I asked. 'Don't you believe me?'

'I do believe you, Nick.' He swung his naked body out of the bed and sat with freckled shoulders hunched, recalling that Sunday morning on the river bank. Now I could stroke the nape of his neck and the line of hairs that curled there like fine links of gold chain.

'Mon beau monstre,' I mumbled, beating my head happily against the taut drum of smooth skin between his shoulder blades.

'So,' he said, 'there was no girl?'

'None. Goodbye to one of crafty Catesby's jolly hunches.'

'Nick.' He half turned and clasped me, peering anxiously into my face. 'Nick.'

'That's better. Can't we have lights out? It must be dreadfully late.'

215

'How much does Mr Catesby know? He's a very decent bloke, as well as shrewd. He's the man to go to. And I don't mind. I'll stand by you, whatever happens, Nick. I promise. Just as if we really were – related. It'll soon be over. You're very young and in the circumstances. Mr Catesby will know what's best to do. He'll treat you fairly, Nick, and we can go together, if you like.'

'Go where?'

'To tell him, of course. He's working on the case.'

'Bob, do grasp that I'm not going anywhere, least of all to see more of Catesby. It's our secret – not his.'

'But, Nick.' He got off the bed, letting me fall back sleepily against the pillow. I watched him pace slowly towards the window, turn and walk back, hardly glancing at where I lay. Warm orange light from the weak bulb under its parchment shade washed his body amber, ochre, tawny, as he padded there: a jungle cat he ought to have appeared but through half-closed lids I was reminded more of a giant agitated moth, trapped in the room and drawn back and back to the source of brightness.

'It's because of my caring so much,' he said, stopping at last, beside me. 'And you'll feel relieved when it's done. I'm really sorry for what happened, Nick, though you yourself … Anyway, thanks for telling me. That was brave. All you've got to do now is keep on being brave, and once Catesby knows the worst is over. What you did upset you, you panicked – it was delayed shock, really. Once it's explained, I hope—'

'Explained? I've contrived so far to fight Catesby off and I'm not capitulating now.'

'But, you'll tell him, Nick?' He sat down on the edge of the bed, looking as perplexed as a doctor trying to diagnose a mysterious ailment and uncertain of the outcome. 'You could write perhaps – put it on paper, first, if you thought that easier.'

'I don't want advice on how to do what I'm not going to do. You can't seriously think I told you for any reason except out of love and honesty, mistaken though I seem to have been? I hadn't anything else to offer you, so I gave you my secret, such as it is. Keep it.'

'We can't do that, Nick, really and truly. This is important,

216

official. Somebody died, don't forget, and we – the police – are investigating it. Of course I needn't say you told me first, as long as you tell Catesby tomorrow. The sooner the better.'

'So much for your professions of love. I thought you'd protect me – not expose me. My mistake.'

'No,' he said fervently. 'You speak up, as you must, and I'd do everything, everything, Nick, I can to protect you. That's the way – it really is. Edna and I won't desert you.'

'And if I've decided not to?'

He looked round the room desperately. Now I had become the doctor, determined to complete the operation on my recalcitrant patient and coolly aware of the necessity for it.

'Well?' I said.

'Oh, Nick ... I'd have to, of course. It's only right. But I'd try to put it as well as I could, you know, the circumstances and so on ... Still, it won't come to that, I'm sure. Don't you be afraid. It's far better your doing it. And you talk well. Everything will be all right, in the end. You'll see.'

'I don't want to see.' I reached up and turned off the light.

He moved uncertainly, I could hear, towards the door.

'Think it over,' he said, pausing.

'Oh, I've thought all right. It's you who needs to start thinking.'

When I went downstairs the next morning mist was hanging like net outside the windows. Bob was already in uniform, standing at the stove. He looked at me fondly enough but it was a weak fondness, irritating if not frightening, as though prompted by a sense of impending separation.

'Nick. Please pay attention. I have thought all night, and we've got to tell Mr Catesby.' Instinctively he adjusted his tunic; perhaps it gave him courage. 'I mean that.'

'For God's sake, shut up. I trusted you – like I might have done my own father. And your only reaction is to bleat on about seeing Catesby. We can't help Philip, and I haven't committed a crime, have I?'

'I don't know ...' he began slowly.

'Oh, maybe you think on reflection I did kill him? Is that where we are? Well, I didn't, but thanks for the suspicion. I'm sure Catesby would take the same line, once he heard. Trust a policeman. And if you're so full of caring, care to wonder about my mother, and other people too, when the whole story came out. What possible good would it do? Now the test of all your boasted affection is simple – keep the secret.'

'I can't,' he said sadly.

'What the hell do you mean?'

'If you don't report it, I must.'

I sat down abruptly at the table.

'By the way,' he said. 'There's a postcard for you, from Edna.'

'Let's get this straight,' I said. 'You intend to go to Catesby, do you, if I won't, and tell him how, putting duty before pleasure, you won my confidence by seduction and have solved the case? God, how could I ever have believed a word you said? And you were meant to be so good and true. And loving. At the end of it all, you'd shop me, wouldn't you?'

'Nick, believe me—'

'Never again. And don't come any nearer or I'll add assault of a police officer to my other felonies.'

'What else can I do?' He gestured at me miserably.

'Turn off the grill before everything goes up in flames. What a suitably symbolic feast you've contrived, literally ashes. Well, you never wanted it to begin, in the first place, I suppose, and now it's certainly over, isn't it? Will I go to prison, do you imagine? Or just a detention centre?'

'Tell Catesby yourself, Nick,' he urged. 'That's best, truly.' He moved closer, and now I felt too weak to resist. Very cautiously he sat down. If he put out his hand I thought I would be lost despite all my talk, but he remained hesitant, almost as if inhibited by the sight of his own sleeve. Mist seemed to be gathering about the room, and the usual breakfast array of china looked forlorn and as neglected as Edna's postcard beside my plate, my place: with a silly yellow raffia napkin-ring she had assigned me and a felt egg-cosy in the shape of a cockerel that had so often greeted me in the mornings.

'I'll come with you,' he went on. 'I'll promise you that. You tell him in your own way … make a clean breast of it. After all, he's been seeing you. He must suspect something.'

'Exactly. He really hates me. And he'll take his revenge.'

'You've got him all wrong, Nick.'

'Have I got you all wrong?' I asked solemnly, raising my

head with deliberate slowness and letting my eyes travel up his row of buttons, his collar, to his flushed and worried face. It was hard to recognise him with his clothes on. 'Have I?' I demanded. 'If I won't go to Catesby, you will? Just let me hear you say that finally, so I am absolutely clear. Nothing I can say or do will alter your decision? No plea, no distress, no blackmail – not even if I threaten to tell Edna about us? You prefer to see me punished than risk your career? Even though I suffer and nobody – repeat, nobody – benefits, except Catesby, of course?'

'I'll do anything, anything at all, to help you, Nick. I am helping you, whatever you think. It's tough for me, but I have to believe that. In a funny way, if I wasn't so concerned about you ... I don't know. Yes, he's got to be told. I know that's right. As for it being me that tells him – well, that's really up to you.'

He pushed back his chair but lingered there as though afraid to leave me alone, or afraid of hearing my decision.

'I see,' I said.

'Nick.'

'There is one thing,' I said calmly. I would not beg. 'Give me the weekend. Do nothing today. Just let me have till Monday – and drop the subject. Let's pretend I never spoke.'

'But on Monday ...'

'It will be resolved, in some way. Don't worry about that. I've decided.'

Before he left, he drank a cup of what must have been tepid tea, almost furtively, yet gratefully too. He pressed my shoulder as he passed, acknowledging our pact, saluting the victim: his hand was so much dead meat on my deader flesh. Perhaps through the misty kitchen I shimmered momentarily for him as the boy-martyr, the plucky school-story hero ('I must tell you, sir, I am the culprit'), led on by the treacherous need to be admired. Bob would admire me, no doubt, if, as he must anticipate, I went to Catesby; and thus I should seem to justify all the feelings he had for me. Poor Bob.

I picked up Edna's card, a deserted village green, sunlit but swimming in sepia tones, with a solitary long-legged child crossing it burdened by a basket of laundry or provisions. Her bold plain handwriting, including a full signature, constituted the message, rather than the few, formal words: 'My village, not much changed, lovely seeing family. Trust all well, back Wednesday. Sincere regards.'

When I thought about the future, I felt sorry for Edna, but in a detached way. She might once have been that child crossing the village green, wearing what looked like black stockings, in the sepia sunshine that seemed so much more poignant for being old and yet perfectly preserved.

I should be very loving to Edna, I determined. We would need each other a great deal during the weeks ahead; and in the end we ought to be happy together, I felt, as I sat on at the table, turning her card over and over, pondering the fact that very shortly Bob had got to die.